THE MEN AND WOMEN OF ABILENE . . .

LUKE TRAVIS: He'd been a fast-shooting U.S. marshal—until he watched his wife die from a bullet meant for him. Now he was looking to start life over again without a gun. But the guns found him . . .

AILEEN BLOOM: A woman doctor in a town full of flying lead, she was out to prove herself in Abilene—and from the day he met her, Luke Travis knew she would . . .

CODY FISHER: While his brother chose the ministry, he chose the road—and a six-gun. Now he'd come home to Abilene, to kill the man who murdered his father . . .

ORION McCARTHY: A rough-hewn Scotsman who owned his own tavern—and played by his own rules. Marcus Donaghue was out to beat him down—but he'd have to kill him to do it . . .

MARCUS DONAGHUE: A governor's pardon had sprung him from prison. Now he fancied himself king of Abilene—and he wasn't about to let Luke Travis interfere with his plans . . .

Books by Justin Ladd

Abilene Book 1: The Peacemaker
Abilene Book 2: The Sharpshooter

Published by POCKET BOOKS

JUSTIN LADD
ABILENE

Book 1

THE PEACEMAKER

™ **BCI** Created by the producers of
**Wagons West, Stagecoach,
Badge, and White Indian.**

Book Creations Inc., Canaan, NY · Lyle Kenyon Engel, Founder

POCKET BOOKS

New York   London   Toronto   Sydney   Tokyo

Another *Original* publication of POCKET BOOKS

POCKET BOOKS, a division of Simon & Schuster Inc.
1230 Avenue of the Americas, New York, N.Y. 10020

ISBN: 0-671-64897-7

First Pocket Books printing June 1988

10 9 8 7 6 5 4 3 2 1

POCKET and colophon are trademarks of Simon & Schuster Inc.

Printed in the U.S.A.

THE PEACEMAKER

Chapter One

———◆———

There was a slight tremor in the old man's hand as he firmly pressed the stubby pencil against the paper in an effort to make his writing bold and legible. After carefully printing the first few words, he paused and rubbed his right hand. The tremors had grown more noticeable of late; he wondered if Dr. Bloom's concerns about his health might indeed have some basis in fact.

A few shuffling footsteps sounded, and an exceedingly youthful voice sang out, "If you'd like, Judge Fisher, you can dictate your message and I'll copy it down."

Lawrence Fisher looked up to see that a man—little more than a boy, actually—had come from the back room of the telegraph office and was facing him across the counter. He did not recognize the clerk, but since being appointed circuit judge for the Abilene district,

Fisher was used to strangers knowing his name, and he gave it little thought.

Glancing down at the slip of paper on which he was writing, the judge shook his head and muttered, "I'll have it for you in a moment." Though he realized that the clerk would have to read the message in order to send the telegraph, Fisher did not want to say the words aloud, as if voicing what so far had only been in his thoughts would be akin to shouting it in the middle of Texas Street.

Fisher began to write more quickly, and the tremors subsided. "There," he pronounced at last, putting down the pencil and hastily folding the paper in half. "It is essential that this be sent at once—while I wait."

The clerk looked at him curiously, then gave a slight nod and took the slip of paper. Opening it, he scanned the words, saying, "It's quite long. It will cost at least—"

"I'll pay, whatever the cost." Fisher plunked down a pair of gold coins on the counter.

"All right," the clerk replied, shrugging his shoulders and starting to turn away. But when his gaze fell on the recipient's name and address at the top of the form, he spun around and exclaimed incredulously, "The governor?"

"I'd appreciate your keeping this in confidence." The judge produced another coin from his coat pocket, this one a twenty-dollar gold piece, and slid it across the counter toward the young man. "This is for your time . . . and for your discretion."

The clerk stared down at the gold coin, then up at the old man, his eyes filling with an eager light. "You needn't do that," he proclaimed in a hushed tone, his gaze dropping and locking on the coin as he placed a tentative hand on the counter only inches away. "We are trained to treat all correspondence with the utmost confidence."

"And so you do. And such conscientious service deserves its reward." So saying, Fisher placed a forefinger on the coin and slid it under the clerk's hand.

The young man closed his hand around the coin. "I'll see to your message at once," he declared. Slipping the money into his jacket pocket, he hurried into the back room.

A few moments later, the telegraph key began to sound. Fisher listened, not comprehending the meaning of the single and double clicks yet knowing they would create quite a stir in the halls of the state capitol. He only prayed that Governor Osborn would understand the seriousness of the message and would do what must be done. For if the state militia was not dispatched at once—if Marcus Donaghue and his henchmen were not stopped—there could be serious and ultimately deadly consequences not only for Judge Fisher but for every law-abiding citizen of Abilene.

As the telegraph key went silent, Fisher lifted his derby hat from the counter and placed it over his curling, silver-gray hair. Though it was warm this mid-June evening, he pulled his suit coat tight against some inner chill and headed toward the front door, not waiting for the clerk to return. He pulled open the door, cautiously stared out into the darkening street, and stepped outside.

Just as Judge Fisher was closing the door, the clerk returned to the main room. The light of the kerosene lamp glimmered on the pair of gold coins that the old man had left on the counter to pay for the telegraph. He had not even waited for his change, the clerk mused, his face breaking into a smile as he pocketed those two coins as well. The company would not miss the funds, he realized, since he had taken care to leave the transmitter turned off while pretending to tap out the message.

With his left hand the young man raised the paper on which the judge had written his message and stared at it. His other hand began to tap the outside of the pocket containing the money, and as he envisioned the additional coins of gold he would get for not sending the message, his smile broadened and he breathed the name "Donaghue."

Quickly he stuffed the slip of paper into his pocket along with the coins. Lowering the lantern wick to a dim glow, he snatched a set of keys from under the counter and hurried to the door. He opened it and stood looking up and down the street until he was certain Judge Fisher was gone. Then he stepped outside, pulled the door shut, and locked it. Dropping the keys into his jacket pocket, he hopped off the wooden boardwalk and went running down the dirt road.

Lawrence Fisher unlocked his office door in the wood-frame building on Texas Street across from the brick courthouse and stepped into its darkened interior. Closing the door and crossing to the large oak desk in the middle of the room, he opened a small metal box and fumbled with the wooden matchsticks inside. His fingers were shaking again, and he made an effort to still them as he withdrew one of the matches and closed the box. He jerked the match head across the rough metal cover, and it sparked once but failed to ignite. He struck it a little harder, and the stick snapped in half. Taking a few deep breaths, he took out a second match and repeated the process. On the third try, the match flared to life, the flame flickering as much from the shaking of his hand as from any movement of air.

Turning up the wick on the desk lamp, Fisher raised the glass chimney and touched the match to the kerosene-soaked wick. He lowered the chimney, blew out the match, and adjusted the flame until the room was filled with a soft, even light. Sighing, he circled the desk and sat in the stuffed leather desk chair, facing the front door.

It was an unassuming office—there was no secretary's desk or outer reception area—but it perfectly suited his needs. A pair of chairs faced the desk on the far side, with a floor-stand ashtray between them, and the only other items in the room were the law books that lined the high shelves along all but the front wall. Fisher had used this office for the private practice he had started upon his arrival in Abilene four years before, and he had continued to use it after being appointed district attorney less than a year later. Now that he was circuit judge, holding sessions both in Abilene and in neighboring towns, he was provided with chambers in the courthouse, yet he kept this office for his personal effects and as a private retreat.

Fisher reached out and touched the picture that faced him on the desk. "Molly," he whispered, still feeling the pain that had led him to seek a new life in Abilene following his wife's death. His finger traced the curve of her face, then moved down to the two inset photographs.

Fisher's gaze fell on the image of his eldest son, Judah—the Reverend Judah Fisher as he was known to Abilene's citizens. The judge was well pleased with his firstborn. At twenty-eight, Judah was a well-respected member of the Abilene community. It was Judah who had convinced his father to come to Abilene following Molly's death, offering him a place to stay at the parsonage of the Calvary Methodist Church. Though Lawrence Fisher had initially accepted the offer, a few weeks after arriving in Abilene he had rented this office space and had taken a room at a nearby boardinghouse, where he still lived.

Yes, Judah has made something of himself, he thought. *Now, if only he'd find a good woman and raise a family.*

As Fisher's gaze fell on the image of his younger son, twenty-four-year-old Cody, his smile grew more melancholy. The eyes that stared back at him were bright, intelligent, and full of life. Yet they betrayed the soul of a vagabond. Fisher knew that his second son had made a sincere effort to succeed in several trades, from farming to blacksmithing to stagecoach driving. When he had graduated from secondary school, he had even considered studying for the law, but one summer working for his father had put him off the idea. It was not just that he hated sitting indoors reading books; it was also that he and his father could barely last a minute without locking horns over even the most trivial issue.

"Just like your mother," the judge whispered, his smile returning, but only fleetingly. He had lost his fiery, passionate wife, and now he worried that he might be losing the boy who reminded him so much of her. He had no idea where Cody was. At last report he had been in Dodge City going by the name Matthew Cody, where a run-in with the notorious Josh Weaver had resulted in a gunfight, leaving Cody wounded and Weaver dead. Now Cody was on the run—not from the law, since his killing Weaver clearly had been a case of self-defense, but from those who would avenge the death or who sought to best the man who outdrew Josh Weaver.

With a gentle sigh, Fisher opened the center drawer of the desk and took out a piece of paper, which he placed in front of him. Removing the pen from a stand atop the desk, he opened the top of the inkwell and dipped the pen inside. In the upper right-hand corner he wrote Saturday, June 17, 1876, then in bold letters centered just under the date, he printed the words LAST WILL AND TESTAMENT.

As Fisher wrote, he tried to empty his thoughts of worry about his sons and the growing lawlessness in Abilene. The will was a simple document, leaving his few possessions and the balance of his bank account to his sons in equal shares, and he found himself pleasantly lost in the formal legal language—so much so that he did not hear the office door open and someone step inside. It was not until he had signed his name at the bottom that he glanced up and saw a shadowed figure standing just inside the doorway.

Fisher gave a slight start, his hand moving toward the desk drawer in which he kept a loaded revolver. But then he seemed to recognize the visitor, because his features relaxed and he rose to his feet, saying, "I didn't hear you enter. Is there something—?"

"I've brought a message from Marcus Donaghue," the visitor said tonelessly, raising his right arm.

It was then that Fisher saw the dull glimmer of gunmetal. He started to raise his hand, his lips fashioning the word *No!* as a shot rang out and a flare of light burst from the barrel of the revolver. His hand shattered from the impact of the bullet, spraying his face with blood. As his arm dropped loosely at his side, a second shot thundered in the small room, and he felt his chest explode and his knees buckle. He did not hear the third shot; it came only as a sharp thud in the center of his forehead and a blinding flash of white. He could feel himself falling. He never felt himself hit the ground.

Chapter Two

Jessica! Nicolette! Saints alive and the Devil be cursed! Move your feet and look alive, dammit! And you, Judith, stop going off in your own direction all the time!"

With a sharp flick of her wrists, the woman gave the team of four mules a taste of the leather reins across their backs. Their gait did not noticeably improve, but the woman seemed temporarily mollified.

"That's better," she pronounced. "Follow Elaine's example. Straight ahead, no dawdling, no looking back."

"But Elaine's the slowest of the lot," a young voice piped in from the back of the covered buckboard wagon. A head of tousled red hair atop a sea of soft-brown freckles appeared just over the woman's shoulder.

"A touch slower, perhaps," the woman admitted,

"but steady. And that's how we'll make it to Wichita —steady and reliable." She glanced back at the boy. "I thought you were asleep, Michael."

"I woke up," he replied, not mentioning that it was due in large part to her urgent protestations to the mule team.

"Would you like to ride with the other children?" she asked. "Perhaps with your sister?"

Michael climbed over the back of the seat and plopped down beside her. Leaning out over the right side of the wagon, he saw the other three wagons strung out behind them on the prairie, following at an equally leisurely pace. While this lead wagon was piled high with crates and carpetbags, he knew that the other wagons contained little more than children, the next in line being driven by his seventeen-year-old sister, Agnes, with the rear two under the command of a pair of boys in their midteens.

"I'll stay here a bit longer, if it's all right."

"But of course," she assured him with a smile.

The boy began to fidget on the seat. "How long until we get there?"

"To Wichita? Quite a few days. But we might make Abilene by nightfall."

"Not at this pace," he muttered.

"What's that? . . . A note of disapproval?" she said in a mocking tone. "And I suppose you could do better?"

"It's just that you're holding them to Elaine's pace, and she's so lazy. Judith is the fastest, and if you'd let up a bit on her reins—"

"Elaine, Judith . . . Judith, Elaine," she said in a singsongy voice. "So now you're a professional judge of muleflesh?" The woman's blue eyes betrayed the smile that she would not allow to touch her lips. She reached over and held out the reins. "I suppose you're also a veteran wagon master. Then here you go, young man. Let's see what a thirteen-year-old jehu can do."

The boy stared up nervously at the woman, uncertain whether or not to take her offer seriously.

"Go on, Michael," she insisted. "Show how it's done."

With a shrug, he placed his right hand over hers, slipping his fingers through the reins in the same manner in which she held them. When he had a secure grip, he nodded, and she released them. He repeated the process with the left ones, then leaned forward and took a deep breath.

"Better get going," she said. "They're beginning to move like molasses." And indeed, while they were speaking, the mules had slowed to a walk.

Michael jiggled the reins very slightly as he squinted and stared along the length of the leathers. Picking out the pair that went to the bit of the front-right mule, he worked them looser with his thumb and forefinger.

"Come on, now," the woman prodded. "If we don't get moving, the other wagons will crash into us."

The boy glanced up at her only briefly, but the mischief in his grin warned her to brace herself. As she grabbed the edge of the seat, he shook the reins and yelled, *"Hee yah!"* Standing up in the driver's box, he slapped the reins harder, all the while shouting, "Get your mule asses moving! You goddamn, good-f'nothing loafers!"

The animals leaped forward at the fierce tirade, the front-right mule taking the lead and setting a brisk pace.

"Atta girl, Judith!" Michael shouted, adding a gleeful, *"Damn!"* He felt himself being pulled back onto the bench, but not from the force of acceleration as

17

the wagon picked up speed. Instead it was the firm hand of the woman as she grabbed hold of the seat of his pants and yanked him down.

"What kind of talk is that, Michael Hirsch?" she demanded brusquely.

Michael avoided looking at her, concentrating instead on keeping the animals at a steady pace as he said cautiously, "It's just—"

"Never you mind," she declared. "You shouldn't be repeating everything you hear from the older children."

His smile returning, he remarked coyly, "Who said I learned it from the children?"

The woman stared down at him, her right eyebrow raising as she considered his comment. Then her eyes narrowed and she gave a slight frown. "I thought you were asleep."

"Father Thomas told us God never sleeps and can always hear what we're saying," Michael pointed out in as innocent a tone as he could muster. "Even what we're thinking."

"You should heed the good father's advice."

"But aren't you worried—?"

"Never you mind about me, young lad. I've a special dispensation for times like this." She gave a haughty toss of her head, then tucked a few stray locks of hair under the white cloth of her wimple.

"From the pope?" Michael asked incredulously.

"Not exactly. But when I took the vows of obedience, chastity, and poverty, I don't remember having to promise anything about profanity!"

"But the third commandment—"

"I wasn't taking the Lord's name in vain. I was merely offering a demonstration of the type of behavior young boys like you should avoid."

Michael knew there was no point in arguing with her. He glanced downward and said, "Yes, Sister Laurel."

She looked at him for a long moment, a broad smile spreading from her lips all the way to her eyes. Patting his shoulder, she added, "Just as you've been demonstrating the proper way to drive a mule team. It seems we can learn from each other. Perhaps I can give it a try?"

His expression brightening, Michael handed her the reins and showed her how he had adjusted the tension on the lines. After a few minutes, Sister Laurel had the wagon going at a lively pace—so much so that Michael had to caution her not to leave the other children in the dust. She settled back on the seat and hummed a lovely French lullaby, the long, black folds of her Dominican habit fluttering in the gentle Kansas breeze.

The curious little wagon train continued to roll west the final few miles to Abilene, from where it would turn due south eighty miles to Wichita. The afternoon was dry and dusty, the mules far more agreeable than Sister Laurel would have dared to hope, given the relentless heat. It was as if they could sense that the trail was nearing an end, and they were pulling hard for the finish.

"Ah, but there's still the run to Wichita," she chided them gently, at which Elaine shook her head stubbornly as if to say, "We will see about that!"

"Is that Abilene up ahead?" Michael Hirsch asked, pointing at something in the distance.

Shielding her eyes with one hand, Sister Laurel squinted into the sun. "No, I don't think so. But there's something there, all right. Looks like a dust cloud." Lowering her hand, she jiggled the reins, picking up the pace slightly. After a moment she said, "It's moving closer. From the speed, I'd say it's riders on horseback."

"Want me to get the rifle?" the boy asked eagerly.

"No need for that. You can climb in back, if you're frightened."

Michael squared his shoulders and pouted. "I'm not afraid. I just wanted to help."

"Then how about taking charge of these mules?"

Sister Laurel handed Michael the reins. As he took control of the animals, she stared ahead again, trying to make out what was coming through the heat waves and swirling dust. As the objects grew larger, she was able to discern four horsemen, riding two abreast and coming on fast. It could be anyone, she realized, from fellow travelers to soldiers, yet something in her stomach warned her that these men were up to no good.

A minute later Sister Laurel could make out the lead riders. The one on the left was bearded and tall, his dark hair worn loose and shaggy, a sombrero hanging behind him from a cord around his neck. He seemed a burly, hulking figure dressed in somber black, and despite his being at a distance and on horseback, Sister Laurel guessed he was over six feet tall and weighed well over two hundred pounds.

In contrast, the man to the right was small and compact, his blond hair trim and his face clean-shaven. He wore a low-slung holster over his tan pants, with a matching beige Stetson and muslin shirt. Everything about his demeanor suggested confidence, and he sat perfectly straight in the saddle, though he was still a full head shorter than his companion. He seemed a natural leader, and Sister Laurel had no doubt that he was the one from whom the others took their orders.

Sister Laurel slipped her right hand into a pocket hidden along the seam of her black habit. The bottom had been cut away, and she felt along her hip until her fingers closed around the butt of a short-barreled Smith & Wesson .38, which rested fully loaded in a small holster strapped to her leg. The revolver had a double-action mechanism; a single pull of the trigger both cocked and fired the weapon. To protect against accidental firing, there was a safety latch that locked the trigger, and now she pushed the lever forward, disengaging the safety. Finally she unsnapped the leather strap that secured the revolver in the holster.

Though she would never use such a weapon to protect herself, Sister Laurel was fully capable of pulling the trigger should the lives of the orphans in her charge be threatened.

Easing her hand out of the pocket, the nun placed her arm on Michael's shoulder and told him to pull up. When the wagon halted, the four riders slowed their horses and came the final hundred yards at a walk. As Sister Laurel had expected, the short man in front was the one to raise his hand and signal the others to stop.

While the other riders sat their horses in a line three abreast, the leader kneed his mount forward and approached the left side of the wagon. "Whatcha got here, Sister?" he asked, his tone impertinent but not threatening.

"We're on our way to Wichita," she replied tonelessly.

"What about them others?" He nodded toward where the other three wagons were just now pulling to a halt in a line behind Sister Laurel's wagon.

"They're with me," she said.

The man lifted himself in the saddle and peered at the other wagons, only to see a dozen or more young faces peering back at him. "Just a buncha young pups. Where's their sires and bitches?" He grinned at what he must have thought was an attempt at humor.

"They are orphans, Mr. . . . ?"

"Now ain't that a shame," the man drawled without divulging his name.

"As I was saying, we're going to Wichita to start an orphanage. If you and your men would be so good as to—"

"Come on, Kincaid," called one of the men. "We're supposed to be in Junction City before—"

"Shut your face, Cooper," the man named Kincaid cut him off. "There's plenty of time for us to show a little hospitality to the good sister here and her young'uns."

Kneeing his horse again, Kincaid rode partway toward the second wagon in line. Seated behind the reins was an attractive young woman still in her teens, with long red hair that had been pinned up earlier in the day but was a bit tousled just now, much of it falling loosely to her shoulders. The girl beside her wore a sunbonnet and could not have been more than eight or nine, and at least three other children huddled behind the wagon seat, looking out through the opening in the wagon cover.

Kincaid turned his horse and headed to the lead wagon. "That one back there don't look like no orphan," he remarked. "Hell, she's pretty enough to be makin' babies herself. What d'ya think, boys?"

Michael jumped up, his knuckles white with rage as he declared, "You leave my sister alone!" Sister Laurel took his hand and eased him onto the seat.

"Oh, she's your sister, is she, boy?" Kincaid moved his mount up alongside the wagon. "I thought this one here"—he pointed at Sister Laurel—"was the only sister around. That pretty filly back there sure don't look like no nun." Chuckling, he turned his sharp-featured, angular face toward Sister Laurel. "No, Sister, that one's too pretty to be a nun. But I hope she's still a virgin like you." As his laughter deepened, it grew more malevolent.

"Mind your tongue!" Sister Laurel demanded, still holding Michael in place with her right hand but wondering if perhaps she should be holding her Smith & Wesson instead.

A shadow seemed to pass over Kincaid's face, erasing any trace of a smile. "This ain't no church, Sister, and we ain't no choirboys, so don't tell us what to do." Glancing at his men, he said, "Bring that pretty one over here, Jeb."

"Sure thing," replied the big, dark-haired man who had ridden beside Kincaid. He started his mount forward and headed around the right side of the wagon.

Suddenly Michael gave such a high-pitched shriek that Jeb's horse reared and nearly threw him. Michael then yanked his arm from Sister Laurel's grasp and leaped at the man. But he had misjudged the distance and slammed the ground hard on his hands and knees. Staggering to his feet, he charged the big man who was daring to touch his sister.

Jeb's revolver was in his hand even before his horse came down on all fours, but instead of firing, he slapped the reins and kicked the horse. The spooked animal leaped forward, barreling into the boy and spinning him aside. As the horse continued on past, Jeb leaned out and swung the revolver, catching

Michael on the side of the head and knocking him senseless to the ground.

It happened so quickly that Sister Laurel had no time to react and could only gasp as Michael fell facedown on the dirt, his left cheek smeared with blood. Just then she remembered the gun holstered to her leg, and she reached for her pocket as she spun around on the seat—only to find herself facing the barrel of Kincaid's revolver.

"You just sit steady," Kincaid commanded in a surprisingly soft tone, apparently not having seen the checked movement of her hand toward her skirt.

Though Michael's sister was a good thirty yards away, the girl had seen what happened and was running toward him, seemingly unaware of the rider in front of her as she shouted Michael's name and raced toward where he was lying.

Jeb holstered his gun and intercepted the young woman. Deftly turning his horse in front of her, he leaned down from the saddle and swooped her off her feet. She flailed her arms and legs, as if running in air, then suddenly turned on the burly man, swinging her arms as she tried to scratch his hairy face. Jeb nearly lost his grip around her waist, but as he tightened his hold he kept grinning and leering, as though he thoroughly enjoyed having her put up a fight. Finally he managed to turn her around to face him, one of his arms pinning her to him, the other clamping her wrists behind her back. All she could do was arch her back and twist her head away as he tried to kiss her lips.

As she struggled weakly against the man, the sound of young children crying could be heard from the other wagons, while a couple of the older boys ventured down from their seats and cautiously approached.

"The boy . . ." Sister Laurel nodded toward where Michael was lying without movement on the ground. "Let me help the boy."

"He's best left lyin' right where he is," Kincaid replied. "Won't get himself in any more fool trouble that way." His smile returned. "And he won't see what me'n the boys have planned for his big sister."

"Leave Agnes alone," the nun pleaded. "She's only—"

"She's old enough. So just keep quiet, and maybe we'll be real nice and take her along, so the young'uns won't have to see pretty Agnes take her vows." He chortled wickedly.

"Please . . . she's so young. I beg you—take me, if you must. But leave her alone."

"You?" Kincaid asked incredulously. "A nun?"

"I'm a woman," she declared simply.

"Hardly. And past your prime." He peered at her more closely, then waved his revolver toward her face. "It's hard to tell behind all that . . . stuff. But you must be forty, pushin' fifty. Hell, you passed your prime the day you put on that outfit and gave up bein' a woman!"

Still holding his revolver on Sister Laurel, Kincaid backed his horse away from the wagon and called out, "C'mon, Jeb! Throw her over the saddle! We're takin' her with us!"

Sister Laurel waited until Kincaid was looking away and then eased her hand toward her gun. But as she sought the pocket of her habit, the sharp boom of a rifle rocked the air. Kincaid and the other two riders fought to control their startled animals, while Jeb released Agnes's wrists and clawed at his revolver. Agnes immediately pushed hard against his chest and broke his grip around her waist. Dropping to the ground, she stumbled, nearly fell, then hiked up her long dress and ran for her brother.

A second rifle shot sounded, and the four men turned in the direction of the gunfire—the rear of the small wagon train—expecting to see one of the teenage boys wielding a rifle. Instead they saw a rider come out from behind the last wagon, the Winchester in his hands pointed upward but ready to be brought into action.

Kincaid signaled his men to hold their fire as the rider approached at a walk. Though he was confident their four guns could easily handle the man, he knew a Winchester was capable of considerable damage before the gunman could be brought down. And Kincaid was not eager to die. Also, the rifleman had not shot at anyone but had fired into the air as a warning. It would be best to determine what the man wanted before risking further gunplay.

Sister Laurel had climbed down from the wagon unnoticed and was kneeling beside Michael and Agnes, her right hand never far from the false pocket of her skirt. The boy's eyes were fluttering open as Agnes held his head cradled in her lap. Sister Laurel gently touched the gash at his left temple and then dabbed away some of the blood with her sleeve. After determining that he was only dazed, she looked up as the man with the rifle approached. He must have been riding toward Abilene and in the confusion had come upon the wagon train from the rear without being seen.

She watched as the man pulled to a halt not far from where Jeb was sitting his horse. The stranger was dressed in a plain blue work shirt and denim pants, which were tucked inside his calf-high riding boots. His tan, flat-crowned hat partially obscured his face, yet Sister Laurel could see that he was clean-shaven, save for a drooping brown mustache. The sandy-colored hair that showed from under his hat was somewhat lighter than his mustache, and it was touched with gray at the temples. The man had a strong yet youthful appearance, and she guessed that he was at least forty.

Something seemed odd about the man, though, and then abruptly Sister Laurel realized that he was not wearing a holstered revolver.

The man sat quite tall in the saddle as he expertly controlled the animal with his legs, his hands cradling the rifle in a nonthreatening but ready manner. He seemed totally unconcerned about the four revolvers that were being held on him. Rather, he took his time as he eyed the big, dark-haired man on the nearest horse and then the other three men bunched in a group beside the lead wagon.

After it became clear that the rifleman was not going to speak first, Kincaid lowered his gun, leaned on his pommel, and said, "Hello, stranger." His lips pulled into a thin, cautious smile.

The rifleman stared at the short, blond-haired man a long moment without reply. Finally he gave another glance at Jeb, who was the closest threat, then turned to Sister Laurel. "What's the trouble, Sister?" he asked in a deep and calm voice.

Sister Laurel stood up and brushed off her skirt, using the movement to slip her right hand casually into her pocket. Struggling to steady her voice, she replied, "These . . . gentlemen . . . were thinking to have a little sport—at our expense."

"Anyone else hurt?" he asked, nodding toward the boy, who was already rising to a sitting position.

As the nun shook her head, Kincaid cut in, "We didn't hurt no one. Fool kid run in front of Jeb's horse, is all."

The rifleman eyed Jeb closely, then said, "A big man like you ought to watch where you're going . . . and who you're laying your filthy hands on."

Jeb's hand immediately tensed, his finger tightening on the trigger. But he held back and glanced uncertainly at Kincaid, confirming that it was the shorter blond man who was in charge. When Jeb again looked over at the rifleman, the Winchester was leveled at his chest.

Kincaid leaned forward in the saddle. "And who're you to be talkin' to us like that?" he demanded.

"The name's Luke Travis," he announced, his eyes holding steady on the big man named Jeb, who seemed unnerved upon hearing the name. "And I'd be right appreciative if you boys left peaceably."

There was a mutter of recognition between the two riders who sat their horses just beyond the blond-haired man. He, too, seemed aware of the name, for he sat up straighter in the saddle and slowly nodded, all the while resting his revolver on the pommel, its barrel pointed away from the rifleman. "Abilene ain't your town, Travis," he finally said. "And this ain't none of your affair."

"Let's just say I'm making it my business. Now ride on out of here—or answer to this Winchester."

Kincaid noted that Jeb had lowered his revolver and was shifting nervously in the saddle. He could not see the two men behind him, but from their mutterings he had no doubt that they were just as apprehensive as Jeb.

Forcing a smile, Kincaid said, "We sure don't want none of the young'uns hurt." Twisting toward the two men behind him, he added, "Maybe we'd best be movin' along, boys."

Turning around in the saddle, Kincaid drew back his hand to holster his revolver. At the last instant, he whipped the gun up to fire. Even more quickly, Travis swung his Winchester to the left and pulled the trigger. The two shots were almost simultaneous, though Kincaid's fired harmlessly into the air as the rifle slug tore through his upper arm and his revolver went sailing out of his hand.

Before Jeb or the others could react, Travis had levered another cartridge into the chamber and was again pointing the Winchester at Jeb's chest. "You'll be next," Travis declared evenly.

Jeb again looked to Kincaid for direction, but the shorter man was busy clutching his bleeding arm and trying to steady his horse as he muttered a string of oaths. Jeb turned then to the other men, who seemed just as uncertain as he—and just as unwilling to go up against Luke Travis's Winchester. After a moment's hesitation Jeb slowly holstered his revolver, with the other men following suit.

"Let's get out of here," he muttered, turning his horse to ride away.

Having regained control of his horse, Kincaid struggled to calm his anger as he scowled at his men. It was clear that they did not have the stomach to back him—at least not here and now. Deciding to leave things as they were for the moment, he glowered at Travis and said, "I told you before that Abilene ain't your town, Travis. You'd do best to keep on ridin' to Wichita, where you still got a few friends." With that he wheeled the horse in a half circle and galloped away, his men close behind him as they headed back the way they had come, thoughts of riding to Junction City all but forgotten.

As the dust cleared, Sister Laurel helped Michael to his feet, while Agnes ran to the rear of the wagon and retrieved a small cooking pot, which she filled from one of the water barrels strapped to the side.

"Are you all right?" the nun asked as she led Michael toward the wagon.

The boy was shaking his head groggily and trying to smile, but his faltering steps indicated that he was still quite dizzy.

"Let's get you up on the seat so I can wash that cut," she told him, inspecting the gash at his left temple.

"I'm f-fine," he managed to mutter, then his smile faded and he added, "I'm . . . sorry."

Sister Laurel pulled the boy close and patted the back of his head. "You were so brave," she whispered. "You put us all to shame."

Michael pulled his head away and looked up into the older woman's clear blue eyes. His smile slowly returned.

"Now, let's get you up on that wagon," Sister Laurel continued, and the boy nodded. But when he reached for the side of the wagon, he started to swoon and had to stop and breathe deeply for a moment.

A shadow passed over Michael, and he looked up to see the tall, sandy-haired rifleman standing over him. "You'd best take it easy for a while, son," Travis said. "That's quite a blow you took. It would've put me down for a week." With that he reached forward, took hold of the boy under the arms, and effortlessly hoisted him up onto the seat.

"Thank you, Mr. . . . Travis, is it?" Sister Laurel asked.

"Luke Travis, ma'am . . . uh, Sister."

"Sister is fine," she assured him as she climbed up beside Michael and started cleaning his wound using the water and a piece of cloth brought by Agnes. "Or ma'am, if you prefer. Just not madam, because I intend to open a house of *healthy* repute. Actually, I'm on my way to Wichita to found an orphanage."

"It's a beautiful city."

"So I've been told, which is why I decided to bring the children there."

"Then you've never been to Wichita?" Travis asked.

"No. But I'm a Dominican, and our order has long wanted to expand our work in Kansas. At least that's what my superiors in Boston told me. I personally suspect it was just a plot to keep me far away and out of trouble."

Travis grinned and nodded. "Trouble does seem to have a way of tracking you down."

Sister Laurel dipped the cloth into the pot of water and looked west across the prairie. "You mean those four?" She frowned. "I've handled worse. But I never doubted that God would pull us through once again." Suddenly she looked with concern at Travis. "I don't mean to discount what you did for us. It's just that God has a way of making these things work out—like bringing you along right when he did."

Travis walked over to where his horse was standing and took up the trailing reins. As he led the animal to the wagon, he remarked, "They say that God works in mysterious ways. Well, if there is a God—and I don't mean to speak poorly of your chosen calling . . . it's just that I'm not sure I understand what his purpose in all this might be."

Sister Laurel looked at him a long moment, trying to read the sorrow that was evident in his eyes. Finally she lifted the wet cloth from the pan of water and continued wiping Michael's face.

"I'm sorry if I sound bitter, ma'am," Travis said, placing his boot in the stirrup and lifting himself into the saddle. "But it was the recent death of my wife—not divine providence—that led me to be riding along this road today."

"I'm so sorry. If there's anything I can do . . ."

"It wasn't unexpected. At least she's at peace." He waved his hand as if warding off painful memories. "I'll be fine. But I would be grateful if you'd let me accompany you into Abilene."

"You don't have to trouble yourself, Mr. Travis," Sister Laurel insisted. "I'm sure they won't try anything more. Certainly not in town."

"You'd be doing me a favor. The road gets awfully lonesome, and being around all these bright young faces will keep me from dwelling on the past."

Sister Laurel did not for a moment think that Luke Travis was making the offer out of concern for his own peace of mind. But though she was convinced the four gunmen would not try such a foolish stunt again, she had to admit that she would feel safer with Travis riding alongside. And it would certainly calm the children's fears.

"We'd be glad to have you along," she said, placing the pot of water in Michael's lap and taking up the reins.

"I left a packhorse beyond the last wagon. I'll go get it and then take up the lead." He pulled on the reins and started to turn his horse.

Agnes had been standing alongside the wagon all this time, and now she stepped forward and raised a hand to stop the rider. "I . . . I want to thank you," she said.

Travis smiled and tipped his hat.

"Mr. Travis," Michael suddenly called out, and Travis turned in the saddle to face him. "How come you're not wearing a gun?" the boy asked.

Travis patted the butt of the Winchester in the saddle scabbard. "I've got all the protection I need right here."

"But what about a revolver?"

"I used to wear one. But that was a long time ago."

"In Wichita?" Agnes put in. "Those men said something about you being from Wichita."

"I lived there once. But that was another lifetime."

"Did you shoot anyone back then, too?" Michael asked, his eyes eager with anticipation.

"Michael!" Sister Laurel exclaimed. She turned to Travis. "I'm so sorry—"

"It's all right," he said, smiling at the boy. "I didn't wear a gun to shoot people, Michael. I wore it to keep them from shooting each other. And, yes, sometimes I had to do some shooting myself. But I wore a badge."

"A sheriff?" Michael said excitedly.

"I was town marshal of Wichita." Travis stared off into the distance. "But as I said, that was a long time ago." He let up on the reins and kneed the horse forward. "A hell of a long time ago." Kicking the animal harder, he rode off toward the rear of the train.

Chapter Three

As the four wagons moved across the prairie under the final rays of the setting sun, droning mosquitoes, fist-sized darning needles, and millions of tiny black gnats were drawn to the white canvas covers. The insects, in turn, attracted a disorganized legion of small hungry bats, which swooped across the backs of the mules and dove at the canvas, only to veer away inches before impact. From inside the wagons, the children could hear the flutter of wings and at times could make out a faint shadow bobbing across the surface of the cloth. The boys and girls huddled together, not in fear but in awe of how massive and endless the great American prairie had proven to be.

The clomp of hooves, clatter of wheels, and incessant flapping of wings was broken by the deep voice of the friendly rifleman—the marshal of Wichita, some of the older boys were saying—as he rode to the opening at the back of each wagon and announced that Abilene was in sight on the horizon. The children quickly gathered behind the driver's seats and peered across the darkening landscape to the twinkling lights in the distance.

For fifteen minutes they watched the lights grow brighter, the buildings more distinct. This was a fair-sized city, they could tell, smaller than Topeka but larger than Ogden or Moonlight or a number of other trail towns through which they had passed. The children hoped it would mean a longer stay—perhaps a day or two—and a chance to play on the hard earth for a while. For certain it meant a visit to the local general store, where each child would be allowed three cents' worth of candy.

As the city grew larger, the hovering insects and swooping bats—even the sparkling city lights—were replaced by a spectacularly colorful array of horehound mints, jelly beans, and licorice sticks, which danced in front of the children's eyes—all the children except Michael Hirsch, that is. Ever since leaving Philadelphia, he had sacrificed the candy so that he could hoard the pennies they were given in each major city. One day he would have enough money to buy himself a pearl-handled Colt Peacemaker revolver— like the one he had seen advertised in the *Godfrey Arms Catalogue,* the picture from which he kept tucked in the bottom of his suitcase. As far as Michael was concerned, this journey could go on forever—or at least until they had passed through enough cities to provide him with the twenty dollars he would need for his purchase.

The dirt road widened and grew better defined as it passed alongside the freestanding buildings at the outskirts of town. Most were clapboard single-story structures that appeared to be private dwellings, though several were brick or stone two-story buildings. There were no streetlamps as yet, the only light spilling from the houses along the way. The taller buildings invariably were dark, undoubtedly warehouses or businesses that already had closed for the evening.

The wagons rolled deeper into town, where the buildings began to be clustered in twos and threes, occasionally with a wide porch or wooden boardwalk connecting them. Soon most of the gaps filled in, until there was a nearly unbroken line of one- and two-story buildings that resembled a crosscut saw with a few of the teeth missing.

Ahead on the right was an open lot with a substantial brick building centered on the lawn. "The courthouse," Travis told Sister Laurel as they passed. Just beyond the next intersection, the street was lit with lamps, indicating the heart of the business district. As the wagons crossed into the light, a pair of smartly painted signs at the corner identified the crossroad as Buckeye Street and the one on which they had been riding as Texas Street.

Here Abilene's main street proved to be a bustling thoroughfare, filled this Tuesday night with carriages, horses, and pedestrians. Most buildings were two or even three stories high, with several boasting lantern-lit signs proclaiming such establishments as the Great Western Store and the Old Fruit Saloon. The wide-plank boardwalk, several blocks long on both sides of the street, was well planned and maintained, providing easy and level passage between buildings. Covered for much of its length, it was a welcome relief from the usual arrangement wherein each business had its own porch, often forcing people to step down into the muddy street between buildings.

As the wagons headed through the business district, Luke Travis obtained directions to the nearest doctor's office, located on the left side of the street beside the Grand Palace Hotel. Just after crossing the intersection of Mulberry Street, Travis saw the hotel's rickety sign—which fronted an establishment that was neither grand nor palatial—and he signaled Sister Laurel to pull the wagons in front of the building just beyond the hotel.

The office was a small two-story cottage that was a curious contrast to the rest of the street. Rather than sitting up against the boardwalk cheek by jowl with the other buildings, it was set back about fifteen yards, with long flower beds lining a brick walk that led directly to the street. There was a break in the boardwalk for the length of the yard, and the house even boasted a grass alleyway on either side, which in daytime would allow some light to penetrate alongside the hotel to the left and Orion's Tavern to the right.

While the other lamps along Texas Street were attached to the edge of the boardwalk canopy, the one in front of the doctor's office sat atop a post at the end of the walk. Suspended from a wrought-iron arm that hung out from the post was a neatly lettered black-and-white sign that in bold letters proclaimed: Dr. Levi Wright, Physician & Surgeon. A smaller sign had been added below the main one and in far smaller lettering read: Dr. Aileen Bloom, Physician.

"A woman . . ." Travis murmured in surprise.

"Yes! Isn't it delightful?" Sister Laurel declared as she climbed down from the driver's seat.

"But I feel fine," Michael insisted, embarrassed by the attention that had been showered on him following the run-in with the man named Kincaid and his three followers. "I don't need a doctor." He held the cloth compress away from his forehead to show that the wound was no longer bleeding.

"We'll let Dr. Wright or Dr. Bloom decide about that," Sister Laurel replied.

Michael looked around uncomfortably and saw his sister, Agnes, approaching after having halted and put on the brake of the second wagon in line. "Tell Sister Laurel I'm fine," he pleaded with her. "I don't need a doctor."

Agnes frowned slightly. "But you do, Michael. You took quite a knocking, and that cut needs proper attention."

Squirming and looking for some other excuse, Michael noticed the lower sign on the nearby post. "But that one's not a real doctor. She's a woman."

Placing her hands on her hips, the nun tilted her head and squinted, her lips drawing into a tight, humorless smile. "I suppose women don't know anything about healing? If that's the case, then we've come to the right place. No one better than a quack to put an end to your clucking!"

As Sister Laurel held out a hand to help him down from the coach, Michael sought out Luke Travis, who was just returning from having tied his saddle horse and packhorse to a hitching post by the neighboring tavern. With a mournful look, he beseeched, "Mr. Travis . . . ?"

"I'm sorry, son," Travis said, shrugging his shoulders and trying to suppress a smile. "Between your sister, the good nun, and this here Dr. Bloom, I'm afraid you and I are heavily outgunned. You'd best take your medicine and save your energy for a battle you can win."

Michael frowned and gave an overly dramatic sigh.

Pointedly ignoring Sister Laurel's outstretched hand, he climbed over the side of the wagon and dropped to the ground. Without waiting for either woman, he shuffled up the walk and onto the porch of the doctor's office, where he stood looking dejected as Travis and the two women followed.

Travis lifted the brass knocker and rapped on the door, then after a few moments knocked louder. On the third try they heard what sounded like hurried footsteps approaching. The door creaked open, and a tall woman wearing a white smock over her brown dress appeared in the doorway. She was far younger and more attractive than Travis had expected, with soft brown eyes and long brown hair that was pulled up in a sweep. A few strands had come loose and hung alongside her face, framing and accentuating her high cheekbones. She could not be much older than thirty, and Travis wondered if she was Dr. Aileen Bloom or perhaps the physician's younger sister or even daughter.

"Yes . . . ?" the woman asked as she peered out.

"It's the boy," Travis began, and Sister Laurel prodded Michael forward. The woman was already opening the door wider as Travis continued, "He took a blow to the temple from the barrel of a revolver. There's a nasty gash, maybe a concussion. Perhaps Dr. Wright could—"

"Dr. Wright is out on call. I'm Dr. Bloom." The woman stepped out and gave the wound a cursory examination, then glanced over at Travis, as if trying to gauge his character. "A concussion, you say?" Her tone was somewhat dubious.

"He was knocked unconscious for a few minutes."

"Did you do this?" she asked him matter-of-factly.

"Saints, no!" Sister Laurel proclaimed. "Mr. Travis came to Michael's assistance. It was some local ruffians—"

"It doesn't matter," the woman said with a wave of her hand. "This needs attending to right away."

Grasping the boy's shoulder, she ushered him in but stopped just inside the doorway and looked down at him. For the first time she smiled, and her expression held an ineffable calmness that soothed the young boy's fears. "My name is Dr. Bloom. And you must be quite a tough young man, Michael. After such a blow, most men would have to be carried here—and they'd probably need a bottle of whiskey and a host of stitches. But it looks like I'll only have to clean and dress the wound. No needles, no bitter medicine. Maybe just a lemon drop or two . . . to put the smile back on your lips." She cuffed his chin, and he started to grin.

Turning to the others on the porch, she said, "If you'll come into the waiting room . . ."

She led them into a narrow room to the right of the front entryway. On the long right-hand wall were two windows that overlooked the front yard. Under the windows, a sofa and a pair of chairs faced three doors, the center one leading to the dispensary, the outer ones to the examining rooms.

The doctor motioned toward the sofa and chairs. "I think Michael and I can take care of this on our own. Can't we, Michael?"

He stood a little taller and nodded.

"Good. Then wait for me in that room on the right. I'm just finishing with a patient in the other examining room." She watched as Michael entered the room. Then she turned to Travis and the other women. "Now, if you'll just wait out here while I see to my patients . . ." She turned, opened the door to the examining room on the left, and disappeared inside.

"Do you think he'll be all right?" Agnes asked as she sat down on the sofa beside Sister Laurel.

"Everything will be fine," the older woman assured her.

Luke Travis sat for a few moments on one of the upholstered chairs, but then he stood and soon found himself pacing the room, holding his hat in his hand. He was not sure what it was that was troubling him, but he sensed something disquieting in the air—something more than the unsettling odors of a doctor's office. Stepping to the door of the room the doctor had entered, he thought he heard a low moan and wondered what was going on inside. Then suddenly he recognized what it was that was disturbing him—and indeed it was an odor, though not that of chemicals and medicine. It was the smell of sweat and horseflesh—the smell of a man who had been riding hard in the saddle. And though Travis had been on the trail for many a day, it was not himself that he was smelling.

Travis heard a doorknob turn and a door swing open somewhere down the hall. Crossing to the waiting room entrance, he glanced down the hall and saw the doctor and her patient step through a side doorway that led directly from the examining room to the hall. His suspicion was confirmed. With Dr. Bloom was the short, blond-haired man Travis had been forced to shoot in the arm. His right sleeve had been cut away, and a tight bandage circled his upper arm, which rested in a wide sling.

The man did not notice Travis standing in the waiting-room doorway. He was nodding to the doctor as she gave him a few final instructions and then reentered the examining room, leaving him alone in the hall. Finally the man turned to leave the office. It was then that he saw Luke Travis stepping out into the hallway.

The man's eyes narrowed, but he did not speak.

"Having a little trouble with that arm, Kincaid?" Travis asked with a thin smile.

"I thought I told you to steer clear of Abilene," Kincaid said coldly.

"I heard what you said. But it's not your town."

"The hell it ain't!" The man's right hand jerked as if going for the gun in his holster. But a spasm of pain must have shot through his upper arm, for he winced and grasped his elbow with his good left hand.

"You'd best let it rest up," Travis said mockingly.

"And you'd best get outta town." Kincaid glanced around, as if feeling naked without his men to back him up. "Next time I won't be alone," he declared.

"Next time I won't aim at your arm."

Kincaid glowered at Travis a long moment and then abruptly turned and stormed out of the building, slamming the door behind him.

Travis stared at the closed door. His own hand instinctively reached for his right hip, seeking the cool comfort of gunmetal. Instead his hand touched denim, and suddenly he, too, felt very naked indeed.

When at last Dr. Bloom and Michael Hirsch emerged from the examining room, Luke Travis was again seated in the waiting room, and he and the women quickly stood.

"My, don't you look dashing!" the nun declared upon seeing the bandage above his left eye.

"Of course he does," Agnes agreed, swelling with

pride. "He's my brother!" Her comment was met by an uneasy shrug from Michael, who looked down in embarrassment.

"He'll be fine," the doctor assured them. "But I'd like him to get some rest in bed. If I could see him the morning after next . . ."

"We'd been planning to push on to Wichita," Sister Laurel explained.

With a look of concern, Dr. Bloom said, "I suggest putting that off for a couple of days. The cut is no problem, but the concussion—"

"Of course we will," the nun interjected. "A few days in Abilene would do us all good."

"Michael tells me you are traveling with seventeen children. Are the others outside?"

"Yes. In four wagons."

"I'd love to meet them. Perhaps when you bring Michael back I could give each a quick examination." Seeing Sister Laurel's hesitant expression, she quickly added, "Of course there will be no charge. I'd just like you to know that all of Abilene is not like the men you encountered today."

"That's so gracious of you. I'd be delighted if you'd examine the children. But I insist on paying for Michael—"

"We'll talk about that the day after tomorrow. About ten o'clock would be fine." So saying, she led the way into the hall and opened the front door, and the group stepped out onto the porch. After they had taken their leave, she called, "Do you know where you will be staying?"

"I suppose we'll head just beyond town and make camp."

"No, I'd like Michael in a warm house and a real bed. Perhaps he should stay here, and—"

"We've imposed on you enough. I'll see to it he has a room at one of the hotels." Sister Laurel glanced somewhat disparagingly at the dilapidated hotel next door. "Perhaps if you could recommend someplace suitable . . ."

All at once the doctor snapped her fingers and said, "Judah Fisher!" She nodded, as if agreeing with her own thought. "Yes, the Reverend Fisher would be delighted to have you as guests. He is a fine young man who is pastor of the Methodist church." Suddenly she turned to Sister Laurel and looked her up and down, almost as if she had not noticed the woman's garb before. "But of course you're a Catholic. Perhaps you and the children would feel uncomfortable—"

"The children come from a variety of religious backgrounds. And like this Reverend Fisher, I am a Christian first, a Catholic second."

Dr. Bloom smiled. "Excellent. You'll find Judah quite delightful, and he always opens his home to travelers." She stepped out onto the porch and led them down the walk to the street, where she pointed in the direction the wagons had been heading. "Just continue two blocks to Elm Street, then turn right across the tracks and stay on Elm until it jags around Mud Creek. You'll see the church on a slight rise to the left, with the parsonage at the back. It's quite large and can accommodate all of you. Just tell Judah I sent you."

"You've been so kind." Sister Laurel offered her hand.

"There's just one thing," the doctor said, shaking the nun's hand. "I had almost forgotten, but Judah's father was killed a few days ago. I'm certain he'd still want you to come, but I thought you should be aware of the situation."

"Thank you. I'll speak with him, and if it seems we'll be in the way, we'll find other accommodations." Sister Laurel turned to Travis. "And thank you, as well, Mr. Travis. We are deeply indebted to you."

"I'll be glad to escort you to the church," Travis began, but she cut him off with a shake of her head.

"You've done more than enough. We'll be fine now."

Agnes helped her brother up onto the seat of the lead wagon and then headed over to her own. As soon as Sister Laurel had climbed aboard, Travis said, "I'm planning to ride on to Wichita in a day or two. Perhaps I could accompany you."

"It isn't necessary . . . but the children and I would certainly enjoy your company."

"Then I'll look in on you at the church." He tipped his hat.

"Thank you again," Sister Laurel said, taking up the reins and releasing the brake. "Both of you."

With a slap of the reins, she started the wagon down Texas Street. Luke Travis and Dr. Bloom stood at the end of the walk, watching as the four wagons clattered down the road.

"Mr. Travis . . ." Dr. Bloom said when the wagons had disappeared from sight.

He turned to her. "Yes?"

"I want to apologize for what I said earlier. It was wrong to suggest you might have been the one—"

"You had no way of knowing. I'm pleased you had the courage to speak as you did."

She gave a slight laugh. "Perhaps it's because there was a nun present. And you aren't wearing a gun."

"Then you should have realized I couldn't have hit the boy with the barrel of a revolver."

"I hadn't thought of that. Again, I'm sorry."

"Don't be, Dr. Bloom."

"You must call me Aileen."

"Aileen," he repeated softly and smiled.

"I hope to see you again before you leave for Wichita," Aileen said casually.

Appearing a little uncomfortable, Travis replied, "That would be nice." He tipped his hat. "Good evening, ma'am."

"That's Aileen, Mr. Travis," she corrected him.

"If you will call me Luke."

"Luke Travis . . ." Her smile faded somewhat, as if the name had brought to mind some disquieting thought.

Unaware of her reaction, Travis walked to the nearby hitching post. As he was undoing the reins of the packhorse and tying them to the back of his saddle, he sensed someone approaching and turned to see that Aileen had come closer.

"Luke," she said hesitantly, her eyes drifting to the rifle in the saddle scabbard. "Is that the gun that shot Bridger Kincaid?" When he looked at her curiously, she added, "The man whose arm I just patched up. I removed a forty-four caliber slug—the same one used by a Winchester."

"You know your weapons," he remarked.

"I've pulled enough lead out of men's bodies to be able to tell a forty-four from a thirty-eight. But, of course, the slug in Mr. Kincaid's arm could have come from a Colt revolver as easily as a Winchester."

"But since I'm not wearing a revolver, you're assuming it was a Winchester."

"I don't mean to sound accusatory, but I thought I heard you two having words out in the hall after I left."

"You did," Travis admitted. "And you're right about me having shot Kincaid."

Aileen nodded, as if her fears had been confirmed. "I never believed it when he said it was an accident, but in Abilene one learns not to question such things too closely."

"You could report any suspicions to the town marshal," Travis suggested.

"To Stacy Parnell?" She gave a humorless laugh. "I'm afraid you haven't met the man. Believe me, it would be a waste of time. Better to patch them up and send them off to finish whatever they started. At least it keeps doctors and undertakers gainfully employed."

"I haven't heard of him. Has he been marshal long?"

"Only a few months. Since Donaghue returned."

"Marcus Donaghue?" Travis asked in surprise.

"You've heard of the man?"

"Of course. But he's in prison over at—"

"He received a governor's pardon about six months ago."

Shaking his head, Travis muttered, "Politicians."

"Exactly. And ever since he's been back, things have gone downhill. Marshal Parnell speaks out against him but doesn't do anything about it. Either he's too young and inexperienced, or else Donaghue has him in his pocket."

Travis nodded in understanding. "And this Bridger Kincaid is connected to Donaghue?"

"They met in prison. Kincaid was released shortly after Donaghue and followed him here. He's been Donaghue's right-hand man ever since."

"Yes!" Travis exclaimed. "I remember him now. Bridger Kincaid. He was working a cattle drive and murdered his trail boss. Happened outside Wichita

three years ago, just after I turned in my badge—"
Suddenly he caught himself. He waited for her inevitable question, but when she remained silent, he said,
"I was marshal of Wichita."

"Marshal Luke Travis. Yes, I know. I came here two
years ago—after you had left Wichita—but folks
were talking about you. They still are."

"How long have you known?"

"Only since you mentioned your first name. Believe
me, if I had known earlier, I wouldn't have accused
you of hurting the boy. I would have realized Bridger
Kincaid or someone like him was the culprit."

"Actually, it was a man riding with Kincaid. A big,
dark-haired fellow named Jeb—part Mexican, I
think."

Aileen shook her head. "I haven't heard of him, but
I think I've seen someone like that hanging around the
Salty Dog Saloon on Railroad Street. That's Donaghue's place."

Travis nodded. For a long moment they stood
looking at each other without speaking. Then finally
Travis said, "I suppose I should be moving along
before all the good hotel rooms in town are taken.
Thank you for your time."

"Not at all," she replied somewhat coolly.

Travis turned and untied the reins of his horse, then
climbed into the saddle. Looking down at her, he said,
"Aileen, there's one other thing. You mentioned a
man being killed—the father of the Methodist minister."

"Yes, Judah's father, Lawrence."

"Lawrence Fisher? Wasn't he the district attorney
who prosecuted Marcus Donaghue and sent him to
prison?"

"Yes. He was later made circuit judge for the Abilene district. Three nights ago he was shot in his office. The funeral was this morning."

"And you think there's a connection to Donaghue?"

"I suppose there are many people who hold a grudge against Judge Fisher, but I'd have to put Marcus Donaghue at the head of the list."

"Yes," Travis agreed. "Well, thanks again." Tipping his hat, he pulled the horse away from the hitching post.

"Luke," Aileen called, and he held up. "I've never approved of grown men walking around town with revolvers strapped to their waists or rifles under their arms. In fact, from what I've seen of lawmen out west, I can't say that I approve of many of them, either. The ones I've met tend to shoot first and ask questions later—leaving it to me and my colleagues to extract the bullets."

"You're saying you don't approve of me."

"I don't really know you. But I've heard that you're different, and though I never fully believed it, now that I've met you I see there may be some truth to the stories."

"I did shoot Bridger Kincaid."

"You did what you thought you must to protect others. My mother was a Quaker, and while I generally don't approve of gunplay for any purpose, I understand what you did."

"But you don't approve," Travis said.

"It is not for me to judge. But I must warn you: If you've made an enemy of Bridger Kincaid, you may wish you were wearing something on your hip besides a pocket."

"I took off my gun three years ago. I've no desire to strap it back on."

She smiled. "I'm glad to hear that. But please, be careful."

"I will." Travis turned his horse to head in the direction he had come. Holding up for a moment, he said, "One other thing, Aileen. Are you a Quaker, also?"

She shook her head. "Only my mother."

"What about your father?"

"He is a convicted murderer," she said flatly. She folded her arms as if suddenly chilled.

"I'm sorry," he muttered.

"Good night, Luke." She backed up a few steps into the shadows.

"Good night, Aileen." He touched his hat brim and headed down the street.

Chapter Four

———◆———

Luke Travis left his horse and packhorse tied at one of the hitchracks along Texas Street, halfway between Mulberry and Cedar streets. Leaving his Winchester in its scabbard, he mounted the boardwalk and approached the swinging batwing doors of the Bull's Head Saloon. Looking over the top, he could see that the Bull's Head was slightly more ornate than the typical frontier tavern. There was a long bar along the right, with round and square tables filling the rest of the floor. Gaudy paintings—mostly of plump, stylized nudes—filled nearly every available inch of wall.

Travis pulled a small pocket watch; it was just past nine o'clock. Inside, the six kerosene chandeliers were turned up full, and the dancing light played across the faces of nearly two dozen card-playing men and a handful of bar maidens. The crowd was relatively well behaved, and it did not appear that the working-women were being bothered in any way. From all appearances, this was a respectable establishment, though if the women on hand did not perform double service as prostitutes, Travis did not doubt that some neighboring business was providing the service in partnership with the Bull's Head management.

After watching the activity for a few minutes, Travis stepped away from the batwings and started toward the jail, which stood across the road and a few buildings down from the Bull's Head. There was no sign of activity within the building, and it was not until he was standing at the door that he noticed a faint light burning inside. Assuming the marshal was on his rounds, Travis almost decided to leave, but then he tried the knob and discovered it was un-locked. As he pushed the door and it creaked open, he saw a man slumped in the chair behind the desk, which faced the door. There was a small lamp on the desk with the wick turned low and the flame only a thin line of blue.

"Marshal?" Travis asked tentatively, but his voice failed to rouse the apparently sleeping man. Deciding upon a more direct approach, he stepped across the threshold, taking care not to muffle his boots, then forcefully slammed the door behind him. With the resulting bang, the slouching man bolted upright in the seat, his hand groping for the revolver that rested in its holster on the desk.

"Marshal," Travis said. "Can I have a word with you?"

Relaxing slightly, the man cautiously moved his hand away from the revolver. Turning up the wick, he squinted at the figure in front of the door and in a faintly slurred voice asked, "Who are you?"

"The name's Travis. I'd like to report a shooting."

"A what?" His tone was suddenly sharp and agitated.

"I was forced to shoot a man several miles east of town. Dr. Bloom already treated and released him."

"Then no one's dead?" the marshal asked, and Travis could almost hear a sigh of relief.

"Just a shoulder wound. But Bridger Kincaid won't be pulling a gun for a while."

"Bridger Kincaid!" Standing abruptly, the marshal lifted his gun belt and hurriedly strapped it on.

As the marshal came around the desk, Travis saw that he was young—no older than twenty-five—and slightly on the short side, though he looked quite muscular and fit. His hair was disheveled and dark, and though he did not sport a mustache or beard, he had what appeared to be several days' growth of whiskers; either he was growing a beard or was badly in need of a bath and a shave. When he came closer, his rumpled clothing, red-rimmed brown eyes, and whiskey-tinged breath betrayed that the latter was the case.

"Bridger Kincaid, you say?" The marshal rested his hand on the butt of his revolver.

"I had no choice. He and his friends had stopped a group of wagons and were molesting some of the occupants."

"That don't sound like Bridger," the marshal replied, and Travis noted that he used Kincaid's first name.

"Well, it was, and the folks in the wagon train and the bullet hole in his arm will confirm that."

"Bridger hasn't filed a complaint."

"And he won't. As I said, Marshal, he was the one who was causing the trouble. That's what I've come to report."

"Maybe I'd best hold you here and get Bridger to explain his side of it."

Losing his patience, Travis blurted out, "Listen, Marshal, this Bridger Kincaid character and three of his *compadres* waylaid four wagons, beat up a thirteen-year-old boy, and tried to rape his seventeen-year-old sister. For heaven's sake, the wagons were carrying a Dominican nun and more than a dozen orphans!"

"A nun? Orphans? That sure don't sound like Bridger," the marshal repeated.

"What is he? Some kind of saint?"

"Now don't be making fun of me or I'll have to hold you in back while I investigate these allegations, Mr. . . . ?"

"Travis. Luke Travis."

The young man's jaw dropped slightly, and he began to rub his stubble. "Marshal Luke Travis?" he finally asked.

Nodding, Travis said, "But no longer a lawman."

Moving his hand away from his gun, the marshal of Abilene stood up straighter and tucked in the tail of his shirt. Making an effort to hold his voice steady and even, he said, "I'm sorry, Mr. Travis. I didn't recognize you."

"I've been away from Kansas for three years now," Travis replied, trying to calm his anger.

"I'm Stacy Parnell." The young man held out his hand, and Travis shook it, noting that it was sweaty and cold.

"Now about this incident with Bridger Kincaid . . ." Travis pressed.

"Yes, I'll look into it at once. No doubt you've got the facts straight, but it does surprise me some. Sure, Bridger's a tough sort, but since he got out of prison he's kept his nose clean." Puffing up his chest, he added, "He knows I'll send him right back if he gets out of line."

"This time he did."

"You say it was a nun and some children he bothered?"

"Her name is Sister Laurel. She and the children will be staying at the Methodist church."

Parnell's eyes narrowed, and he looked thoughtful for a moment. Finally he said, "I'll go over there in the morning and get the story from this Sister Laurel. If she wants to press charges, I'll follow through from there."

"Fine." Travis started to reach for the doorknob.

"And about that shooting . . . I see you're not wearing a revolver."

Turning around, Travis replied, "I used a Winchester."

"Well, I suppose I can just let this one lie. From what you say, you were justified, and it sounds like Bridger isn't gonna make a complaint." He paused a moment, then added, "Just be careful. The man's got friends."

Travis again nodded and reached for the door, but this time Parnell stepped closer and laid a hand on his arm. "Mr. Travis," he said, his voice cautious, "you planning on staying in Abilene long?"

"Only a day or two. I'm heading on to Wichita as soon as Sister Laurel is ready to travel."

Parnell let go of his arm and smiled, then covered his obvious delight by saying, "It's not that you aren't welcome in Abilene. It's just that with your reputation —and with some folks already riled at you—well, I'd hate to have a bunch of greenhorns coming to town to try to brace you."

"Don't worry," Travis reassured him. "I'm not looking for trouble. That's why I don't wear a gun."

"Good. As you know, we lawmen like to keep things quiet in our town."

Glancing over at the desk chair, Travis had the urge to say something about the quietude of whiskey-induced sleep. But he could see that the young man was trying to create a sense of camaraderie, and so he thought better of it. Instead he merely said, "Good night," and headed outside.

Travis walked down the boardwalk and found a place in the shadows, from where he stood watching the jail, curious whether or not the young lawman would go back to sleep. If he did, it would support the idea that he was inexperienced and out of his element as Abilene's marshal. Surely any responsible lawman would be walking the streets at this time of night—and certainly he would not be hitting the bottle. On the other hand, if Parnell headed out—if he made a beeline for the Salty Dog Saloon—it would lend credence to Dr. Bloom's suggestion that he might be involved with Marcus Donaghue and his bunch. Of course, he might simply be investigating the shooting incident by seeking out Bridger Kincaid, so Travis would have to follow and determine his relationship with both Kincaid and Donaghue.

In less than a minute the office lamp dimmed again. Travis waited until he was certain Parnell was not coming out, then he turned and walked away. He felt a curious mix of relief and regret. He was relieved that early evidence did not support the notion that the young marshal had been bought off, since he apparently was not rushing off to warn Donaghue of Travis's visit. But that relief was tinged with the regret of knowing that an officer of the law was so inept and unprofessional that he would get drunk on the job and would do nothing to investigate a reported shooting in his jurisdiction. If things had not already gone downhill in Abilene, as Dr. Bloom had indicated, they surely would soon with a man like Stacy Parnell in charge of keeping the peace.

At the corner Travis turned left onto Cedar Street and headed toward Railroad Street, which traversed Cedar at an angle only a short way up the block. There was no boardwalk here, and only two major establishments were situated on the left side of the street: G. B. Seely General Goods and the Northcraft Drug Store just beyond it. The other side of the street was dominated by the Alamo Saloon, the well-known drinking and gambling establishment in front of which Marshal James Butler Hickok accidentally shot and killed his own deputy during a gunfight with gambler Phil Coe. That was on October 5, 1871, during the early boom days when "Wild Bill" Hickok first cleaned up the streets of Abilene. Travis had been doing the same in Wichita then, and he and Hickok had met on several occasions. Though far from being cut from the same cloth, Travis and the flamboyant Wild Bill had developed a bond that was built upon mutual respect.

Travis stood looking at the Alamo, smiling with thoughts of those days when he and Wild Bill had taken on and tamed the streets of their respective cities . . . days when Travis had thought himself immortal and indestructible. But that was before his beloved Sarah had been paralyzed by a bullet meant for him. Before he had spent three years watching her shrink and waste away despite the efforts of the best physicians in the East. Before he had discovered just how fragile and precarious life really was.

Travis visualized Sarah's smile, which had kept them optimistic right until the end and which continued to comfort him in the weeks since her passing. He tried not to be bitter, for he knew that Sarah had never felt sorry for herself and would want him to be happy now. And despite the pain and the loss, he found himself smiling again.

Turning away from the Alamo, Travis continued to the nearby corner and made a right onto Railroad Street, which fronted the tracks of the Kansas Pacific Railroad. He passed two more saloons, the Elkhorn and the Pearl, and stopped in front of the Salty Dog. A quick glance through the window confirmed that the place was quite busy with what appeared to be a fairly rough crowd, though the management seemed to have things under control. Still, the patrons—a mix of hard-drinking, go-for-broke cowboys and impeccably dressed, unscrupulous high rollers—were the type that would erupt given the slightest provocation.

Fleetingly Travis wished he was wearing his familiar walnut-handled Colt Peacemaker or had his Winchester at his side, but he knew either could ignite the passions of men like Bridger Kincaid, and tonight he had no desire to stir up trouble. He wanted only to see what the situation here in Abilene was shaping up to be. Such information had been a key to his success and longevity as a lawman, and since he was here, he intended to stay ahead of any threat to himself or Sister Laurel and her children.

Travis had just decided to enter the Salty Dog and was approaching the batwings when they swung open and a dark-haired man stepped out—the man Bridger had called Jeb. He was as tall as Travis—about six foot two—and even broader shouldered and more muscular, though with a slight paunch.

"What the hell do *you* want?" Jeb said, recognizing Travis.

"A whiskey. Why? Are you the bartender?"

Jeb narrowed one eye. "He don't serve bastards."

"Is that why you're leaving?"

Even as he said the words, Travis regretted them, and he was not surprised when without warning Jeb cursed and took a swing at him. The big man was not set for the punch, and Travis had plenty of time to feint to the right and deflect the blow with his left arm. He followed with his own right to the waist, and he felt a keen satisfaction as his fist sank deep in the man's belly, doubling him over.

Travis stepped to the side and let Jeb stagger across the boardwalk. He almost stumbled into the street but caught hold of an upright post and held on, catching his breath. Clearly the blow had surprised as well as stunned him, and Travis knew that if the fight continued, he would not get such an opening again.

Jeb stood away from the post and glowered at Travis. Clenching his fists and lowering his head, he shouted, "Bastard!" and charged across the boardwalk.

Travis had only an instant to brace himself before the big man barreled into him, shoulder first. The impact lifted Travis off his feet, and the two men went hurtling through the saloon's plate-glass window and sprawling across a table covered with cards and cash. Shards of glass showered over them as their momentum propelled them over the table and onto the floor.

The cardplayers leaped from their seats and scattered, while other patrons dashed over and formed a circle around the two fighters, who were rolling back and forth across the floor, locked in a bear hug. Though no one was quite sure yet who was fighting or what the dispute was about, they started shouting their encouragement to both men, with quite a few dollars already being wagered on the outcome.

Travis was on his back, struggling to breathe as the big man managed to lock his hands behind Travis's back and attempted to crush the life out of him. Travis tried to find his own hands, but he could not quite reach around the man's broad back. Instead he slipped them under the man's chin and pushed upward. The crowd began to call Jeb's name now, and Travis knew they were surrounded by the man's friends.

Jeb was gritting his teeth and growling as Travis pushed against his chin. As the big man's head was forced farther and farther back, the strength drained from his hands. All at once his hold was broken, and the two men rolled away from each other and struggled to their knees.

Travis was the first one on his feet, and he had only a moment to gauge the crowd and determine that they showed no signs yet of wanting to interfere. Apparently they were enjoying the spectacle and the unexpected opportunity to gamble. Travis caught a glimpse of someone pushing through the crowd and recognized the sling on the man's right arm, but before he could confirm that it was Bridger Kincaid, Jeb was back on his feet and ready to charge.

This time Travis was prepared, and he darted to his left and took only a glancing blow. As Jeb spun around, Travis met him with a hard left to the nose, then a right uppercut to the chin, driving his head back and splattering the spectators with blood. Jeb's knees almost buckled, and he stood tottering, his hand trying to stem the blood that was spurting from his nose. He shook his head to clear it, then came at Travis with both fists flailing.

Travis took a left to the jaw, then a crushing blow to the stomach, doubling him over. He came up at once with a pair of uppercuts to the chest and neck, driving Jeb backward and momentarily halting the onslaught.

It was then that a pair of men appeared from behind and grabbed Travis's arms. He did not have to look to know that they were the other riders who had accosted the wagon train. He tried to spin away, but he was exhausted and their grip was too solid. He steadied himself, planning his strategy for the moment that Jeb would attack. The hold of the man on his left did not seem as strong, and so he decided that he would kick the man's shins as he spun toward him, trying at the same time to break the hold of the man on his right.

Jeb took his time. He wiped his bloody nose with his sleeve and grinned at Travis like a spider anticipating a fly caught in his web. Finally he raised his fists and took a step forward.

"Eno' o' this!" a voice called out in a thick brogue.

To Travis's left, a squat, powerful-looking man forced his way though the crowd and stepped forward. He was at least fifty, with an abundance of red showing through his graying hair and bushy beard. He seemed to be smiling, but there was no trace of humor in his fiery green eyes.

"This ain't your show, Orion," Bridger Kincaid said as he, too, stepped out from the crowd.

"This show is over!" the man named Orion declared. "'Twas an even match till these boys stepped in. Now I say they'll be backing off!"

"This ain't Orion's Tavern," Kincaid shot back. "You won't be callin' the shots here."

Orion stepped over to one of the overturned chairs and snatched it up. Everyone watched as if mesmerized as he raised it over his head and brought it down on the glass-strewn table, smashing the chair to pieces. Wielding one of the legs like a club, he turned to Kincaid.

"Ye call 'em off, or we'll settle this a'tween we two—ye arm in a sling or no!"

"It's all right," Jeb interjected, waving off the two men who were holding Travis. "I don't need no help to finish off this son of a bitch." Again waving them away, he said, "Let him go."

The two men glanced over at Kincaid, who gave a slight nod and stepped back to the edge of the crowd. As the men released Travis's arms and backed away, Orion stood nearby brandishing the club, making it clear that anyone who interfered in the fight would have to deal with him.

Jeb's smile faded somewhat, and he touched his bloody nose. Then he took a cautious step forward. With his left hand down to protect his still-tender belly, he drew back his right and looked for an opening. Travis gave him one—a clear shot at his jaw—and Jeb took it. But Travis had been expecting it, and instantly his left hand was up and parried the thrust.

Travis swung his own right then, holding nothing back. He caught Jeb on the tip of the chin, and there was a bone-jarring crack as Jeb's head was knocked back. This time Jeb's knees gave way, and he dropped to the floor. He lay there on his back for several seconds, unmoving, while the crowd cried out for him to stand. He opened one eye, tried to lift himself onto an elbow, and fell back down. A couple of men standing nearby grabbed his arms and helped him to his feet, and he stood there, propped up, trying to shake away the dancing lights in his head.

When it looked as if the men were going to push Jeb back into the fight, a booming voice shouted, "Hold up! That's enough, now!"

The crowd parted, and a burly, black-haired man stepped through. He was as big as Jeb, as powerful-looking as the man named Orion, but dressed in the tailored brown suit of a businessman. Immediately Travis recognized Marcus Donaghue.

"Luke Travis, isn't it?" Donaghue said with an insincere smile. "I haven't seen you in . . . what is it? Four or five years?"

"And I hadn't expected to see you in at least another seventeen. Isn't that about right?"

Donaghue's smile hardened. "I served my time. The governor was satisfied with three years. Who was I to argue?"

"And now you're back."

"I'm a businessman." With a sweep of his hand he took in the room. "I've a business to run, and you and this fellow here"—he pointed at Jeb, who was finally standing under his own power, swaying slightly on his feet—"are disrupting it. And causing quite a bit of damage in the process, I might add."

"I'll be glad to pay for the—"

"You already have, Travis," Donaghue said, patting his pocket. "I'm one of the few who bet on you." He paused, then added, "The next fight, however, the odds may change."

"I'm not looking for any more fighting," Travis answered sincerely. "As one of your associates pointed out, this isn't my town. But I do have some friends here, and their well-being *is* my concern."

"You're speaking of the nun and her flock."

Donaghue chuckled. "This is a rough land for the meek. What they need to inherit around here is some backbone. But don't worry about the orphans. I've put the word out, and there won't be any more such . . . indiscretions." He glanced over his shoulder. "Isn't that right, boys?" His question was greeted with silence. Turning to Travis, he said, "There, now. That ought to put this thing to rest."

Travis looked at him closely. "I hope it does. Those children and I are planning to move on to Wichita in a day or two. I'd hate to be delayed here in Abilene."

"Nobody wants that. I'm certain your friends in Wichita are looking forward to seeing their beloved Marshal Luke Travis come home. So you let me handle these hotheads. I'm certain they won't get out of line again."

Travis started toward the door. Coming abreast of the man named Orion, he said, "I appreciate what you did."

As Travis headed through the swinging doors, Donaghue turned to Orion and said, "You might as well join your friend. I'd say our own business is concluded."

Orion merely glowered at him, then turned and pushed through the batwings. As they swung shut behind him, he started down the boardwalk, calling, "Mr. Travis. Wait up."

Travis waited for the shorter man to catch up. "The name's Luke," he said as Orion approached.

"Aye, 'n' we have'na been properly introduced. I'm Orion McCarthy, a Scotsman born 'n' bred, by God."

Travis smiled. "Somehow I had that idea." He shook Orion's hand and noted that his grip was exceedingly firm.

"An' tell me, Lucas, from where hails the Travis clan?"

"Our family came over before the Revolution. I'm sorry to have to tell a Scotsman, but we're originally English."

"Surely a misfortune o' birth, but once overcome, a badge o' character. Like tha' tin star ye used t'wear."

"That was a long time ago," Travis said thoughtfully.

"Aye, but still talked about in these parts."

"And best left to rest." Wishing to change the subject, Travis glanced over at the Salty Dog and said, "I hope I didn't cause you any trouble back there."

"Wi' Marcus Donaghue?" Orion turned and spit into the street. "Damned Irishman! No, there's nothing more t'be said a'tween the likes o' him 'n' me." Stroking his beard, his eyes suddenly lit up, and he declared, "Eno' talk of Irishmen. Instead, I'm ginna treat ye to a drink o' the only real Scotch whisky in Abilene!"

"And where might we find that?" Travis asked as Orion clapped him on the back and led the way down the boardwalk.

"Why, dinna be daft, man! At Orion's Tavern, by God!"

Chapter Five

The four wagons clattered along Elm Street, a hard-packed dirt road containing only a smattering of darkened buildings, to where the road jagged around a bend in a fairly wide creek on the left. Mud Creek, Dr. Bloom had called it, and though it was too dark to see more than the faint outline of the creek's banks, Sister Laurel's sense of smell was evidence enough that it was as murky as its name.

Sister Laurel led the wagons up the street to where a small hill separated the road from the creek. At the top of the rise stood an imposing white church with a square, flat-topped bell tower. Set back and to the right was a smaller two-story parsonage in matching white clapboard. Farther to the right, a long, low-roofed carriage house with six bays faced the side of the church, so that a large parking area was framed on three sides by the buildings.

The lead wagon turned up the long drive, which curved past the church door before entering the parking area. Sister Laurel pulled the mules to a halt in front of the parsonage, then signaled the other wagons to head over to the carriage bays. Handing the reins to Michael, she said, "Park this with the others while I meet with the minister." Then she climbed down and approached the front door.

The lantern outside the door was not lit. But Sister Laurel could see a faint glow through the windows to the left of the door, so she raised the brass knocker and rapped three times. She waited a few moments, but there was no response. Standing on tiptoe, she peered through the small octagonal window centered fairly high on the door and saw that it opened into a hallway, with rooms to the right and left and more at the back. On the right side of the hall, a fairly wide, bannistered stairway led to the second floor. The entire house seemed dark except for the light that spilled through the partway-open door on the left.

Sister Laurel knocked several more times and waited, again without response. Glancing over her shoulder, she saw that the children were talking to one another in the open lot, while Michael, Agnes, and the other two drivers were backing their wagons into the bays. She turned back to the door, banged the knocker a final time, then tried the knob. It was unlocked, and she cautiously pushed the door open.

"Hello?" she called tentatively. "Reverend Fisher? Are you home?"

There was no reply. Hiking her black skirt slightly, she stepped over the threshold and entered the hall. Leaving the front door slightly ajar, she approached the door on the left and rapped on it lightly.

"Reverend Fisher? I'm a friend of Dr. Bloom's."

The only sound was a slight creaking as she swung the door wide and looked into what appeared to be the parlor. It was bathed in the soft, flickering light of a kerosene lamp, which sat on a stand between two plush chairs that faced the fireplace on the far wall. The room appeared empty, until she noticed the shadow cast by the lamp on the right-hand wall. It was a profile of one of the chairs, seated in which was the shadow of a man. It was then that she noticed an arm hanging off the left side of the chair.

Something about the way the hand was dangling sent a shudder through Sister Laurel, and she hurried to the chair, praying the minister was merely asleep, fearful that, like his father, he was dead. As soon as she came around the chair, she realized that neither was the case. His head was hanging to the side, his chest gently rising and falling, his mouth open wide. His right hand was in his lap, clutching a bottle of amber-colored liquid, some of which had spilled on his starched but wrinkled shirtfront. He was snoring, and each gusting breath reeked of alcohol.

"Drunk as a piper!" she declared, folding her arms and shaking her head sadly.

"Sister Laurel?" a soft voice called, and the nun looked over to see Agnes Hirsch in the front hallway.

Hurrying out to the hall, Sister Laurel pulled the parlor door closed behind her. "Yes? What is it?"

"I thought you might need some help. Is the reverend at home?"

"W-why, uh, yes," she stammered. "I was just speaking to him. I'm afraid he isn't feeling too well."

"Because of his father?" Agnes asked, remembering what Dr. Bloom had said.

"Yes, I'm certain that's it."

"The children were wondering if we'll be staying—"

"Yes, we can stay the night." She ushered Agnes outside and stood blocking the front doorway. "Have the boys unhitch the mules and tie them in the vacant stalls. And make certain they are watered and fed. Meanwhile, I'll see to our accommodations."

Agnes stood trying to look beyond Sister Laurel, as if she sensed there was something wrong.

"Well . . . ?" the older woman finally said.

"I'll see to it at once," Agnes replied, then turned and headed to where the other children were waiting.

Sister Laurel closed the front door and engaged the locking bolt. With her back leaning against the door, she turned toward the parlor and sighed. "Good Lord," she muttered. "The man is as polluted as Mud Creek!"

While the mules were unhitched and bedded down, Sister Laurel made a complete inspection of the parsonage. It was quite large, with four cavernous rooms upstairs that seemed unused. Three of the rooms each had several stripped beds and empty dressers, while the fourth had but a single bed and a nightstand. Each room had a kerosene lamp, which she lit. Downstairs the house boasted a large kitchen and adjoining formal dining area. Across the hall from the parlor was a larger living room, and beyond it was a fair-sized room, which the minister apparently used as a bedroom. While the room was not untidy, the bed had not been made, and some of the minister's clothes were tossed over the back of one of the chairs.

Sister Laurel unlocked a back door leading outside from the kitchen, then headed down the hall and exited through the front door. She called the children over, and as they gathered around, she told them, "Tonight we have a real treat. We will be staying upstairs in the parsonage—and the girls will have the chance to sleep on real beds."

"The girls? Again?" complained one of the older boys, who had been driving the far wagon. "They had the beds last time." He shot a glare at one of the older girls, who was grinning smugly at him.

"That was weeks ago, Cameron," Sister Laurel replied. "I should think that you and the other boys would be gallant enough to insist they get the mattresses."

The boy frowned and looked down at the ground.

Sister Laurel turned to the girl who had been teasing Cameron and said, "Muriel, I'd like you and the other older girls to double up with the young ones."

Paying no attention to Muriel's petulant expression, she started walking toward the carriage house, waving for the children to follow. At the wagons, she helped the children gather bedding, bedclothes, and clean outfits for the next morning, as well as necessary toiletries. She cautioned them that the minister was quite ill and just now was resting in the front parlor. Then, with an admonition to be as quiet as possible, she led them around the building to the back door and brought them to a narrow back stairway hidden behind a door in the far corner of the kitchen.

"Use these stairs if you need to visit the outhouse out back," she whispered as the children filed past her.

Following them up, she divided them among the rooms, placing the older boys in a front room that looked out on the carriage house. It had the single bed, which Michael would use because of his head injury. The girls and younger children took the three rooms with the beds and dressers. Once the beds were ready, she assigned each of the younger children to one of the older girls and supervised them as they went downstairs in pairs to use the outhouse and wash up in the kitchen, which had a pump in the sink.

It took more than half an hour to get everyone settled down for the night. Once the lights were out, Sister Laurel stood alone in the tiny hall between the rooms and listened to make certain the children were going to sleep. Finally she headed down the front stairs and entered the parlor.

Judah Fisher had not moved since Sister Laurel had left him. His right hand still clutched the bottle on his lap, and she had to pry open each finger to get it away. She gave the liquid a sniff and muttered, "Whiskey." Searching around, she saw a small cabinet with one door slightly ajar. Inside was a set of four glasses, which the minister had not bothered using. The cork stopper was sitting atop the cabinet, and she forced it into the neck of the bottle, then placed the whiskey inside the cabinet and shut the door.

Returning to the easy chair in which the young man was slumped, she stood wondering what to do. He was not heavy but seemed quite tall; she was certain she could not lift him alone. His face was youthful and pleasant enough, though just now it might be the whiskey that gave him such a peaceful demeanor. His hair was a sun-bleached brown, and he wore a pair of black wire-rimmed spectacles that gave him a slightly more mature look. Still, he could not yet be thirty, she estimated, though certainly old enough to know better where whiskey was concerned.

Sister Laurel shook her head sadly as she recalled Dr. Bloom's saying that the man's father had been killed recently. She found herself wondering if it had been an accident or murder, and suddenly she realized how lonely it must be for a young minister, alone in the world, to lose his father. Men like Judah Fisher were comforters, leaders of the flock, and often there was no one there for them when they needed comforting. And so he had sought solace in a bottle. She only hoped that this was not his usual response to the loneliness of his calling.

Kneeling beside the chair, Sister Laurel took the young man's hands in her own and rubbed them. "Judah," she said softly. She continued rubbing and whispering his name, but his only reaction was when his head lolled to the opposite side. Finally she stood and patted his cheeks, calling his name louder. This time his eyes fluttered, and he moaned slightly; then his head sank down, and he resumed snoring.

The nun jumped with a start at the sound of a creaking door, and she looked up to see Agnes Hirsch standing in the doorway. The seventeen-year-old girl had a blue robe over her nightgown, and her red hair fell loosely to her shoulders. The soft lamplight danced in her large green eyes, highlighting her soft, round features. Sister Laurel stared at her, speechless, suddenly realizing that Agnes was no longer a child and that what once had been baby fat was now the curves of a woman.

"I knew you'd need help with the minister," Agnes said matter-of-factly.

"I . . . uh . . ." the older woman stammered, stepping away from the chair slightly.

"I heard him snoring when I came in earlier," Agnes explained. "I figured he wasn't just sleeping."

Sister Laurel shrugged and sighed. "You may as well give me a hand. We'll see if we can get him to bed."

Agnes came across the room and circled the chair.

She was not sure what to expect, and when she saw the tall minister slouched in the seat, half smiling and oblivious to the world, she let out a giggle.

"This is serious business we're about," the nun gently reprimanded her. "And not a word to the others. The poor man's lost his father; he should be allowed some liberties."

"I'm not making fun. But he looks so . . . so cute."

Sister Laurel shuddered slightly at the thought of the first of her orphans becoming an adult. "He won't look so cute in the morning," she said abruptly. "He'll look like a rumpled mattress, and he'll feel a whole lot lumpier. All we can do is get him to bed and let time do the rest."

She directed Agnes to the opposite side of the chair, and then each woman grasped the man under the arm and lifted him from the seat. He came up with surprising ease, but then his legs turned to rubber and he began to sink. The women had to lift his arms over their shoulders and prop him up on either side to keep him from slipping to the floor.

The young minister began to hum, almost as if he was about to sing, and his head lolled back and forth. Once, his eyes opened slightly, and Agnes could see that they were an unusually pale blue. He smiled at the young woman under his arm and whispered something that sounded like "Ah, Mama," and then his eyes fluttered closed again.

"He thinks you're his mother," Sister Laurel commented.

"I thought he said Mona."

"Never you mind. Let's just get him to bed."

The women half dragged, half carried the young man out of the parlor and down the hall to his room, where they eased him to a sitting position on the bed.

As soon as they let go of his arms, he flopped backward and lay sprawled on top of the covers, his legs dangling over the side.

Sister Laurel lit the lamp on the dresser, then stooped down beside the bed and said, "His shoes." She untied and removed the right one while Agnes took care of the left.

"What about his clothing?" Agnes asked somewhat eagerly as she stood again.

"He can bloody well sleep in it," the older woman replied somewhat testily.

"Let me at least loosen his collar," Agnes insisted, kneeling on the bed to undo the top few buttons.

When Agnes had opened the second button and was reaching for the third, Sister Laurel reached out and pulled her arm. "Enough of that, now. Let's cover him up."

Working together, the women got him turned around and lifted his feet up onto the bed. With some effort they pulled the blankets out from underneath him and covered him with them. A contented smile immediately formed on the young minister's face, and he rolled sideways and curled up under the blankets, sound asleep.

"There, that should do it," Sister Laurel declared as she lowered the lamp. She led the way into the hall, which was dimly illuminated by the light spilling from the parlor.

Turning to look through the door at the shadowed figure on the bed, Agnes asked, "Do you suppose one of us should stay here and—?"

"Certainly not, young lady," the nun cut her off. "It's scandal enough that we had to drag a drunken pastor off to his bedroom and tuck him under the covers. No one mentioned such goings-on to me at the convent."

Agnes gave a barely audible sigh. "I suppose he will sleep well enough now."

"And if he doesn't, the saints be praised. There's nothing like a little morning nausea to put a man back on the straight and sober."

Staring compassionately at the sleeping man, Agnes said, "But his father . . ."

"All our fathers die one day. But liquor is never enough to fill the emptiness."

"It helps us forget."

"We must never forget. It is for the living to remember."

Agnes shivered slightly, as if suddenly chilled. "You make it sound so . . . severe."

Sister Laurel wrapped her arm around Agnes's shoulder. "You're right," she whispered as she pulled the young woman away from the doorway. "I'm a heartless old goat. Even a minister has a right to put on a drunk once in a while."

Agnes looked up and smiled at her. "As long as it isn't every day."

"Exactly. But that remains to be seen."

"I'm certain Dr. Bloom wouldn't have sent us here if the minister were a drunkard," Agnes pointed out.

"Of course not. But the devil that lives in a bottle is a wily beast. He can knock a man low one night, then turn around the very next day and put a cherubic smile on his face and a glib word on his tongue. Believe me, I've known men of the cloth who could charm the last dollar out of a congregation, and it was never them, but the bottle preaching." She pulled the minister's door closed and led Agnes through the kitchen to the back stairs. "You run along and get some sleep. I'll close things up down here."

"But where will you sleep?" Agnes asked, suddenly realizing that no arrangements had been made for the nun.

"I'll be perfectly fine in the parlor."

"But there isn't a bed—"

"After weeks on the hard seat of that buckboard, any of the chairs in that room look like heaven itself."

Agnes was about to offer her own bed, but seeing the look of determination on the older woman's face, she realized it would be a futile gesture. Leaning forward, she surprised Sister Laurel with a kiss on the cheek. "Thank you for letting me help you. I won't tell anyone."

"I know you won't, my dear. Why, you're almost a full-grown woman, aren't you?"

Blushing, Agnes turned and hurried up to her room, while at the foot of the stairs Sister Laurel stood shaking her head and smiling.

Chapter Six

———◆———

Michael Hirsch was facing a snarling, blond-haired man wearing a low-slung holster. The man's hand hovered over the butt of his revolver, his trigger finger twitching with anticipation. *Smith and Wesson,* the boy thought disdainfully. Nothing, he knew, could stand up to the fury of his pearl-handled Colt Peacemaker.

Suddenly the man went for his gun. As if by magic, the Peacemaker leaped into Michael's hand, and in a smooth, effortless motion he brought it up and fired. Once. Twice. Again and again until the cylinders were empty and only smoke came from the barrel.

The man's gun never fully cleared his holster, and as his hand lost all feeling, the weapon clattered to the ground. The man staggered forward a step, then tottered back as he stared down at the blood spurting from his chest. He looked up at Michael, his arm reaching in supplication. And then his legs buckled, and he fell to the ground. A sudden wind poured down the street, and dust began to swirl around the lifeless body.

Michael raised the Peacemaker and blew away the smoke, a smile touching his lips. Bridger Kincaid was dead; it had been a good day. Suddenly a board creaked behind him, and he remembered the dark-haired man with the sombrero who had accosted his sister. In one fluid motion he whirled around and swung the gun toward this new threat. But the swirling dust was so thick that he could not make out his adversary.

"It's only me," a voice called through the darkness. "Go back to sleep."

Michael rubbed his eyes and struggled to see. Somehow he had been transported to a strange, unfamiliar room, empty save for the bodies lying around him.

"I'm just going to the outhouse," the voice said.

Lifting his head, Michael saw someone standing in the doorway, and as his eyes adjusted to the thin moonlight spilling through the window, he recognized the older boy named Cameron. Michael suddenly realized he was lying on the single bed in the upstairs room of the parsonage, and the bodies scattered around him were the bedrolls where the other boys were sleeping. The creaking boardwalk was merely Cameron crossing the room on his way to relieve himself.

Michael nodded and lay back against the jacket he was using as a pillow, watching as the older boy pulled the door shut and disappeared down the stairs. For a long while he just lay there, thinking of his dream and wondering if he would ever face someone in such a showdown. After a few minutes, he decided that as long as he was up he might as well visit the outhouse once Cameron returned. Standing, he pulled on his pants and shoes and walked over to the window.

The yard was bathed in blue moonlight. At first all seemed still, but then from the corner of his eye he caught a flicker of movement near the carriage house. Pressing his face against the glass and shielding his eyes to block his own faint reflection, he peered down at the open bays where the wagons were parked. Someone was indeed moving near one of the wagons, but it was not until the person emerged into the yard that Michael recognized Cameron.

Michael immediately backed away from the window so that he would not be seen. The older boy was examining something in his hands—transferring items from one hand to another as if counting or sorting. Then he looked around him, pulled his coat tighter, and started down the walk toward the street.

Without hesitating, Michael grabbed his jacket off the bed and headed into the hall. Moving as swiftly and quietly as possible, he made his way down the back stairs and out the kitchen door. Donning his coat, he circled the parsonage, cautiously stepping out into the parking area after determining that the older boy was gone. Then Michael started running, pausing every now and then behind a tree and searching for a glimpse of Cameron.

Michael was well down Elm Street when he saw Cameron walking briskly over the train tracks. Following at a distance, he soon crossed the tracks and turned left onto Texas Street. Though it was certainly late—probably after midnight—the streetlamps remained lit and many buildings were aglow with evening revelers. It seemed as if half the buildings were saloons, and none were at a loss for patrons.

A block and a half down, Cameron stopped in front of a building—the saloon beside Dr. Bloom's office—and as Michael watched from down the street, he pushed through the batwings and entered. Michael waited until the batwings stopped swinging, and then he cautiously approached and took up a position in a shadowed doorway directly opposite the saloon.

The sign above the door read Orion's Tavern, and Michael guessed that Cameron had looked it over while they were at the doctor's office. But why had he returned in the middle of the night? "To drink, of course," he whispered to himself. He recalled several occasions when Cameron had bragged about buying a shot of whiskey in one of the trail towns while the other children were off buying candy. He had even prodded the other boys to join him, though Michael did not think any had taken up the challenge.

Michael knew that Sister Laurel would be upset—and furious—to learn that one of the children had sneaked off to a saloon. He also knew that most of the children would hate him if he turned Cameron in. Yet he was genuinely concerned about the older boy. After all, Abilene was considered a rough town, and somewhere out there Bridger Kincaid and his cronies were lurking about, licking their wounds and probably eager to get back at someone for having been run off. In fact, Kincaid had been at the doctor's office earlier and could well be in Orion's Tavern this very minute, nursing his injured arm over a bottle of whiskey.

Michael knew he could not turn in the older boy. Yet he also could not leave and simply crawl back to bed. The least he could do was to check out the tavern and make sure Cameron was not in any trouble. Leaving the shadowed doorway, he slowly crossed the street and stepped up onto the opposite boardwalk. He was slipping past the batwings to look in one of the windows when suddenly the doors swung open and a tall man nearly barreled into him.

"What are you doing here?" the man said in surprise, and Michael looked up to see Luke Travis.

"I . . . er . . ."

"Does Sister Laurel know where you are?"

"Not exactly, but . . ."

"Oh, of course," Travis said as if all at once he understood what Michael was up to. "You were on your way to see Dr. Bloom."

"No," he replied, then quickly regretted having said it.

Travis placed his hand on Michael's shoulder and led him away from the door. Stepping off the boardwalk so that they would be at closer heights, he looked down at the boy and said, "Why not tell me what's going on? Are you in some kind of trouble that I can help with?"

"It's not me," Michael began, wondering if telling Travis was the same as tattling to Sister Laurel. But this was the man who had helped them before; surely he would know what to do. "It's one of the other boys," Michael finally admitted. "I followed him here without his knowing."

"He's in the saloon?"

"Just went in a few minutes ago."

"I didn't see him at the bar, but it's pretty crowded in there. But if he's only a boy, the bartender won't—"

"He's sixteen."

"Then he's almost a man, and if Orion refuses to serve him, there's probably plenty inside who'll buy him a drink. Or is it gambling he's come for?"

"I don't know. I'm just worried, and I wasn't sure what to do."

"You've done the right thing," Travis reassured him. Mounting the boardwalk, he moved to the window. "Come over here and see if you can find him."

It took a moment, but then Michael pointed toward the back of the room and said, "That's Cameron talking to those two men. He's got black hair and is wearing a blue jacket."

Travis looked where Michael was pointing and saw the teenage boy engaged in conversation with two ragged-looking young men. He was nearly as tall as they were and could easily pass for eighteen or so. "I see him," he said, turning away from the window. "Now here's what I want you to do. No one knows you're here, right?" When Michael nodded, Travis continued, "Then return to the church and go to bed. I'll take care of Cameron."

"You will?" the boy asked in surprise.

"I said so, didn't I? I'll send him on his way, and I won't even let on that you spoke to me, so no one need know."

"What about Sister Laurel?" Michael asked hesitantly.

"You don't have to tell her, if you don't want. This is something we men should take care of, don't you think?"

Michael nodded eagerly and began to smile.

"Now run along." Travis clapped him on the back.

Michael looked up at him a moment, his eyes betraying his gratitude. "Thanks, Mr. Travis," he finally mumbled. Then he turned and raced off down the street.

Travis waited until Michael rounded the corner of Elm Street and disappeared from sight. Then, with a bemused grin, he pushed through the swinging doors. He headed straight to where the youth named Cameron was seated at a square table in the corner with the two young men, who themselves could not have been much older than eighteen. The three of them were laughing and smirking as they played a game of stud poker. Cameron was dealing what seemed a friendly game, since there was no money on the table.

Coming up from behind, Travis said in a casual tone, "Cameron, what are you doing here?"

The boy nearly jumped out of his seat in surprise. Spinning around in the chair, he dropped the cards and nearly toppled a shot glass of whiskey. Recognizing the tall man standing over him as the one who had come to the aid of the wagon train earlier that day, he abruptly stood and stammered, "H-how did you know my n-name?"

"Sister Laurel mentioned it when you were driving the wagon. You remember me, don't you?"

"Uh, Mr. Travis, right?"

Nodding, Travis placed a hand on his shoulder and said, "Relax, son. I didn't mean to spoil your game."

Nervously, the teenager turned and gathered up the cards, including the ones he had begun to deal. As he fumbled with them, one of the cards flipped over, and he quickly swept it up and shoved it back among the others. Its face was visible for only a moment, but long enough for Travis to see a highly realistic and detailed full-color sketch of a voluptuous woman wearing garters, a pair of dark stockings—and nothing else. The only other markings were a diamond and the numeral four, indicating the card's value.

Trying to suppress a smile, Travis pulled out the single empty chair to Cameron's right. "You fellows mind if I join your game?"

The two older ones looked unperturbed and merely shrugged. Cameron, on the other hand, began to sweat noticeably. Clutching the cards in his fist, he said, "We were just finishing, Mr. Travis. I . . . I have to be heading back now."

"Don't be silly. It's barely one o'clock. Surely you can stay another game. How old are you anyway, Cameron?"

"Almost eighteen," he lied.

"Then it's settled. Here, let me deal."

Before Cameron realized what was happening, Travis snatched the deck from his hands and expertly began shuffling them.

"Five-card draw, all the ladies are wild," Travis declared tonelessly, upon which Cameron's jaw dropped open. "The queens . . . they're wild," Travis explained, smiling at the uncomfortable youth as the other young men snickered. Travis picked up his cards and sorted them, and Cameron reluctantly followed suit. As Travis examined his hand, he saw that every card featured a different woman, each exotic, each completely naked, and some in the most daring of poses.

"Your move," Travis said, turning to Cameron. At first the boy seemed too nervous to play, but under Travis's prodding he finally discarded three cards and was dealt three new ones. Each player made his exchange, ending with Travis, who chose to stand pat.

"Since no one seems to be betting, let's see what everyone's got," Travis declared, turning first to Cameron.

"Nothing. I fold," he blurted, placing the cards facedown on the table and covering them with his hand.

"Nonsense," Travis told him. "You needn't fold when there's no money on the table. Even an empty hand could be a winner." So saying, he reached to his left, grasped Cameron's wrist, and lifted the boy's hand off the cards. Sliding them out and flipping them over on the table, he announced, "Two pair, aces and eights. Why, that's a great hand for draw poker. Never fold with two pair." Turning to the other players, he asked, "What have you boys got?"

The first young man had a pair of jacks, the second had missed a straight by one card despite having one wild queen.

"See, Cameron?" Travis told the boy. "You've bested both of them, and if not for the wild cards, you would've got me." He spread his cards faceup on the table. "Four kings—two naturals and two wild ladies." He pushed the cards into the center of the table and leaned his chair back on two legs. "So what do I win?" he asked innocently.

In an exceedingly faint voice, Cameron said, "We were just playing for fun."

For the first time, one of the young men spoke. "Fun? Hell, you charged us a shot glass each to see those cards."

"Let's not bicker, boys," Travis urged as he leaned forward and swept up the cards. "After all, the fellow holding the deck gets to name the stakes." Tapping the cards into a neat pile, he placed them in front of Cameron.

"It was just for fun," the boy repeated even more softly, his eyes downcast and a frown on his face.

"And that's exactly what we had," Travis assured him. "But I guess it *is* getting time to head home." Pushing back his chair, he stood and turned to the two young men. "A bit of advice, boys. Don't pocket any of the cards while you're playing. Someone less friendly than Cameron or I might think you were cheating."

Reaching over, he plucked a card out of the shirt pocket of the nearest man and dropped it faceup on the table, revealing the queen of spades, depicted by an exotic-looking woman with dusky skin and the most ample bosom Travis had ever encountered. "I'll be damned—a queen. It would have completed your straight," he exclaimed. He turned to the second man, who reluctantly emptied his own pocket of the two cards he had stolen.

"That's better," Travis declared. "After all, you wouldn't want our friend Cameron to be playing without a full deck."

Cameron glowered at the two young men who had been buying him drinks in order to view his cards. Snatching up the missing cards, he added them to the deck and then stood and stuffed them in his pants pocket.

Tipping his hat, Travis said, "It's been a pleasure, gentlemen." He stood without moving, waiting to see what Cameron would do. The boy merely nodded, his eyes filled with a blend of anger and embarrassment, then turned and stalked out of the saloon.

"C'mon," one of the young men said to his friend. "Let's go home."

The other fellow gave a dejected shrug, and the two of them stood and filed out, each carefully avoiding Travis's eyes. As soon as they were gone, Travis shook his head and headed for the bar. Grinning, he called out, "Orion, set me up one final whiskey."

"Call it Scotch, man!" the rambunctious barman insisted as he produced a bottle from under the counter and uncorked it. "Whiskey can be anything from rye t'corn. If it be good malted barley ye want, it's got t'be Scotch!"

Cameron walked quickly down Texas Street, ashamed at having been confronted by Luke Travis and enraged at the young men for having taken advantage of him. The two feelings began to merge, with his anger shifting to Travis. Obviously the man had been trying to humiliate him in public, treating him like a child and even suggesting that he could not handle those other fellows without assistance. *Hell, I'm almost as old and just as big,* he thought. *And so what if they steal a few cards? I've got plenty more.*

After turning onto Elm Street, Cameron slowed his pace considerably and pulled the deck of cards from his pocket. As he crossed the tracks and headed up the street, he began to count them to confirm that the only one missing was the jack of diamonds, depicted as a young girl in the first flush of puberty looking over her shoulder to examine her naked body in a mirror, thus revealing her buttocks as well as her newly emerging breasts. He had sold that one in Junction City for a dollar to the very grocer from whom the other children had purchased their candy. The little man had pasty skin and the sweatiest hands Cameron had ever seen, and from the way he had fawned over the orphan girls and patted their hands as he handed them candy,

Cameron had known he would find that particular card of special delight.

Cameron had counted to forty-three when a harsh voice called out, "I'll take those."

Spinning to his right, Cameron saw one of the young men from the saloon standing in the shadows a few feet away.

"Hand them over," a second voice demanded, this time from behind him.

Cameron looked around quickly, knowing he was surrounded but frantically seeking some means of escape. He was only a little more than a block from the church. Perhaps he could outrun them if he caught them off guard.

"Uh, sure, here they are," he said meekly, holding out the deck as he approached the first one who had spoken. He saw the young man take a step forward and reach for the cards, but when Cameron drew within range, he lashed out with his foot and caught the fellow squarely on the knee. As the young man howled and dropped to one knee, Cameron heard the other one curse and then come rushing from behind. Cameron quickly turned and took off up the road, stuffing the deck of cards in his pocket as he ran.

The teenager could hear the pounding of footsteps close behind him, and he only made it about fifty feet before a firm hand gripped his shirt and nearly yanked him off his feet. Another hand collided solidly with the side of his head, stunning him and dropping him to his knees. Cameron felt steely fingers grab hold of his hair and start to pull his head back, but the youth twisted around and drove his head forward, right into his attacker's belly, knocking the air out of him and causing him to release his grip. Cameron started to scramble to his feet, but the other fellow had come limping up by now, and he drove a solid fist into Cameron's lower back, doubling him over in pain. The punch was followed with a sharp blow to the head, knocking him facedown on the ground.

The two young men were both on their feet now, one on either side of Cameron, and they relentlessly kicked him in the sides as they cursed at him. All he could do was cover his head and pray they would not kill him.

"Enough!" one of them shouted, and then a pair of hands grabbed his shirt and rolled him onto his back. The fight was completely out of him, and he made no effort to resist as they reached into his pocket and pulled out the deck of cards. With what little strength remained, he struggled not to give them the satisfaction of seeing him cry.

"We're *borrowing* these," one of them said facetiously as he smirked at the youth sprawled in the dust of the empty street. "If you want 'em back, just look us up . . . if you've got the guts."

"Let's get back to the shack," the second young man told his partner, and the two of them started to walk away from the moaning teenager.

Just then there was the sound of quick footsteps approaching from farther up the street, and a voice called, "Hey, you! What's going on?"

"Let's get outta here!" one of the young men said, and in a flash they took off at a run down the street and disappeared into the darkness.

Cameron rolled on his side and looked up just as someone knelt beside him. "M-Michael?" he moaned as he recognized the bandage on the boy's forehead.

"What happened?" the younger boy asked, placing a hand under Cameron's head and helping him to a sitting position.

Cameron sat for a moment with his eyes closed, holding his stomach and sides and trying to catch his breath. "Help me up," he finally muttered, and Michael wrapped an arm around him and helped him to his feet. "I'm all right," he declared, pushing himself away and standing on his own.

"Who were they?" Michael asked.

"A couple of toughs who thought I had money."

"Did they steal anything?"

Cameron paused a moment. Shaking his head slightly, he said, "No. I think you scared them off."

"What were you doing out here, anyway?"

"Just taking a walk. Enough questions, okay?"

"Sure," Michael replied.

Cameron stood up straighter and took a deep breath. Letting go of his sides, he turned to the younger boy and asked, "And what're you doing out here?"

"I had to go to the outhouse," Michael lied, not wanting to admit that he was hanging around outside to make sure Cameron returned from the saloon. "I thought I heard something, so I came to check it out."

Cameron forced a smile. "Well, thanks."

"It's okay. But we better get back before somebody else comes looking."

Nodding, Cameron took a step forward.

"Need a hand?"

Cameron waved him away. "Let me do it myself," he said and started to walk toward the church.

Michael glanced down the street in the direction the assailants had fled, but all seemed quiet. As he turned toward the church, something on the ground glinted in the moonlight. He reached down, expecting to see a coin dropped by Cameron during the scuffle. Instead his fingers touched the smooth surface of a stiff card, which he lifted and held in front of his face. He could not make it out clearly in the thin light, but it looked like a playing card from a deck. He thought he saw the image of a woman and assumed it was a queen. With a shrug, he stuffed it in his pocket and started up the street after Cameron.

Chapter Seven

———◆———

Aileen Bloom poured the strong, black coffee and sat holding the warm cup in her hands. She flexed the fingers of her right hand, still chilled a half hour after arriving at the office from her boardinghouse room several blocks away. It had turned unusually cold and windy for this time of year during the night, and with the sun just beginning to rise, the chill had not yet left the air. With stiff fingers, she awkwardly flipped the page of the magazine she was reading. Raising the cup to her lips, she shivered slightly, as if the blast of predawn wind were still chasing her down the streets of Abilene.

Aileen drained the cup and placed it on the tray that Dr. Levi Wright's housekeeper, Mrs. Finnegan, had prepared. Then she glanced at the clock above the apothecary cabinet. It was nearly seven; Dr. Wright soon would be returning from the house call that had taken him away in the middle of the night. A note from the elderly doctor had been left for her on the tray: "It's five o'clock Wednesday morning, and old Tim Price let one of his milking cows knock some sense into him. His son thinks it's a broken leg, so I've gone to set it. Think you can handle opening the office without me?"

Aileen gave an inward groan at his final comment. Ever since her arrival in Abilene two years before, Dr. Wright had poked fun at the idea of a woman being a physician. He had continually denigrated the abilities of women to handle even the simplest tasks—such as opening the office. His most acerbic comments were directed at the notion of a woman surgeon. It might be all right for her to assist in the office—change bandages, prescribe fever powders, and the like—but the idea of a woman performing surgery was inconceivable to him. Therefore he had scrupulously kept Aileen from handling any of the more challenging assignments that came to the office. It was his practice and his prerogative, Aileen realized, but she hoped that one day she would earn his trust and be able to serve more fully.

Looking at the note again, Aileen smiled. Perhaps she was being too hard on the doctor. She knew that despite his crusty exterior, he was really quite kindhearted. After all, he had hired her in the first place, and that alone was more than almost any other man in his position would have done. Of course he had said it was because there was a shortage of trained physicians, but in the time she had been there, he had had several opportunities to replace her with a man and had not. "Takes too long to train another young upstart," Wright had grumbled each time, but Aileen did not believe it for a moment. Despite all that he said, she was certain that he had faith in her abilities. He had even stopped complaining when she found an opportunity to remove a stray bullet or two from someone's arm, such as the night before. And wasn't that surgery? "In Abilene, it's like taking someone's temperature," he would have argued.

Aileen put down the note, took another sip of coffee, and picked up the magazine. Before closing the office and leaving the night before, she had cleaned and laid out the instruments and had readied the examination rooms on either side of the dispensary for the morning patients, so she was taking a few minutes to read an article in the *Lancet* on Dr. Joseph Lister's controversial theory about the use of antiseptics to prevent infection. Fascinated by the account of one of his recent lectures, she did not hear any approaching footsteps before a doorknob turned and the back door leading to the kitchen creaked open. Startled, she dropped the magazine into her lap and spun around.

"Got your nose in *Godey's Lady's Book* again?" a deep, gruff voice called. The physician, a tall and imposing man of sixty-eight with gray hair and a trim beard, shook his head disparagingly as he walked to the dispensary counter, where he deposited his black surgical bag and began thumbing through the appointment book.

"No, Dr. Wright," Aileen replied, slipping the magazine onto the table. "It's the *Lancet*—a fascinating article on Lord Lister's work with carbolic—"

"Antiseptics," the doctor muttered with a slight note of disdain. "You'd think they'd discovered the Fountain of Youth. Well, thirty years ago an old frontier sawbones like me could've told those fancy English physicians that it's plain common sense to

clean your hands and instruments before cutting into somebody."

"Yes," Aileen whispered as she stood and approached the counter. She opened the older doctor's surgical bag and checked that it was properly supplied. As she restocked some of the items, she cautiously continued, "But Dr. Wright, if his germ theory is correct, then the use of antiseptics could be the key to eliminating infection."

The doctor shook his head and turned to face the young woman. "Miss Bloom . . . you're almost thirty now?"

Aileen looked at him curiously. "I just turned twenty-nine. But I don't see—"

"And you're certainly attractive enough—though Mrs. Finnegan says you'd do better at getting a husband if you piled those brunette locks up in a sweep and used a little more rouge. She's not keen on your long skirts, by the way—says the Paris style is well above the ankles these days. She's nearly forty, but she still keeps a sharp eye on what the fashion magazines have in mind for the women of America. Only way she'll get another husband, she insists."

"I still don't see what—"

"What I'm getting at?" he cut in. "Just this: If you spent a bit more time reading *her* magazines than *mine,* you'd have a better chance to secure a comfortable future." He chuckled. "And if Mrs. Finnegan would spend a bit more time doing her job and a bit less poring over *Godey's,* her future as my housekeeper might be more secure."

Aileen checked her temper as she put the last of the items in the surgical bag and began to close it. The clasp was as stiff as her fingers, and she had difficulty snapping it. As she struggled, she said in a firm but calm voice, "That's just what I'm trying to do, Dr. Wright—my job." She gave the clasp a final jab, but it would not shut.

"And you do it exceedingly well." He reached over and took the bag from her. "Except when it comes to delicate operations like this." In one precise motion, he pushed the clasp into place, then gave a satisfied smile. "It takes the hands of a surgeon," he said smugly, only to see the clasp pop open again. "Damned contraptions," he mumbled, throwing his hands up and turning away. He pretended not to notice when Aileen finally succeeded in securing the clasp.

Aileen placed the bag at the edge of the counter near the back door so that it would be at hand should Dr. Wright be called out unexpectedly. Turning to him, she asked, "How was Mr. Price's leg?"

"It was his foot. The old fool let a damn cow step on it and break a few toes. He won't be walking for a few weeks, but I told him he's not hurt so bad that he can't hobble in here and pay his bill for the past ten years."

Aileen suppressed a smile. "What about Mrs. Lanford? Did you see her last night?"

He nodded brusquely. "And a damn waste of time. It's as if she's simply refused to have that baby. You'd think after six sons she'd be a bit more punctual about dropping the seventh. Instead she keeps me riding all the way out there near every day for three weeks past her due date."

"I hope you don't have to go there again this morning. The way the wind's picking up, I'd say we're in for a storm. Not at all a pleasant day to be out visiting patients."

Dr. Wright gave an exaggerated sigh. "Ah, well,

such is the life of a country surgeon. Be glad I leave you the office duties and spare you such discomforts. You can sit in the cozy warmth of the office and—" he paused, waving a hand toward the tray on the table "—and sip hot coffee and such. That's why doctoring is really for men. Women just aren't cut out for the realities of the profession."

Again Aileen restrained her temper. Forcing herself to speak calmly, she replied, "There have been women physicians for nearly thirty years—"

"This is 1876, not 1849, and nothing's happened in all those years to change my opinion. It may have been a noble experiment when they allowed that Blackwell woman to attend medical college, but it hasn't changed the fact that folks just don't feel confident with a woman when it comes to matters of life and death. They want somebody with a clear mind and steady hand. Women are far too . . . emotional." He waved at the air, as if brushing off any dissent. "But enough of this talk, Miss Bloom. I well realize how much you admire Elizabeth Blackwell and her cohorts, but remember I hired you because a suitable man wasn't available—not because I wanted an authority on medical ethics. So let's keep our mind on the task at hand, all right?"

Setting her jaw, Aileen coolly replied, "Yes, Doctor."

"Fine. Now, if I'm not mistaken, it's time to see if we have any patients out there." He nodded toward the door across the room that led to the waiting area. "That is, if you're all through with that magazine." Without waiting for an answer, he strode to the door, threw it open, and found himself staring at a tall, gangly youth of about thirteen. The boy wore overalls and held a knit cap in his hands.

"Simon?" the doctor asked. "I just left your mother last night."

"Ma's real sorry," the boy muttered, staring with some embarrassment at his muddy farm boots, "but she said to tell you it's finally time."

"Have you been standing out here long?"

"She said not to disturb you during breakfast, and—"

"Hell, boy, doctors don't have time to eat. Do we, Miss Bloom?"

"Of course not," she agreed with a slight grin. "We don't even have time to read a magazine."

Looking at her askance, Dr. Wright said mischievously, "Or saddle our own horse, so why don't you take care of that for me, Miss Bloom? The gelding got a good workout this morning, so I'll take the mare. I'll wash up and meet you out front." Spinning around, he proclaimed, "Let's go, son. It's time to greet the seventh little Lanford boy."

As Dr. Wright and Simon headed through the waiting room to the front hall, Aileen grabbed her coat and made her way out back to the small horse barn. She quickly saddled the doctor's gray mare and led it to the front of the house, where Simon's chestnut mare was tethered. As she waited for the doctor to emerge from the house, she glanced up the street to the west. The wind was strengthening, the sky dark with clouds. The air was still quite cold, and it carried the first traces of rain.

Soon the front door opened and Dr. Wright appeared, bundled in a black rain slicker and hat. "Be back as soon as I can," he called as he climbed into the saddle and took the reins from Aileen, while Simon raced down the stairs and mounted his own mare. "If there are too many patients for you to handle, tell some to return tomorrow," he added as he pulled on the reins and turned the horse. "You can close at five if I'm not back." He kicked the horse into a trot and started west down the street, Simon riding close behind.

As soon as the horses disappeared from sight, Aileen hurried up the walkway and into the house. No patients had arrived yet, and so she hung her coat in the dispensary and began to gather the supplies needed to prepare a fresh supply of belladonna cough syrup, which was in demand whenever the weather turned foul for any length of time.

Fifteen minutes later, she had just finished mixing the first batch when she happened to glance at the other end of the counter. She almost took no notice of the object sitting near the door, and then suddenly she realized that Dr. Wright had forgotten his surgical bag. Aileen decided at once to bring it out to the Lanford homestead. Though she realized that the birth would likely be routine and no special supplies would be needed, there was always the possibility of complications.

Aileen wrote a hasty note informing prospective patients that the office would be closed until later that morning and hung it outside the front door. Then she donned her gray coat and one of Dr. Wright's wide-brimmed hats, grabbed the leather bag, and headed to the horse barn, where she saddled the doctor's spirited brown gelding and strapped the bag to the back of the saddle.

The rain was still light but was coming down steadily as Aileen led the horse to the front yard. She wished she were wearing riding clothes, but there was not enough time to go home and change. Nor would she attempt an awkward sidesaddle position, so she hiked up her long skirt, put one foot into the stirrup, and lifted herself into the saddle, straddling the animal. She knew some might disapprove of her style, but at least her dress had enough material that only her lower calves were visible.

Aileen was about to ride out of the yard when a man on a large brown horse pulled to a halt in the street in front of her. He tipped his hat slightly, and the rain ran off the brim. "Morning, Aileen," he said, and she recognized him as the gentleman from the night before.

"Mr. Travis," she replied with a smile.

"That's Luke," he corrected her.

"Yes, Luke."

"Not a fit day to be riding."

"I have no choice. I must deliver some supplies to Dr. Wright at a farm several miles northwest of here."

"Perhaps I could make the ride for you," he suggested.

"I appreciate the offer, but the Lanford place is off the main road and hard to find. It's best if I go myself."

"Then at least let me ride along with you."

"I couldn't ask you to do that. Surely you have business of your own—"

"I already had breakfast and was just giving my horse a little exercise before the weather gets too bad. I'd love to accompany you."

"But you needn't go to so much trouble. . . ."

"No trouble at all," he insisted. "It would give me a chance to see some of the area around Abilene. And when a storm is brewing, folks shouldn't be out riding alone."

"It seems there's no arguing with you, Luke," she said with a shrug and a smile. She pulled a pair of gloves from her coat pocket and put them on. "Shall I lead the way?"

With a gallant sweep of the arm, Travis signaled her to pass. She took off like a shot, and he had to kick his horse into a gallop to keep from being left in the dust—*or in this case mud,* he thought ruefully.

As the riders left town and turned northwest into the gathering darkness, the rain began to mix with small pellets of hail that danced on the ground all around them. Aileen pulled down the brim of her hat to shield her face—she knew Mrs. Finnegan would never approve, but just now she was happy to be wearing something with a brim wide enough to protect her from the pelting sleet. She was equally pleased she was not wearing a fancy pair of Parisian narrow-heeled button shoes but had on her plain flat-heeled boots.

The black clouds rolled so quickly across the landscape that three miles outside of town it looked as if night had fallen. The sleet was lessening, but the wind howled all the more furiously, and it was all Aileen could do to make out the small road on which they were riding, forcing her to keep their horses at no more than a brisk walk.

Travis's horse pulled alongside, and he shouted above the din, "Maybe we should turn back!"

"We're almost there!" she called back, and he nodded. Ahead they spied the silhouette of what appeared to be a stand of trees, and she shouted, "We're at the border of their property!"

"What's that?" he suddenly yelled, raising his arm and pointing into the near distance, where a huge black object seemed to traverse the road. "Looks like a tree!"

Slowing her horse, Aileen shielded her eyes from

the biting wind and cautiously approached. As she neared the scene, she could see the giant tree and was able to discern the forms of two men moving about it. Beyond them was what appeared to be a buckboard wagon. She called out as she rode closer, but the men either could not hear her above the wind or were too intent on what they were doing to give her any notice. Suddenly she realized why. A massive pine had snapped near its base and had fallen across the road, crushing a horse beneath it. The horse was motionless, and the two men did not seem to be paying it any attention. Their efforts were concentrated upon a much smaller figure—a man, whom they were pulling from the wreckage.

As Aileen and Travis leaped from their horses, the men on the other side glanced up only briefly, then continued extricating the victim. While Travis tied their horses to a branch of the fallen tree, Aileen ran around the shattered stump toward where the men were working. One of the men quickly intercepted her, blocking her way.

"Nothin' you can do, ma'am!" the fellow shouted, grabbing her by the shoulders.

Though Aileen could not make out the young man's features beneath the hood of his rain slicker, she realized he was only in his teens. Leaning forward, she shouted into his ear, "I'm Dr. Bloom, and Dr. Wright is nearby—at the Lanfords'."

The boy hesitated, then glanced at his companion. Looking back at her, he shook his head and said, "Sorry, ma'am, but he never made it to our house."

Aileen felt her whole body stiffen. She stared blankly at the boy in front of her, then shifted her gaze to the twisted mass of limbs and leaves. With a shock, she recognized the body of a gray mare underneath.

She already knew but heard herself asking, "Is it . . . is it . . . ?"

"I'm afraid so, ma'am. They never saw it coming."

Just then Aileen made out the form of a second horse buried under the tree. A body lay on the ground nearby. "Simon?" she whispered, motioning toward the body.

The boy nodded grimly. His voice broke as he replied, "When my brother didn't return with the doctor, Will and I came looking. We pulled them out, but it was too late."

"You mean . . . ?" She tried to pull away and approach the site, but he held her back.

"I'm sorry."

"Are y-you sure?" she stammered, and she felt her body go limp as he nodded.

"Are you all right?" a deeper voice asked from behind her, and Aileen felt Travis's hands on her shoulders.

Aileen nodded, and he relaxed his grip. She slowly walked forward to where the other teenager was just pulling the body of Dr. Wright clear of the tree. As he laid it on its back, she stepped closer and grasped the boy's arm.

"I'm Aileen Bloom—Dr. Wright's associate," she said in a surprisingly steady voice. "I must examine him."

He nodded and backed away from the body.

Aileen knelt and began to wipe mud from the doctor's face. Placing her ear by his mouth, she pulled the glove off her right hand and gently pressed his neck with two fingers. "My God," she whispered, glancing up at Travis and then over at the two boys huddled nearby. "He's alive."

A quick examination revealed that the elderly man

had suffered a bad concussion but did not seem to have any broken bones. She told the boys to wrap him in a blanket from the wagon. Then she hurried to where Simon was lying a few feet away. The whole top of his head was covered with blood, and she had no doubt that his skull had been crushed.

Just as she was about to feel for a pulse, Simon drew in an audible breath, and Aileen jumped with surprise. Without looking up, she called, "Luke, get the surgical bag from my saddle!" Then she tore a clean section from the hem of her soaking dress and began to wash the head wound.

A few moments later, Luke placed the bag beside her. Fumbling with the clasp, Aileen breathed a sigh of relief when it opened without its usual stubbornness. She reached inside and quickly found the surgical probe. Holding it in her right hand, she carefully felt the entire surface of the boy's skull until she isolated the damage to the top front of the forehead. With a silent prayer, she slipped the probe into one of the gashes near the edge of the torn mass of flesh and bone and started to pull.

Aileen held her breath as the whole surface of the wound lifted away, like a flap of skin being peeled from an orange. As expected, she saw the gleam of white bone underneath but was horrified to discover a jagged gaping hole near the center. A section of skull nearly two inches in diameter was missing. It had been shattered by the impact of the tree, and the broken shards had come away with the skin. Beneath, the gray mass of the brain lay exposed. Aileen gasped and turned away from the dreadful sight.

Travis knelt beside her and touched her arm. "What can I do?" he asked.

Aileen stared up at him, then glanced at the buckboard wagon. All the while, her thoughts raced through the medical books and journals she had been reading in her spare time. Finally she said, "If we try to move him, he'll surely die. I must operate at once—right here and now."

"But how?" he asked.

Looking over at one of the teenage boys, she called, "Do you have any more blankets?"

The boy thought for a moment. "There's a canvas tarp in the wagon."

"Perfect. Bring the wagon right up beside here and stretch the tarp between it and the tree, so I can work underneath. Do you have a lantern? And a hammer in the toolbox?" she asked, and the boy nodded. "Fetch them both and get that wagon over here. There's no time to waste."

While Travis and the boys readied the wagon and tarp, Aileen reexamined Dr. Wright and verified that his injuries were not more extensive than she had first thought. He remained unconscious, and so she wrapped him snugly in the blanket and made sure he was well protected under the tarp.

Fifteen minutes later, the makeshift operating theater was completed. The boys, one of them holding the lantern, huddled beneath the tarp near their brother's head, while Travis knelt beside Aileen, ready to assist as needed. She began by handing him several of the surgical instruments. Then she took out a bottle and removed the rubber stopper.

"This is carbolic lotion," she explained as she poured some onto her hands and began to wipe them. "To prevent infection, we have to rinse everything with it." She gave Travis the bottle. "Just pour it over each instrument before you hand it to me, all right?" When he nodded, she continued, "Now give me the scalpel—that's the long-bladed knife." He started to hand it over, and she said, "Douse the blade first, and don't touch anything but the handle."

Taking hold of the disinfected scalpel, Aileen deftly began to cut away the crushed pieces of bone and the most damaged sections of tissue, pausing every so often to blot up the seeping blood with some cotton. Simon stirred once, but a moment later his body relaxed, and Aileen continued her work. Soon all the bone fragments were removed, and she folded the skin over the skull to make sure enough remained to close the wound. Finally she leaned over to make sure the unconscious boy was still breathing regularly.

The boy holding the lantern had been staring in wide-eyed amazement throughout the procedure. Now he cleared his throat and ventured to ask, "Is that all, Dr. Bloom? Are you going to sew him up?"

As Aileen turned to answer, she realized that her hands were shaking. Forcing a smile, she replied, "I'm afraid we can't leave that hole in his skull—it would never heal." Seeing their concerned expressions, she added, "We're going to put Dr. Wright's lucky twenty-dollar gold piece to work for us—and find out just how lucky it really is."

The brothers were too surprised by all they had seen to question her. Instead they watched in awed silence as she felt around inside the surgical bag and produced a bent gold coin, which she held aloft.

"Dr. Wright has had this since the Civil War. See this dent?" She pointed at a prominent bump near the center. "A rebel bullet made this at Gettysburg. It saved his life, and he's carried it in this surgical bag ever since. Now give me that hammer," she asked the boy holding the lantern.

The boy quickly pulled the hammer from behind

his belt and handed it to Aileen, who placed the coin on the surface of a flat rock and proceeded to bang away at it. Travis and the brothers watched, transfixed as she pounded the malleable metal into a two-inch-wide disk. Holding it out for them to see, she said, "I read an article in a medical journal about a new procedure they are using in England when the skull is damaged. They simply mold a thin metal plate to cover the area and then sew the skin right over it."

"How do they get it out?" Travis asked.

"They don't. It stays there forever."

Aileen turned to her patient and carefully held the flattened coin over the gaping hole. Determining that it was a little too small on one side, she placed it on the rock and pounded it into the appropriate shape. In a few minutes she had a thin gold plate that was nearly a perfect fit, and she then doused it with carbolic lotion.

After laying the disk over the damaged area, Aileen chose one of the surgical needles, placed it in the needle holder, and cleaned both with the lotion. She threaded it with a length of fine catgut ligature, then handed it to Travis to hold. Using forceps and several surgical clamps, she stretched the flap of skin over the plate and clamped the edges together. Finally, after again cleaning the needle, she began a series of delicate stitches to bind the skin together. Ten minutes later, the last of the clamps was removed. The operation was finished.

Aileen leaned back and sighed. She started to gather the instruments and return them to the surgical bag, but her hands were so shaky that she dropped several on the ground.

"You'd make a damn fine surgeon," a thin, quavering voice intoned.

With a start, Aileen spun around to see Dr. Wright raised up on one elbow. Her mouth dropped open in surprise.

"That is, if you learn to hang on to your instruments." He gave her a pained smile.

"How long have you—?"

"Since you started sewing my lucky gold piece inside his head. Where did you learn that little trick?" She was about to reply when he cut her off, saying, "Don't tell me. The *Lancet,* right?"

"But why didn't you say something?"

"There was no need. You were doing just fine without getting a case of the nerves from having a crusty old physician like me looking over your shoulder."

The doctor glanced at the boys kneeling nearby and said, "We won't be sure for some time, boys, but I think Dr. Bloom has just saved your brother's life." He turned to Aileen. "Now you leave me and these gentlemen to finish up here. You'd best ride on to the farmhouse. If I'm not mistaken, there's a woman in labor over there—and who better to attend her than a woman physician?"

Aileen stared at Dr. Wright for a long moment, her eyes and smile communicating her gratitude. Then she turned to Travis and said, "The patients can be moved now, so you and the boys had best get started. I'll meet you at the house. You heard the doctor; there's a baby that needs delivering."

Chapter Eight

———◆———

Judah Fisher was unbearably hot and sweating profusely as he tossed left and right, his fists clenched tight, his eyelids clamped shut. His clerical collar seemed to be choking him, and he reached up and pawed at it. He heard voices crying and laughing—his congregation mocking him—and with a sharp gasp he bolted upright on the bed. "My God!" he cried, his breath coming in ragged pants.

Judah blinked his eyes and tried to focus in the dim light. He was in his bedroom, and the closed curtains gave enough of a glow to tell him it was well into the next day—making it Wednesday. He tried to recall the events of the night before. With a groan he remembered the loneliness and pain of his father's death, the somber funeral service at which he had officiated in a daze, the bottle of whiskey he had drunk in an attempt to drown it all. Somehow he must have stumbled off to bed—even removed his shoes, he noted as he stared down at his stockinged feet. But he remembered nothing beyond the dull forgetfulness that the whiskey had afforded. That much he recalled all too clearly now, for it was being hammered into his brain like a runaway train colliding over and over against the inside of his skull.

Leaning forward and placing his head in his hands, Judah tried to still the pounding and clear the fog that filled his ears and brain. Slowly the pain subsided until it was a dull, annoying throb. But the noise inside his head refused to lessen. Instead it grew louder and more distinct, until he was certain people were laughing at him, mocking him for his weaknesses.

He cocked his head and listened closely. Yes, there was laughter, but it was not imaginary. This raucous babble was coming from somewhere in his own house, and it was neither a dream nor the whiskey mocking him. Furthermore, he detected the unmistakable odor of bacon being fried.

Judah groped around on the nightstand until he found his black wire-rimmed glasses. Putting them on, he stood and shuffled to the window on unsteady legs. Opening the curtains, he looked out and saw rain falling steadily, with a stiff breeze throwing the droplets against the glass. The sky was a fairly bright gray, so either the storm was a gentle one or the worst of it had passed.

Awkwardly making his way to the bedroom door, he opened it a crack and placed his ear near the opening. The laughter that floated down the hall was clearly that of children, and it sounded as if they were gathered in the kitchen. He pulled the door open wide, took a deep breath, and headed down the hall.

Judah thought it odd that the door to the kitchen was closed; he never shut it, and neither did Mrs. Eastman on the mornings she came to clean. And indeed there was a babble of voices on the other side, and the rich aroma of bacon seeped under the door. He reached for the doorknob but then pulled back and stood listening, suddenly feeling awkward, as if he were an intruder in his own home. When he heard the patter of feet racing up the back stairs, he decided to investigate more surreptitiously before barging into the kitchen—his own kitchen, no less.

Hurrying down the front hall as quickly as his unsteady legs would carry him, Judah mounted the main staircase and emerged in the hallway that separated the four unused upstairs rooms. The doors were open, and he glanced in the nearest one. With a shock he saw that the beds were unmade and several bedrolls were on the floor. The second room had been used, as well, and he turned to check the third, wondering what army had invaded his private sanctuary.

Just then a small child came dashing from the room, barreling into the minister and nearly knocking him off his feet. The little girl, who could have been no older than four or five, gasped with surprise and jumped back, clutching her rag doll to her chest.

"Who are you, child?" Judah asked in as calm a tone as he could muster. When the girl did not reply, he knelt in front of her. "What are you doing here?"

The girl's eyes widened, and she lifted a thin hand and pointed at Judah's clerical collar, which was crumpled and a bit crooked. "Are you my father?" she asked ingenuously.

Judah found himself smiling. "Not exactly. But where is your father?"

"He art in heaven."

Judah looked at her curiously. Then he nodded and said, "Ahh . . . you mean he *is* in heaven."

"No, our father who *art* in heaven," she corrected him.

"I see." He tried not to chuckle. "And where is your mother?" he asked gently, but the girl merely shrugged. "Surely you must be with someone. Who brought you here?"

"We came with a sister."

"Good," he proclaimed. "Can you take me to her?"

The girl gave a slight nod. "She's downstairs. I came up to get Henrietta." She turned the rag doll so that Judah could see its face. "She's awfully hungry."

"Then let's get her something to eat," Judah said, standing. "And you can introduce me to your sister."

The little girl smiled. "My name is Emily," she said, dashing around Judah to the doorway that led downstairs. She waited until he came up behind her, and then she took his hand and led him down to the kitchen.

At the foot of the stairs, Judah emerged into a world awash with children of every age and size. Most were huddled around the big table that dominated one side of the room, while others stood at the sink or stove. The tallest boy was holding an armful of firewood just inside the rear door, and Judah noticed he had a purple bruise on his cheek, as if he had been in a fight. Nearby, the oldest-looking of the girls stood in the open pantry doorway, and Judah thought he saw someone inside the pantry gathering food.

The children who were facing the stairway immediately fell silent and began to shake or prod the ones whose backs were to the door. The silence spread like a wave through the room, until everyone was facing the minister in stockinged feet who was holding little Emily's hand.

"Oh, dear," the oldest of the girls whispered.

"What's that, Agnes?" a woman called from the pantry, and then a dark figure appeared behind the teenager and moved past her into the room. "What's going on out here?"

Judah's mouth dropped upon seeing that Emily's sister was actually a Roman Catholic nun. As if to confirm the fact, Emily tugged his arm and said, "That's Sister Laurel."

Her face breaking into a broad smile, Sister Laurel clasped her hands and approached the minister. "Reverend Fisher," she declared, "I'm so glad you're feeling better." Stopping a few feet in front of him, she turned to the children. "Boys and girls, this is the Reverend Judah Fisher, who has been so kind as to open his home to us."

"I—I'm not sure I understand," he replied hesitantly.

"Of course not. You were feeling so ill, and I did not want to disturb you. These children are all orphans under the care of our Dominican order. We are on our way to Wichita to found an orphanage, but one boy"—she signaled Michael to stand so that Judah could see his bandage—"was injured yesterday. Dr. Bloom insisted he spend the night in a bed, and she suggested we come here. I hope I didn't—"

"Of course not," he cut in with a wave of his hand. "I'm only sorry I was not well enough to greet you myself last night." He smiled cautiously.

"Let's not speak of last night again," she proclaimed. "Today is a new day, and I'm certain a good hot meal is just what you need to set your *spirits* right." She grinned mischievously, and Judah averted his eyes.

Sister Laurel spun around and circled the room, motioning the children to continue what they had been doing. Most were finished eating, but there were still plenty of eggs and bacon on the stove ready to be fried. A place was quickly set for Judah at the head of the table, and before he knew what was happening, Emily and some of the other smaller children had dragged him over and plopped him down in the seat. In short order, a steaming plate of food and a mug of black coffee were placed in front of him.

The final shift of children seated at the table all picked up their forks, waiting for Judah to begin. He gave them a thin smile, then gingerly picked up his own fork and took the first bite. Immediately the others dove at their own plates, and within moments the kitchen was alive again with the sound of children laughing and talking, seemingly all at the same time. Judah seemed to forget how unsettled his stomach had felt only minutes before, and he ate heartily. He could not remember the last time he had such a delectable meal, and when Sister Laurel brought a platter of bacon and eggs around, he allowed himself to be served a second heaping portion, which he quickly consumed.

"Delicious," he declared, totally forgetting the slight throbbing at his temples as he put down his fork. "I don't think I ate yesterday. I . . . I had a funeral to attend."

"Yes," the nun said. "I'm so sorry about your father."

Judah nodded. "I guess I was hungrier than I thought."

"Then have a bit more." She scooped up several thick strips of bacon and dropped them onto his plate, then pushed the plate in front of him.

"I shouldn't," he said, but then he picked up his fork and added, "but I suppose one more wouldn't hurt."

He was wrong. The feeling came over him quite suddenly, between the second and third strip of bacon. At first it felt as if a large lead weight had been dropped from the top of the church tower directly into his stomach. But then the weight came alive and began to roil around inside him like a gathering hurricane. His stomach caught fire as the hurricane became a volcano, with the lava threatening to erupt.

"Is something wrong?" Sister Laurel asked, standing over him with the plate of bacon almost directly under his nose. "Perhaps another piece . . . ?"

"I . . . I th-think n-not," he managed to stammer, his face turning sheet white and his eyes bulging at the sight of the crisp, greasy bacon. He gave a rumbling belch, and his eyes opened even wider.

"Oh, dear," Sister Laurel whispered. "I hope—"

The second belch was louder and deeper. "Ex-excuse me," he blurted as he pushed the platter of bacon away and stood on shaky legs. He almost knocked over the chair as he backed from the table.

"Quick! The door!" Sister Laurel called to one of the children, who yanked open the back door.

Judah turned and headed across the room, his stockinged feet slipping on the polished hardwood floor. Grabbing the doorjamb, he pulled himself through and went stumbling through the rain across the muddy backyard.

The children gathered at the rain-splattered windows and watched Judah stagger through the outhouse doorway. The moment the door closed behind him, the most god-awful, gut-wrenching noises reverberated across the yard, as if Vesuvius itself were spewing forth from the very bowels of the earth.

"Oh, dear," Sister Laurel muttered as she stood in the kitchen doorway and stared across the yard, shaking her head with pity. "The saints be spared!"

Judah Fisher spent the rest of the morning resting in his room and wisely decided to skip lunch. He had washed and changed his clothes and felt much better as he sat in a chair near the window and read his Bible, seeking appropriate passages for the upcoming Sunday service.

There was a gentle knock at the door, and he called, "Yes? Come in."

The door creaked open, and Sister Laurel entered carrying a small tray. "Some tea and a slice of fresh bread," she said, approaching and placing the tray on the stand beside the chair. "It will settle your stomach."

"Thank you," he replied, looking a bit sheepish. "I'm sorry about this morning. . . ."

"No need to apologize. We are intruders in your home."

"This is supposed to be God's home. I'm afraid I'm not a very worthy caretaker."

"Just because you got a bit sick——"

"Drunk is the word," he corrected her.

"I got drunk once, myself. How else can we understand the ways of the world to which we are trying to minister?"

Judah stared at her a long moment, as if gauging her character. Then he motioned her to the chair by his desk. When she was seated, he said, "I haven't gotten drunk just once. When I was younger, I was drunk much of the time."

"Before you took up the cloth?" she asked, and he nodded. "But you were a different person then."

"I've been sorely tempted since."

"The bottle is a powerful seductress."

"And once since becoming a minister I *was* seduced by the bottle—after my younger brother strapped on a gun and left home. I should have been stronger."

"You blamed yourself," she said knowingly. "And with your father's death, you feel that same guilt. But why?"

Judah sighed. "My father was murdered by Marcus Donaghue, and I should have seen it coming."

"So they've caught his murderer?"

"Donaghue?" He laughed bitterly. "He practically owns Abilene. No one will touch him, and anyway, they could never make a case stick. He may not have pulled the trigger, but he paid the man who did."

"But how could you be to blame?"

Judah picked up the warm mug of tea and held it between his hands. "I've spoken against him from the pulpit, urging my parishioners to do what they can within the bounds of the law to see him brought to justice. But it isn't enough—I realize that now. I should have been speaking out on the streets, not hiding behind an altar. I left my father out there to fight alone, and they killed him for it."

"It sounds like you were fighting—in your own way. We are each given our own pulpit—and yours is in this church. Dr. Bloom said your father was a judge?" she asked, and he nodded. "Then his was in the courtroom. It could have been you who took that bullet, but your father must have had this Donaghue fellow more worried—enough to kill. Don't turn your anger at Donaghue against yourself. There are millions of Donaghues in this world, and God will judge each."

"Are you saying I should do nothing?"

"Not at all. But you were right not to sink to Donaghue's level. Any action you take must be within the law and with the support of the people. There is no profit in defeating one Donaghue and creating another."

He waved his hand in an offhand manner. "Oh, I know what you say is true. But the problem runs deeper."

Sister Laurel leaned forward in her chair. "Just what do you mean?"

"I want to kill the bastard," Judah said bluntly. "Slowly. Without mercy."

The words settled into a heavy silence. "But you won't," she finally said, a statement more than a question.

"I just don't know. It goes against everything I believe. But perhaps my faith isn't as strong as I had thought. Maybe . . ." His voice trailed off.

"Maybe you are a man, Reverend Fisher, with the natural feelings of a man. A man who is being far too hard on himself. You must first forgive your desire for vengeance before you can hope to forgive others."

"I will never forgive Marcus Donaghue," he said flatly.

"He, too, is a man—a very weak man. Don't let him make you weak, too."

"I let him murder my father."

"God allowed that, as well. Don't expect more from yourself than you do from God."

"I know," he muttered, taking a deep breath. "But this desire—this anger—it feels so unchristian."

"It's human, and so are you. Accept your weaknesses. Just don't magnify them."

Judah nodded, then took a sip of tea. "Thank you," he said at last, putting down the mug. He forced a smile but still looked somewhat troubled. "I'm afraid my mind is a whirl of thoughts that I'll have to sort out. But it was good to talk with someone about all this."

Sister Laurel stood and headed to the door, then looked back and said, "By the way, the children and I will be leaving shortly. We'll be taking lodgings at—"

"No," he cut in, standing and raising his arm. "You must stay here."

"We've imposed—"

"Not at all. I insist. Your funds must be saved for the journey ahead. You're going on to Wichita?"

"Perhaps tomorrow—after Dr. Bloom examines the children."

"Then you will stay here until you leave," he declared, and she smiled and nodded. "And one other thing," he added as she started out into the hallway. "I should be able to put myself to bed tonight."

"I hope the same holds true for me," Sister Laurel replied with a broad smile. "It's been a long journey, and now I know where you keep your whiskey."

"I'm afraid you'll have to settle for communion wine. I poured out the whiskey this morning." When Sister Laurel pouted, Judah shrugged apologetically and added, "They say there's no one more falsely pious—or troublesome—than a reformed drunk!"

"Yes there is, Reverend Fisher," she insisted, "and pray you never see it."

"What's that?" he asked, his dark eyebrows arching above his wire-rimmed glasses.

"A tipsy nun!"

Chapter Nine

The rain had stopped and the wind had diminished by the time Luke Travis and Dr. Aileen Bloom returned to Abilene from the Lanford farm late Wednesday afternoon. Young Simon had regained consciousness and was resting peacefully in his own bed. He had not yet spoken, and only time would tell if his injury had caused serious brain damage. Dr. Wright was feeling better but would spend a day or two at the farm, both to recuperate and to keep an eye on the teenage boy and his new baby sister.

After helping Aileen bed down her horse for the night, Travis led her around the house to the front door.

"I'd like to invite you in for some tea," Aileen said as they stood on the porch, "but I have to visit some of the patients who came while the office was closed."

"That's quite all right," Travis assured her. "But

eventually you'll need some dinner. Perhaps you'd be my guest at one of the local restaurants?"

"I'd like that." She smiled gently. "But I don't know when I'll be back. I'd hate to keep you waiting."

"I've got nothing to do. I'll just check in every hour or so."

Aileen shook her head and said, "I've a better idea." She pointed at the kerosene lantern on the wall beside the front door. "When I get back, I'll light this lamp."

"Fine. Until later, then." He tipped his hat, then waited while she unlocked and opened the front door. As she started inside, he said, "Aileen, what you did this morning was quite impressive—and took quick thinking."

She blushed slightly. "I didn't have any choice."

"You could have stood there and done nothing."

"No." She slowly shook her head, and her eyes looked into the distance. "You see, I'm a physician."

"Yes, you are. And you're fortunate to be so sure of who you are."

Detecting a slightly despondent tone, she said, "Surely the famous Marshal Luke Travis knows full well who he is."

"Who he *was*. I'm no longer so sure who or what I *am*."

"How long has it been?" she asked.

"What do you mean?"

"Since your wife's death."

Travis looked down. Drawing in a deep breath, he said, "Only a few weeks."

"Give yourself time. You'll discover soon enough where you're headed."

"I'm not eager to take up a badge again. I've seen enough of death."

Aileen placed a hand on Travis's forearm. "One year out of medical school I felt the same way. I was working at a women's hospital in New York City during a cholera outbreak, and the poor women kept dying despite our greatest efforts. Then one day a pregnant woman died, and I could still hear the heart of her unborn baby beating inside her. I cut the woman open and brought the child crying into the world. I wondered if I'd done it a service, but when I handed that baby to its father and saw the joy in his eyes, I knew there was a reason I had become a physician. Perhaps just for that one child, or maybe the boy today."

"But you never knowingly took a life."

"And you must remember the lives you've saved," she reminded him, withdrawing her hand.

He looked at her closely. "Are you saying I should put on a badge and strap my gun back on?"

"Not at all. But you were meant to have served as marshal of Wichita, just as I am meant to be a physician. And in time you'll know what you're supposed to do next."

"I hope so."

"And what will you do until then?" she asked.

"I suppose I'll continue on to Wichita—try to pick up the trail I left three years ago."

"Maybe you never left it, Luke. Maybe you're on it right now."

Travis grinned. "Just so long as it takes me to a comfortable seat at one of Abilene's finer eateries."

"Yes, I'd like that."

Travis waited as she stepped over the threshold and disappeared inside. Then he turned and looked out toward the street, watching as a wagon crossed in one direction and a pair of mounted cowboys passed the opposite way. Travis found himself smiling. He had hardly spoken about his feelings since before Sarah had died—and it felt good. The only thing that just now might feel as nice was a warming drink from the special supply behind Orion McCarthy's bar.

"Who goes there?" a weirdly high-pitched voice called as Travis entered Orion's Tavern.

Travis looked around but did not see the big Scotsman. "Orion? Is that you?" he asked as he stepped up to the long mahogany bar that ran along one wall.

"Dinna be daft, man!" the thin voice with a strangely lilting brogue replied.

Travis jerked his head around, looking for Orion. But he was neither behind the bar nor in the large main room, which was empty save for a quartet of poker players at a rear table who looked as though they had been in from the range for several days and were taking a breather between one drunk and another.

"Orion?" Travis called, turning toward the bar.

"Gone fishing!" the squawky voice answered.

Furrowing his forehead, Travis leaned over the bar to look down at the floor. "You down there?" he asked.

"Dinna be daft! Gone fishing, I say!"

Travis heard a ruffling sound, and he looked up quickly to see a beautiful green bird fluffing its feathers on a perch that stood on the rear shelf of bottles.

"You down there?" the bird suddenly spoke, perfectly mimicking the tone Travis had used.

"Well I'll be damned!" Travis muttered.

"Dinna be damned!" the bird replied, cocking its head to one side.

"So ye met Old Bailey," a voice called, and Travis

turned to see Orion coming through a door at the far end of the bar. He stepped up to the perch and put out his finger. The bird hopped aboard, and Orion swung around and held him out to Travis. "I'd have introduced ye two last night, but Bailey boy was upstairs in his cage, catching some sleep."

"I'll be damned!" the bird squawked, and Orion gave a hearty laugh, which the bird immediately imitated, though an octave or two higher.

"Ye ginna have t'mind ye language around Old Bailey, Lucas. He picks things up as quick as ye say 'em, but fortunately forgets 'em just as fast."

"Dinna be daft!" came the reply, and both men laughed.

"Well, maybe not everything," Orion admitted, returning Old Bailey to his perch. Choosing a glass from the back shelf, he slapped it down on the bar and then reached below and produced a bottle. "Well, ye have'na come here just t'ruffle the feathers of me pet parrot. A drink, perhaps?"

"Straight up," Travis declared, taking hold of the glass as Orion poured. Lifting the glass to his lips, Travis took a sip and savored the warmth.

"An' one f'me, if ye not be averse t'drinking wi' a Scotsman."

"An' one f'me!" a small voice echoed as Orion turned to get himself a glass.

Orion lowered one eye and glowered at the parrot, then turned to the bar and poured a shot glass for himself. As he downed the contents, the small glass seemed to disappear momentarily within his abundant red beard. He banged the empty glass atop the counter, filled it again, and downed it just as quickly. "C'mon, man," he prodded Travis, who was still nursing his first drink. "Ye kinna get there from here less'n ye kiss the barleycorn wi' a bit more passion." He tipped the bottle and filled Travis's glass to the rim.

Keeping a serious expression, Travis lifted his glass and swallowed the Scotch in one gulp. He felt a delayed kick in his stomach, then allowed himself a smile. When Orion raised the bottle to pour another, Travis covered the glass with his hand.

"Dinna tell me ye drink like an Englisher, too!"

"A bloody Englisher!" the parrot exclaimed in as mocking a tone.

"I'm having dinner with Dr. Bloom," Travis explained.

"Now there's a looker," Orion pronounced with a wink. "But a strange one. Keeps t'herself, though ne'er at a loss for suitors." He took another drink, then added, "Ye be a lucky man, Lucas."

"It's just a friendly dinner," Travis protested.

Orion winked knowingly. "I'll pray tha' it is."

"Who goes there?" the parrot piped in, and the two men turned to see the batwings swing open. In strutted Bridger Kincaid, his tan pants and shirt looking freshly laundered, his boots polished to a high shine. Even his broad white sling, which covered his right arm from above the elbow to over his hand, looked newly pressed and starched. Entering the tavern, he pulled off his hat and casually tossed it onto the nearest table, then ran his fingers through his trim blond hair. As he approached the bar, a pair of men shouldered their way through the batwings—the same two who had tried to interfere in the fight at the Salty Dog Saloon. The man named Jeb was nowhere in sight.

"Good evenin', Orion," Bridger said with a smirk. He leaned against the bar several feet away from Luke Travis.

"What d'ye want?"

Looking the former marshal up and down with disdain, he replied, "We've come to ask Mr. Travis, here, why he ain't taken our *suggestion* that he move on to Wichita." He glanced across the bar and squinted one eye at Orion. "And there's the question of that money you owe Mr. Donaghue."

As he spoke, the other two men walked over to where the cardplayers were seated and began to remove cards from the stunned dealer's hands, placing them faceup on the table. The dealer started to object, but he was quickly silenced by the menacing expressions he received from the two gunmen.

"I'd say this game is about over," was all one of Bridger's men had to say for the players to get the hint and fold their hands. They quickly pocketed their winnings and a moment later were gone from the tavern.

"Now about that money . . ." Kincaid said as soon as the poker players were gone.

"I'll be damned a'fore I pay one red cent for wha' I dinna need."

"Dinna be damned," the bird chirped, but no one paid it any attention.

"I'm sorry you see things like that," Bridger replied. "But don't be so sure you don't need our services." He glanced around the tavern, taking in the tables, chandeliers, and long rows of bottles and glasses. "It looks like you've put a lot into this place, Orion. I'd hate to see you lose it all in some drunken brawl by a bunch of rowdy cowboys." He gave Orion a smug grin.

Orion's face began to redden as he glowered at the

man. "Get out, I say!" he suddenly blurted, and in a high screech the parrot echoed, "Get out! Get out!"

"Mr. Donaghue only wants to keep the peace in his—"

"His city? Ye tell him tha' I'll be damned a'fore I pay protection money t'the likes o' him!"

"Dinna be damned!" came Old Bailey's plea.

"Have it your way," Kincaid said, waving his good hand as if to show his lack of concern over Orion's decision. "But there's still the question of Mr. Travis." He turned to the former lawman and smiled. "I see you ain't left town. I also see you ain't wearin' your gun."

Travis glanced at the gun strapped around Bridger's waist, then looked the man in the eyes and calmly but firmly said, "I'll be staying in Abilene just as long as I choose." As he spoke, he was aware of the other two men circling the room to come up behind him. Still looking at Kincaid, he leaned away from the bar and gave himself some room, though he made no effort to protect his back.

"That's your choice, I suppose," Kincaid drawled, "but not a healthy one. Mr. Donaghue may be patient, but I ain't." His grin widened as he looked over Travis's shoulder at his approaching men.

One of the men was moving up alongside the bar, behind and just to Travis's right. Without warning, Travis lifted his right arm, clasped hands, and drove back his elbow, catching the man full force in the belly and doubling him over. As Travis spun around, he brought up his left knee under the man's chin, snapping his head back and dropping him to the floor. The other man moved in with a wild haymaker, but Travis raised his arm and deflected the blow, throwing the man off balance. Travis followed with a left jab and a solid right that connected with the man's nose. There was the crunch of bone, and the man's knees buckled and he sank to the floor, blood spurting from his nostrils.

"Sorry," Travis apologized, "but you boys shouldn't have crowded me." He heard the double click of a hammer being cocked and spun back around, surprised to see that Kincaid's sidearm was still holstered.

"And *you* shouldn't have crowded *me,*" Kincaid said flatly, his smile gone as he pulled back the sling to reveal a hidden revolver, its muzzle pointed at Travis's chest.

Travis could hear shuffling noises behind him and knew that Kincaid's men were pulling themselves up off the floor. "I'm unarmed," he said, lifting his hands away from his hips and showing his palms.

"But I'm not," Kincaid pointed out, his finger tightening on the trigger.

There was the rasp of metal and another set of clicks. "An' neither am I!" Orion declared as he brought up a sawed-off, double-barreled shotgun from behind the bar.

Keeping his revolver trained on Travis, Kincaid eyed the barkeep uneasily.

"The first barrel's for ye, the second for ye friends," Orion announced, glancing over at the two men, who were finally on their feet but not looking at all steady.

Kincaid grinned again and raised the barrel of his revolver toward the ceiling, uncocking it at the same time. With his left hand he took it from inside the sling and jammed it behind his gun belt. "Another day, perhaps," he said amiably. He walked over to the table near the door and retrieved his hat, while the two men picked up theirs from the floor and followed him to the swinging doors.

Kincaid ushered his men outside. But as he started through the batwings himself, he turned at the last moment and said, "You ain't too smart, Orion. Donaghue don't like folks like you sidin' with an outsider. And he sure as hell hates when a man don't pay what's due."

"Ye tell Mr. Donaghue tha' there will be no gunplay in Orion's Tavern—especially agin an unarmed man. An' ye kin tell'm as well tha' I've no need for his protection." He waggled the shotgun at Kincaid. "I kin protect me own self 'n' mine without help from the likes o' him!"

"Have it your way," Kincaid replied, shrugging his shoulders. "Good day, gentlemen." He pushed his way through the doors and was gone.

"Good goddamn day!" Old Bailey squawked as the batwings swung back and forth and slowly settled into place.

Orion was breathing heavily, his face still mottled with rage as he uncocked the shotgun and placed it behind the bar. Without speaking, he slapped a fresh pair of shot glasses on the bar and unstoppered the bottle of Scotch. Filling the glasses to the brim, he slid one to Travis, and both men downed their drinks in a single gulp.

"Ahh!" Orion sighed as the liquor went down. "Here's t'seeing the last o' tha' man!"

"Agreed!" Travis declared. He held out the glass for a refill, and again the two men drank.

"Easy now!" Old Bailey piped in. "Steady as she goes!"

Both men laughed heartily, and they were still

laughing when the doors swung open and a few of the regular evening patrons filed in and took a table in the middle of the room. One of the men signaled Orion, who called, "Be right up!" then began to line up several large mugs on the bar.

"I'd better head to my hotel room to freshen up," Travis said as Orion filled the mugs with foamy beer from the tap.

"Aye, ye will want t'be as fresh as the little lady will allow." Orion gave a wink.

"Enough," Travis declared with a mock frown.

"Just remember t'tell ye good friend Orion all about it in the morning."

"Don't count on it."

"Aye, tha' I do. Now get out o' here. Ye should'na keep a lady waiting."

Travis smiled and started to turn from the bar. He stopped, looked at Orion, and said, "I hope tonight's little entertainment won't cause you any problems."

"Kincaid? He's nothing I kinna handle."

"Don't underestimate him."

"I dinna get t'be fifty by turning me back on the likes o' him. But dinna worry. I'll be careful."

Travis nodded and headed across the room. As he pushed through the swinging doors, he heard a voice call out, "Be sure t'give her a kiss, Englisher!" Though the voice was a fairly high-pitched Scottish brogue, he could not be sure if it was Orion or his parrot squawking at him.

Just after two in the morning, Orion McCarthy ushered the last of his patrons through the batwings, then circled the room, turning down the kerosene chandeliers. "Think I'll be leaving mop 'n' broom till tomorrow," he told himself as he lowered all but one lamp behind the bar. "An' this is for me old friend Bailey," he added, opening a tin of crackers and holding one out for the parrot.

"Thank ye! Thank ye!" the bird chirped as he always did when offered a treat. With his beak he snatched the cracker from Orion's fingers and proceeded to chip away at it, steadying it with one foot.

"Aye, 'twill be good t'hit the sheets." Orion placed the last couple of used glasses in the small sink behind the bar. Grabbing the key ring from the metal cashbox, he headed around the end of the bar to lock up the tavern.

The heavy double doors, which closed behind the swinging batwings, were held open by wooden wedges on the floor. Orion moved a chair that had been left in front of the right door, kicked the wedge free, and swung it closed. Just as it was closing on the jamb, it was abruptly forced back against him, making him stagger backward. The shadows of a pair of men filled the doorway as both batwings were thrown open, and before Orion could fully regain his balance, Bridger Kincaid's two henchmen came storming in, one carrying a shotgun, the other wielding a club.

Orion made a break for the shotgun behind the bar, but before he had taken the first step, something smacked against the side of his head, throwing the room into blackness and knocking him to his hands and knees. He heard wood cracking, and his vision cleared enough to see the man with the club bringing it down on a nearby tabletop, then swinging it against the overhanging chandelier.

Through the ringing in Orion's ears he heard Old Bailey screeching and cursing. It must have annoyed the intruders, because as Orion's vision continued to clear he looked up to see the man with the shotgun raising the weapon toward the parrot's perch behind the bar. The man was only a few feet in front of Orion, while the other man was busy circling the room, smashing everything in sight. Forcing his feet up under him, Orion leaped at the back of the shotgunner's legs. He caught the man around the ankles and knocked him forward just as the weapon blasted. The squawking of the bird abruptly ceased, and Orion feared the worst.

The shotgunner was lying on his stomach, and Orion tried to stand up away from him, but he had only struggled to his knees when the other man came racing over and brought the club down on his back, knocking him facedown on the floor. The man then began to kick him brutally in the sides. Orion tried to curl up and protect his face as he turned toward Old Bailey's perch. His vision was obstructed by the shotgunner scrambling to his feet, but as the man came around the other side, Orion caught a glimpse of the perch. It was empty, and he thought he saw a few feathers settling around it. Then the shotgunner grabbed the barrel of his weapon and swung it in a wide arc, bringing the butt crashing against the side of Orion's head.

The hardwood floor seemed to hurtle away from Orion as he was propelled into the darkest of space. He felt things striking his head and sides, but the sensation was muffled and not overly painful. Then it stopped, and he was left to float away alone. He thought he heard faint, distant explosions, as if worlds were colliding somewhere beyond his consciousness, and he fleetingly envisioned the curious image of furniture collapsing and rows of bottles bursting on a shelf. But then the spraying shards of glass became the twinkling of a million stars, and Orion eagerly flew through them, following a shimmering green bird that soared ahead, its luminescent body a meteor lighting the night.

Several blocks away, Cameron pulled the collar of his blue coat against the stiff night breeze and continued east along the tracks that divided Railroad and North Second streets. The tall, lanky youth had no idea how long he had been walking the streets, but he guessed that by now it must be a couple of hours after midnight. He knew he should head back to the church, but the idea of returning empty-handed gnawed at him. It was bad enough being treated like a child by Sister Laurel. It was worse to have his youth and inexperience confirmed by a couple of hooligans who thought themselves better because they were a year or two older and who hid behind each other, afraid to face him one on one.

"We'll see who has guts," Cameron muttered as he touched the long kitchen knife under his belt and envisioned himself disemboweling each of the young men, spilling their intestines onto the dirt. Then reality struck home: He had been walking the streets for several hours and had come no closer to finding the shack one of his attackers had mentioned to the other last night after beating him up. It could be any shack, anywhere in Abilene—and so many of the buildings looked like shacks.

Cameron was well beyond the main business district, near the stockyards of the Great Western Cattle Company. Buildings were going up all around the stockyards, and he guessed that within a few years the loading docks would be moved farther east and this part of town would become indistinguishable from the rest of the downtown area. He was about to head back when he noticed a dilapidated wooden structure perched in an overgrown field just beyond the stockyard fence. As he approached he saw a sign hanging on one hinge over the porch, but it was not until he was within twenty feet or so that he made out the fading letters in the thin moonlight: THE LINE SHACK. Smaller signs in the windows announced that the establishment was a purveyor of fine whiskey for drovers who had been long on the trail.

The building was obviously an abandoned saloon of sorts—an exceedingly tiny one made to look like a typical line shack found on the perimeter of a large ranch. It probably had served the influx of cowboys during Abilene's early boom days as a cattle shipping center but had quickly succumbed to the more substantial establishments that had sprung up with the coming of the railroad.

Cameron stepped up onto the rickety porch that fronted the shack. The creak of the planks was magnified by the stillness of the night, and he paused a moment to listen for any sounds from inside. All remained quiet, so he approached the front door, turned the rusty knob, and thrust it open. There was an abrupt cry of surprise, accompanied by the sounds of people stirring and bedsprings squeaking.

"Whaa?" a muffled voice cried. "Who is it?"

Cameron heard several people getting up, as well as what sounded like a gun being cocked. He quickly backed away from the open doorway and stepped off the porch, his hand clutching the knife handle and drawing the blade from his belt. A moment later a dark silhouette appeared in the doorway, then a lantern came on inside the shack, lighting the back of the figure and obscuring his features.

"Who's out there?" the person called.

Trying to steady his nerves and voice, Cameron replied, "I'm looking for two guys I played cards with last night."

"Who are you?"

"My name's Cameron. If they're in there, these fellows will remember me. They stole my cards."

Someone handed the lantern to the young man at the door, who held it out over the porch, bathing his face in light. Cameron saw that this fellow was not one of the ones he was seeking, though he was about the same age—eighteen or so. Cameron realized that he also was being illuminated by the lantern, so he lowered the knife from sight.

"Are you crazy coming here like this?" the young man said as a half-dozen others began to pile out of the shack behind him, all wearing longjohns. "For a deck of cards?"

"Then this is the right shack? The bastards are here?"

Suddenly one of the others pushed to the front and blurted, "Just who're you calling a bastard?"

Recognizing him as one of the cardplayers, Cameron squeezed the knife handle and replied, "You. Bastard!"

Suddenly the young man jumped off the porch and charged Cameron, who brought up the knife and thrust it forward. Seeing the flash of metal, the young man twisted aside at the last moment, and the blade grazed along his side, tearing his longjohns and making a long gash along his skin. As much from surprise as pain, he went down on one knee, clutching his bleeding side. "Damn!" he muttered, looking up and realizing for the first time that Cameron was armed with more than his fists. The others on the porch seemed just as shocked, and it took them a moment to react. Then they started to advance, cautiously at first, wary of the long blade in Cameron's hand.

Remembering the earlier sound of a gun being cocked, Cameron figured that at least one of them might be armed with something more effective than a knife. Trying to keep the advantage, he turned to the young man who was still down on one knee. Taking a quick step forward, Cameron lifted his right leg and kicked the wounded man full force under the chin, knocking him onto his back.

The others started to rush him, but Cameron leaped forward and straddled the unconscious young man, gripping his hair and pulling back his head with one hand while pressing the tip of the knife blade against his neck with the other. "Get away!" he shouted.

"Take it easy," the fellow with the lantern urged as he signaled the others to hold back. "Let Marty go."

"Not till I get my cards."

"Hell, is that all?" The young man spun around, seeking one person among the group, and called, "Get 'em and give 'em back, Jake." When Jake stood his ground, he shouted, "Now!"

Jake glowered, but he seemed unwilling to buck the apparent leader of the group, and finally he cursed under his breath and stalked into the shack. A moment later he returned with the cards.

"Give 'em here," the leader said when it looked as if Jake was about to throw them at Cameron, and reluctantly Jake complied. Then the leader, still holding the lantern, walked forward alone and held out the cards.

Cameron let go of Marty's hair and cautiously reached up, snatching away the deck and stuffing it into his pants pocket, all the while keeping the blade at Marty's throat.

"Now what're you gonna do?" the leader asked.

Cameron looked at him curiously. "What do you mean?"

The young man nodded toward the others standing in a half-circle behind him. "How are you gonna get out of here? Drag Marty all the way with you?"

For the first time, Cameron looked noticeably nervous. He glanced around and seemed to realize the awkwardness of his position. His best hope was to make a break for it and disappear in the darkness. But he needed a head start. Grabbing Marty's hair again and pressing down slightly on the knife, he said, "I want all of you to get back in that shack. And close the door. If you come out before I give the word, your friend's as good as dead."

The leader started to grin. "You don't really think that's gonna work, now do you? We've got rifles in there. We could plug you before you got two feet away."

"I . . . I'll take my chances. Just do what I say!"

"Easy now. Maybe there's another way." The young man paused, as if giving Cameron time to get more nervous and confused, then said, "My name's Ryan, and these are some of my friends. It's good to have friends, don't you think?"

Cameron stared at him, not knowing what to think. "I don't know what you're trying to do, but—"

"Hold on," Ryan cut in. "I'm just saying it's good to have friends who'll stand by you in a fight. Is that why you came alone? You ain't got friends who'll back you up?"

"I don't need friends."

"What about your family?"

"Never had one—and I don't need one, either."

"An orphan, eh?" When Cameron made no reply,

Ryan added, "Marty said he heard something about a Sister Laurel. Ain't you a little old to be traveling with a nun and a bunch of orphans?"

"I can leave whenever I want," he replied defensively.

"So why don't you?" Ryan pressed, and Cameron shrugged his shoulders. "'Cause you ain't got nowhere to go. And you ain't got any friends."

Cameron could feel Marty stirring beneath him. "You better get back in that shack like I said," he demanded, his voice betraying his fear.

"Forget Marty," Ryan said. "He deserved what you did. And it showed you got real guts." He noted the way Cameron seemed to swell with pride, so he added, "Yes, real guts. I could use a friend like you. We all could—even Marty."

Cameron eyed him closely. "I don't understand. . . ."

"Look, forget what happened tonight. You got your cards back, and you can go. No one's gonna hurt you. I promise. But maybe you should consider staying."

"Staying? Here?"

"Exactly. Me and my friends have been making a pretty good living for ourselves. There's plenty of easy work to be had—if you know the right people and ain't afraid of a little excitement now and then. What do you say?"

"I . . . I don't know."

"You said you ain't got any friends. Here you'll have friends and money, instead of a bunch of little orphans and a nun telling you when to put on your socks." Ryan reached over and laid a palm on Cameron's knife hand. "C'mon, what do you say? Let him up. No one's gonna hurt you."

Cameron glanced down and saw that Marty's eyes

were open wide now, staring up at him in fright. He felt the muscles of his hand relax, and he allowed Ryan to pull the knife away from Marty's throat.

"That's better. Like I promised, no one's gonna hurt you." Ryan stood and pulled Cameron up by the forearm. Looking down at Marty, Ryan said, "Get back inside."

Marty crawled away slightly, then clambered to his feet and hobbled over to the others, clutching his bleeding side, his fear slowly being replaced by a look of anger.

"Forget him," Ryan said, wrapping an arm around Cameron's shoulder. "He'll get over it." He looked Cameron directly in the eye. "So how about it? You want in?"

Cameron stared at the group of young men in front of the shack, then glanced at the railroad tracks behind him. He thought of Sister Laurel and the orphans and remembered how childish he felt around them. Turning back, he realized that he was almost as big as Ryan, even though he was only sixteen. And Ryan did not treat him like a child but like one of the group. Jamming the knife behind his belt, he smiled sheepishly and then found himself nodding.

"Good!" Ryan clapped him on the back. "And the first thing we're gonna do is introduce you to Marty and Jake, so there'll be no hard feelings." With his arm around Cameron's shoulder, he started toward the waiting group, then suddenly paused and put his hand to his chin. "Oh, yes, there's one other thing."

Cameron looked at him questioningly and asked, "What?"

Smiling, Ryan removed his hand from around Cameron's shoulder. "This," he said in a steely tone as he abruptly drew back his right arm and swung his fist full force into Cameron's unprotected stomach, doubling the youth over and knocking the breath out of him.

Gasping and clutching his belly, Cameron looked up, his eyes widening with wild rage. Straightening, he sputtered, "You b-bastard!" and clawed at the knife in his belt.

"Take it easy!" Ryan shouted as he grabbed Cameron's wrist and held it locked in place. "I just wanted to see if you really got guts . . . and you do." He stared at Cameron a long moment until he was certain the youth would not do anything foolish, then released his wrist. Backing up a few steps, he raised his hands palm forward. "Sorry, but I had to see what you're made of." He grinned. "And you needed to know the same about me."

Cameron was still clutching the handle of his knife. Slowly he relaxed his grip and let the blade settle in place behind his belt. A thin smile touched his lips, and he muttered, "You really are a bastard, aren't you?"

"You're damn right," Ryan declared as he stepped closer and again clapped Cameron on the back. "But coming from someone who don't know his ma *or* his pa, I'd call that a compliment." Laughing, he led Cameron through the circle of young men and into the shack.

Chapter Ten

The cool morning fog was burning off as the sun rose in the sky; the only remaining evidence of yesterday's storm was an occasional patch of mud along Texas Street. There was a great deal of commotion in front of Dr. Levi Wright's office this Thursday morning as his associate stood in the doorway and ushered sixteen youngsters into the waiting room so that each could be given an examination.

"Is that everyone?" Aileen Bloom asked as the last of the children crossed the threshold.

"I wish it were," Sister Laurel replied, her tone betraying her concern. "Cameron, our oldest boy, has not been seen all morning. I'm afraid he's run off."

"Perhaps he went for a walk."

Sister Laurel shook her head slowly. "He left in the middle of the night. Soon after going to bed, one of the boys saw him leave, and he hasn't been back."

"I'm sure he'll turn up. We're a small community, and he couldn't have gone far."

"I hope you're right," the nun responded.

"And when he returns, you just bring him over, and I'll be glad to examine him, as well."

"Thank you. And thank you also for sending us to Reverend Fisher's. He's been so accommodating. In fact, he's out looking for Cameron right now."

"Then everything will be fine," Aileen pronounced confidently. "Shall we go in and get started?" She held the door wide for Sister Laurel to enter.

"Can I leave the children here for a while? The older ones will take care of the younger."

"Of course."

"I'd like to find Mr. Travis, if I can."

Aileen smiled fleetingly as she recalled the pleasant dinner they had had the night before, but then her smile faded. "I think you'll find him next door at Orion's Tavern."

Seeing Aileen's look of displeasure, Sister Laurel assumed she disapproved of Travis frequenting the saloon at such an early hour. But she also wondered how Aileen knew he was there, and she asked, "You've seen him this morning?"

"I'm afraid so. There was a bit of a brawl last night. Luke—uh, Mr. Travis wasn't involved, but his friend Orion McCarthy was beaten senseless and his tavern ransacked. Mr. Travis found him early this morning and brought him over. I patched his head, but I couldn't convince him to rest. The two of them are in there trying to clean things up."

"Oh, dear," Sister Laurel muttered. Then she thanked Aileen again and headed down the walkway.

Approaching the tavern, she realized it had been

quite some time since she had entered such an establishment. Suddenly she felt very self-conscious in her nun's habit, but she took a deep breath, made a silent prayer, and pushed through the swinging doors. She must have looked like the shade of death standing in front of the batwings in her black outfit, for there was no response from the two men for a full ten seconds after they turned to look at her. Then the stocky tavernkeeper declared, "The Devil be damned!" His words were instantly echoed in a weird, high-pitched squawk.

"And that he will . . . if Sister Laurel has anything to say about it," Luke Travis said, grinning broadly as he recognized the visitor. "Orion, I want you to meet the nun I told you about. Sister Laurel, this is Orion McCarthy. And that's Old Bailey." He pointed to the green parrot sitting on a splintered, lopsided perch in front of the shattered mirror. "He's lost a few tail feathers, but he's no worse off than his master, who's lost a few red hairs."

Sister Laurel noticed that a narrow bandage circled Orion's head. As she approached the bar, she quickly took in the destruction all around her. Tables were overturned, chairs and chandeliers shattered, and virtually every bottle on the back shelf knocked down and smashed. The entire room reeked with the pungent fumes of whiskey and kerosene.

"Thank God no one lit a match," she commented as she stepped up beside the two men at the bar.

"Aye," Orion agreed, nodding. "An' just let 'em try. Then they'll know a Scotsman's wrath!"

Sister Laurel guessed from Orion's tone that this had been no usual tavern brawl. Not wanting to pry, she said, "So you're from Scotland?"

"Born 'n' bred. 'Tis a pleasure t'meet ye." He held out his hand and was surprised at the woman's firm grip.

"I'm Irish," she said matter-of-factly.

"An Irisher?" Orion's eyebrows rose. "Ye dinna speak wi' the tongue o' the blarney."

"I was born in America. My parents came from Ireland."

" 'Tis sorry I am," he said with genuine feeling, and Sister Laurel did not know whether he was referring to her birthplace or heritage. He smiled again and went on, "Lucas tells me ye are bringing t'Wichita a dozen or more bairns." Seeing her confused look, he said, "Bairns . . . wee ones."

She smiled and nodded. "Yes. Seventeen orphans."

"How is Michael doing?" Travis asked.

"Fine. Dr. Bloom is examining him now," she replied, though her eyes betrayed a concern of sorts. "It's . . ."

"One of the others?" Travis asked.

"Yes. Our oldest boy, Cameron. He seems to have run off, and I have no idea where or why."

Remembering the incident at the tavern the night before last, Travis nodded sympathetically. He assumed that Sister Laurel was unaware of what had occurred, and he was about to tell her when she asked, "Do you think you could help look for him before we leave for Wichita, Mr. Travis?"

Deciding to wait before betraying the boy's trust, he said, "Have you spoken to the marshal yet?"

"No, not yet. After all, he may have just taken off for a few hours. But if you think I should report this—"

"No, you're probably wise in waiting," Travis cut in. "I'll be glad to look for him, and if I don't turn up anything, then we'll bring in Marshal Parnell."

"Thank you so much," she replied with evident relief.

"How long has he been gone?"

"Since shortly after going to bed last night."

"Then I'd better get started at once."

"I know you're eager to be on your way to Wichita," she said, "but I'm afraid I can't leave until I find Cameron. So if you need to be going . . ."

He waved off her concern. "It really makes no difference when I get there. Right now the important thing is to find out what's become of Cameron."

"Bless you," she whispered with such genuine feeling that Travis found himself blushing.

"The Devil be damned!" Old Bailey piped in, and Sister Laurel spun toward the parrot and replied, "My sentiments precisely!"

Michael Hirsch was the first to be examined by Dr. Bloom, who pronounced the gash on his skull all but healed. She removed the bandage and cautioned him to keep the area clean, then ushered him out of the examining room so that she could see the rest of the children.

For a while Michael sat with the others in the waiting room while his sister, Agnes, accompanied the younger ones in to see the doctor. Growing bored, he headed into the front entryway and then slipped out through the front door. Standing on the porch, he saw Sister Laurel and Luke Travis come out of the tavern next door. Then a voice called the nun's name, and the minister from the Methodist church waved at them and started across the street.

Michael casually stepped off the porch and wandered across the yard, his toe kicking a pebble as he tried to make out their conversation. At first it was apparent that Travis was being introduced to the minister, but then their voices deepened and grew more serious, and Michael had to risk getting closer to hear.

". . . and I've asked everywhere, but no one's seen the boy," Judah Fisher was saying as he shook his head sadly.

"I don't understand it at all," Sister Laurel put in.

"Has he ever done this before?" Travis asked.

"Cameron's always been on the wild side, but he's never run off. I've caught him playing poker and drinking a couple of times, but that's been the extent of it."

Remembering how he had betrayed Cameron to Travis the other night, Michael suddenly felt very guilty. He backed away slightly and stooped down to play with a stick, though he was still close enough to hear what was being said.

"I'll check the other saloons," Travis offered. He looked at the nun's black habit and Judah's clerical collar, then glanced down at his own jeans and dusty boots and smiled. "It looks like I'm better dressed for the part."

"I'm certainly willing to go into a saloon, if that's what's needed," Judah said.

"So am I," Sister Laurel insisted.

Travis raised a hand. "I think I'd be less conspicuous and might find out something you couldn't. You must admit you'd create quite a stir—especially you, Sister Laurel."

"Which is exactly what I intend to do the moment I find out where that fool boy has run off to!" So saying, she turned to head toward the doctor's office. "If you gentlemen will excuse me, I must check on the children."

Still stooping nearby, Michael realized there was not enough time to leave, so he turned away and continued to play with the stick. When Sister Laurel approached and saw him idly poking the stick into the ground, she asked, "Michael, how is your head?"

"Uh, my head?" he asked with some confusion as he spun around and looked up at her. Then he realized what she was talking about, and he touched the sore spot and said, "It's better. The doctor says I don't need a bandage no more."

"Anymore," she corrected him, then smiled and continued up the walkway to the front door.

As soon as she disappeared inside, Michael looked over at the two men. They were shaking hands, and then the minister headed down the street toward his church. Luke Travis turned to Michael and smiled. With a nod, he started down Texas Street in the opposite direction.

Before Michael realized what he was doing, he jumped up and called, "Mr. Travis!" and started after the tall man.

The former marshal had just stepped onto the boardwalk in front of the Grand Palace Hotel, and he turned and waited for the boy. "What is it?" he asked as Michael came over.

Looking a bit guilty, Michael scraped his boot against the boardwalk planks and said, "I, uh, didn't mean to listen in, but I heard you talking about Cameron."

Placing a hand on Michael's shoulder, Travis asked directly, "Do you know where he's gone?"

"No. But something happened the other night."

"What?"

"It was after you went into the saloon to get him. I went back to the church but hadn't gone inside yet when I heard something—people fighting." He looked up into Travis's clear green eyes and seemed to decide that he could trust the man, because he went on. "It was Cameron—in a fight with two older boys. I think they were the ones in the saloon with him."

"They beat him up?"

Michael nodded. "Not too bad, though. They ran off when they saw me coming. Cameron was real mad and swore they'd pay for it. He said they didn't steal anything, but later he called them a couple of thieves. I don't know why . . . unless . . ." He looked down at his feet.

Putting his finger under Michael's chin, Travis gently forced him to look back up. "Unless what, Michael?"

"Well . . . I found something in the street, and I think one of them may have dropped it." His hand slipped into his pocket as if he was about to reveal the object in question—or perhaps was trying to protect it.

"Can I see it?" Travis held out his hand and waited as Michael looked at his feet again, frowned, then hesitantly pulled out a playing card. Travis did not have to see the face to know it had a nude woman painted on it. Trying not to grin, he said, "They must have stolen the rest of the deck. And you think Cameron's gone to get it back, right?"

Still looking down, Michael nodded.

"Any idea where he's gone?"

Michael shook his head, then said, "Except for something the other two fellows said when I came running over." He looked up now. "I heard one of them say, 'Let's get back to the shack.'"

"The shack?"

Michael shrugged. "Maybe it's where they live."

"Do you think Cameron heard them?"

"He must've. He was lying right there, and he wasn't unconscious or anything like that."

Travis nodded slowly. "That's a very good lead, Michael. If I can find that shack, perhaps I'll discover what happened to your friend."

Michael suddenly looked very worried. "You don't think they—"

"Let's not presume the worst. The thing right now is for me to find that shack."

"Maybe I could help," the boy suggested.

"You've helped already. I think I'd better take over from here. Sister Laurel is worried enough about Cameron."

"I might be able to—"

"Don't worry about Cameron—I'll find him. And if I need any help, I'll let you know." He patted the boy on the shoulder and turned to leave.

"Uh, what about this?" Michael asked, his tone dripping with guilt.

Travis looked back and saw the boy holding out the playing card. "You said you found it in the street," he replied. "It could be anyone's, so you might as well keep it. What good's one card without the rest of the deck?"

"It's not a normal card. Maybe you should look at it."

"I don't need to, Michael. I've seen a naked lady before." Grinning, Travis headed down the boardwalk, whistling as he walked away.

Michael stood looking at the queen of hearts. He felt his own heart quicken as he stared at the alluring woman, who was clad only in a gauzy red scarf that had fallen away from her ample breasts and only barely covered her lower abdomen and the secret place between her legs. How he yearned for a magic eraser that could remove the offending garb and unveil the mysteries beneath!

It was late afternoon, and traffic was picking up at the Salty Dog Saloon as other businesses began to close and the first cowboys arrived from the range. Marcus Donaghue was playing poker at his usual table against the far wall, near the door that led to his private office. He was already dressed for the evening in a dark-gray suit with a matching vest and a ruffled white shirt. It had been a warm day, and despite the faint breeze that drifted in around the batwings, his forehead was beaded with sweat. He would wait a little longer before closing the top button of his shirt or knotting the string tie that hung undone from his collar.

"Two pair, jacks high," he announced, placing his cards faceup on the table. One by one the other three players folded their hands, and he grinned broadly and raked in the pot. "Don't look so gloomy," he declared, shuffling the deck. "The night's young, and there's plenty of money to be won. So why not raise the limit to, say, five dollars?" He stared from one player to the next. "This just might be your hand. . . ." He tapped the cards, then began to deal.

The other players grumbled their assent, and the hand was played. As Donaghue had predicted, one of the other men won this hand, and the saloon owner congratulated him and again suggested they raise the betting limit.

"Too rich for me," mumbled a young cowboy whose expectations far exceeded his wallet. He pushed back his chair, picked up his sweat-stained hat, and left the game.

"Anyone want in?" Donaghue asked as a small crowd began to gather around the table. "Or is a ten-dollar limit too rich for the rest of you?"

A man in a brown business suit took up the challenge and dropped into the seat. Producing a wallet from his inside coat pocket, he removed a small bundle of bills. "I'm ready," he said, nodding toward the cards. "Deal."

"Gentlemen?" Donaghue asked the other two players. They indicated that they were ready, and the deal began.

Donaghue was just picking up his cards and fanning out his hand when he was startled by a loud banging as the batwings flew open and cracked against the walls on either side of the doorway. Looking up to see a stocky, muscular man step inside, he muttered, "McCarthy."

"Marcus Donaghue!" the man in the doorway called out, gaining the attention of the room. "I want a word wi' ye!"

Donaghue's eyes narrowed as Orion McCarthy started across the room toward his table. Though it was easy to see that the Scotsman was angry, Donaghue could not tell whether he was threatening violence. Out of the corner of his eye, the saloon owner saw one of Bridger Kincaid's men moving toward the table, and he waved the man back, then turned to Orion. "You've found me. Now what do you want?"

"Wha' I want is t'break ye neck. But I'll be satisfied wi' a hundred dollars."

"What are you talking about?" Donaghue asked, genuinely confused. "A hundred dollars?"

"Aye. For repairs t'me tavern."

"I don't know what you're—"

"Ye know damn well wha' I'm talking about!" Orion stepped up beside the businessman in the brown suit and slammed his fist against the table, upsetting a couple of shot glasses and totally petrifying the businessman. "It dinna take much brains t'figure out tha' the order comes from ye own mouth when the likes o' Bridger Kincaid 'n' his lackeys smash up me tavern 'n' try t'kill me Old Bailey!"

"You're crazy."

"Aye, 'n' I'll be crazier still if ye dinna give me the money I ask."

"I'm not paying anything I don't owe. If you've got a complaint, take it up with the marshal."

"We both know wha' good tha' will do. No, I want no part o' the law in this. Wha' I want is one hundred dollars t'fix the mess ye boys made o' me tavern."

"I said I'm not paying anything, and if you don't get out of here, I'll have you thrown out." Donaghue sat back and nodded at one of the men standing to the side. The man drew and cocked his revolver.

Orion looked at the man with the gun, and a broad grin spread across his face. Turning to Donaghue, he commented, "'Tis said ye are a betting man. No?"

Donaghue narrowed his eyes but did not reply.

"An' a cautious man." Orion waved a hand toward the gunman. "Aye, there's no doubt o' tha'." He placed both palms on the table and leaned toward Donaghue. "A cautious, betting man. So wha' say ye to a sure bet?"

Donaghue cocked his head slightly. "What kind of bet?"

"Ye are a big man—bigger than me, t'be sure. Let's put away the guns 'n' resolve this a'tween just we two."

"If you think I'm going to engage in some common brawl with the likes of you—"

"Not a brawl, Marcus Donaghue. Wha' we'll do is clasp hands o'er tha' bar there 'n' see who kin put down the other's hand."

"Are you serious?" Donaghue asked incredulously, and Orion grinned and nodded. "For one hundred dollars?"

"Aye. The cost o' repairing me tavern."

"But I had nothing to do—"

"Call it wha' ye will, but if I win, I get me hundred."

"And if I win?"

Orion reached into his pocket and slapped five gold coins onto the table.

Seeing the twenty-dollar gold pieces, Donaghue smiled. "You've got your bet, Scotsman." He rose and removed his jacket, then rolled up his sleeves, revealing muscular arms. He was several inches taller than Orion and a good thirty pounds heavier, but Orion did not seem at all concerned as he rolled his own sleeves and headed toward the bar.

The patrons crowded around, exchanging money and placing bets as the two men took up positions across from each other at the bar. The immediate area was cleared of bottles and glasses, and then Donaghue placed his elbow at the center of the bar and unclenched his fist, ready to clasp Orion's hand.

The Scotsman started to place his elbow beside Donaghue's, but then he pulled back and grinned at the bigger man. "Wha' say ye t'raising the stakes?"

"More than a hundred dollars?" Donaghue asked, removing his arm from the bar.

"Not the wager," Orion replied, shaking his head. "But the contest." He reached into his pants pocket and produced two stubby, inch-high candles, which he placed about three feet apart on the bar—at the precise spot that either hand would come down. He took out a match, struck it across the surface of the bar, and lit each candle, saying, "The loser is the man whose hand goes down or who blows out the flame."

The crowd began to whisper in excitement, and the betting dramatically increased. Donaghue looked at the crowd, then at Orion, whose face became an expressionless mask as he placed his elbow between the candles. Donaghue's own features hardened, and he took a few deep breaths. "I'll see your bet," he declared as he positioned his elbow beside Orion's and firmly grasped his opponent's hand.

As if on a signal, the two men started to push. Their knuckles whitened, their hands vibrated, but there was no movement to the right or left. As the seconds passed, their biceps swelled and the veins on their forearms began to protrude. A few beads of sweat rolled down Donaghue's forehead and into his eye, forcing him to blink, while Orion's lips quivered and parted, revealing clenched teeth through his bushy red beard. The crowd cheered them on, softly at first but then with increasing intensity, with the majority favoring the owner of the Salty Dog. The clamor must have had an effect because, imperceptibly at first, Donaghue's hand began to come down over Orion's, slowly driving the Scotsman's arm toward the candle.

All of Orion's concentration was focused on his hand, as if willing it to change direction and head back over the top. But the descent continued, the back of his hand drawing ever closer to the candle. As if mocking him, the flame rose higher, until the yellow tip was but inches from his flesh. His eyes widened as the hair on the back of his hand began to singe. The acrid smell touched his nostrils, and he could see a circle of black soot forming on the flesh. He turned away and stared directly at Donaghue, whose attention was still focused on the flame. A faint smile formed on Orion's lips, and then he closed his eyes, his expression inexplicably calm, as though he were no longer aware of the pain. It was as if the heat were filling his arm with renewed strength, for his hand slowly began to move away from the flame.

Donaghue could see his advantage slipping, and his eyes widened with surprise and fear as his hand approached the apex. With a grunt he tightened his grip and put all his strength into driving Orion's arm down. Their hands shook uncontrollably, the corded muscles of their arms bulging and quivering. And then Donaghue's wrist weakened, and Orion's hand came over the top, relentlessly driving the other hand toward the opposite flame.

"B-bastard!" Donaghue blurted in an attempt to summon the strength to regain the advantage. He looked up at Orion, hoping to see something that would give him an edge, but Orion's eyes remained closed, his expression a serene, unreadable mask. "Bastard!" he muttered again as the first lash of heat touched his skin.

Donaghue watched, transfixed with horror as the flame lengthened and leaned toward his approaching hand as if seeking some new source of nourishment, unaware that it was merely following the currents of air that were being disturbed by their hands. He forced himself not to curse again as hair and then skin began to singe. He knew he could hold out for only a few seconds more, just as he knew he no longer had the strength to reverse the tide and defeat the accursed Scotsman. But he would not give Orion the satisfaction of seeing him blow out the flame, nor would he give in prematurely to the heat. He would endure to the last of his strength, until the flame itself was licking his flesh. And then he would see Orion McCarthy in hell!

"Give it up!" a voice shouted, and Donaghue saw the tall, former marshal of Wichita push through the crowd and step up beside Orion. "Let it go!" Luke Travis demanded.

Donaghue merely gritted his teeth and pushed all the harder, and for a moment his hand began to rise away from the flame, but then it started to come down again, until it was but an inch away.

"Damn you both!" Travis cursed, and he reached out and swiped away the candle, dousing the flame as wax splattered across the surface of the bar.

Despite the obvious relief to his hand, Donaghue's eyes communicated a burning anger at having been denied the chance to prove that, though he might lose the wager, he could endure the pain. And lose he did, for suddenly his arm gave out and his hand smashed against the top of the bar. "Bastard!" he repeated, this time directing the word at Luke Travis as he rubbed his wrist and hand. He glanced over at the bartender and said, "Pay the man." Then he turned to Orion. "Don't think this is finished."

Orion glared at him but held his tongue. He walked over to Donaghue's table and retrieved his own gold coins. Returning to the bar, he received an equal amount from the bartender and stuffed the coins in his pocket.

"Let's get out of here," Travis said, placing a hand on Orion's shoulder.

"Aye," the Scotsman muttered, turning to go.

"Yes, you'd better get out of here," Donaghue said,

pointing the forefinger of his burned hand at Luke Travis. "And I don't mean my saloon. I want you out of Abilene." He swung his finger toward Orion. "And you . . . just remember that this isn't finished."

"Dinna be threatening me," Orion said, holding his ground. "An' dinna be sending the likes o' Bridger Kincaid t'be doing ye work." He turned to address the crowd. "I say it in front o' ye all. I will'na pay a single cent to any man for protection I dinna need nor want. An' any man who tries t'lay a hand on me or mine will have this Scotsman to answer to!" Turning to the bar and glowering at Donaghue, he reached toward the candle that was still flickering and pressed the wick between his thumb and forefinger, smothering the flame. Then he stalked off through the parting crowd and pushed through the batwings.

As Travis turned to follow, Donaghue called after him, "You've got exactly two hours to get out of town."

Travis paused, and as his hands settled against his hips, he was painfully aware that he was not wearing a gun. Without looking back, he replied, "I hear you." Then he continued through the crowd and followed Orion through the still-swinging doors.

Precisely two hours later, Luke Travis stood alone in the middle of his cramped, second-floor hotel room, looking down at the small valise that lay open on the iron bed. He started to reach inside, then pulled back his hand. *What would Sarah think?* he wondered. *What would she counsel me to do?*

"She would stand beside me," he said aloud. "She'd tell me to do what I thought was best."

And he knew that leaving Abilene was not what was best—for himself, for Sister Laurel and her children, for the people of Abilene. Though his search that day had not turned up the missing orphan boy, Travis had asked enough questions to confirm that Marcus Donaghue was at the head of a growing crime network that would not hesitate to murder anyone who stood in its way. And if the local citizens sought assistance from Marshal Stacy Parnell, they quickly found him either too incompetent or too scared to do much about the situation—or else he was receiving a more lucrative offer from Donaghue to look the other way.

The story, as Travis had been able to piece it together, was that when Donaghue returned to Abilene after being released from prison, he discovered that some of the men who had taken over his operation were not willing to give it back. There was a bloody struggle for control, but that had not concerned the local populace so long as it was confined to the town's lawless elements. But when Bridger Kincaid arrived on the scene, the situation escalated. Soon Donaghue had firm control over Abilene's underworld, and he began expanding his operations. Local businesses were forced to pay protection money so that they would not be the target of so-called random violence, which in actuality was carried out by some of the town's tougher youth, hired by Donaghue himself. Those who would not pay, such as Orion McCarthy, soon learned that the cost for refusing was high.

During the previous week, the remaining opposition to Donaghue had begun to collapse. The catalyst was the murder of Judge Lawrence Fisher, who had been working actively to bring Marcus Donaghue to justice. Few in town doubted that the crime leader had ordered the murder, but Donaghue had been attending a dance-hall review at the time of the shooting and had been seen by a large number of citizens. While he easily could have hired someone to do the job, Marshal Parnell was unable to turn up any evidence. Even Bridger Kincaid had an ironclad alibi, since he had been playing cards all night—in Orion's Tavern, no less.

Luke Travis walked to the window and looked down at Texas Street. It was early evening, yet the street was strangely empty, as if people sensed what was about to take place. Gazing toward the saloon district, he saw a group of four men approaching down the middle of the road. Though none of them appeared to be wearing a sling, Travis was certain Bridger Kincaid was among them.

Returning to the bed, Travis stared into the valise a final time. Then he whispered, "Help me, Sarah," and reached inside, pulling out a well-worn leather gun belt. Grasping the walnut butt of the holstered Colt Peacemaker, he slid the gun out and hefted it, remembering the familiar feel. Dropping the belt onto the bed, he opened the chamber of the gun and spun the cylinder, making sure it was empty. Then he picked up the gun belt again, strapped it low around his waist, and tied the thongs around his thigh. Sliding the gun into the well-oiled holster, he eased it in and out a few times, then took a stance facing the bureau mirror.

As quick as lightning, Travis drew the gun, cocking the hammer as he brought it up and then squeezing the trigger, all in one fluid motion. Satisfied that his continued practice during the past three years had kept him from losing too much speed, he removed six bullets from the belt and loaded the gun. Tonight he would not take the precaution of leaving empty the chamber under the hammer; he knew that it would be empty soon enough.

As Travis made his way downstairs and stepped into the fading sunlight, he saw that the four men who had accosted Sister Laurel's wagon train were waiting for him. Directly across the street from the hotel, Bridger Kincaid, no longer wearing a sling, sat on the boardwalk railing, smoking a thin cigar, a Winchester cradled in his lap. Jeb and the other two men, each wearing a low-slung holster, stood farther to Travis's right, spaced six to ten feet apart.

Kincaid took the cigar from his mouth and dropped it to the ground. "I see you're wearin' an iron," he drawled. His mouth quirked into a smile. "You should've taken Mr. Donaghue's advice."

"Never was much good at taking advice . . . especially from a couple of bastards like you and your boss," Travis said evenly as he positioned himself so that he could draw and fire from left to right, starting with Kincaid and moving down the line.

Kincaid's smile faded, and though his rifle was still pointed away from Travis, his finger closed around the trigger. "I'm givin' you one last chance to ride out of here," he declared, his voice betraying an edge of fear. When Travis stood his ground, he added, "No one's gonna help you. The marshal's been called out of town on business."

By Marcus Donaghue, no doubt, Travis thought, though he was uncertain whether the marshal had been duped or had gone along willingly. In any case, Travis never expected assistance from that quarter, and he replied, "I'll leave when I'm ready. Make your move."

Travis, knowing Jeb and the others would not fire

before their leader, watched as Kincaid smiled again and then slipped down off the railing. Seeing Kincaid's eyes narrow slightly, he knew the play was beginning, and he was ready. Even before the muzzle of the Winchester came up all the way, Travis's Peacemaker had cleared leather and roared for the first time, the bullet thudding into Kincaid's chest and throwing him backward over the railing.

Moving his arm in a smooth arc, Travis swung his gun to the right and took out the first of Kincaid's cohorts as the man was drawing his gun. Realizing that the other two would be palming theirs by now, he leaped at the ground and rolled just as their guns fired. One of the bullets creased his left arm, but he paid it no mind as he came up in a crouch, carefully but quickly aiming at the next man in line—the one named Jeb. He fired, and Jeb dropped his gun and threw his hands to his neck, blood spurting between his fingers. He tried to scream but made only a choking, gurgling sound. Then his legs gave way and he fell to the dirt.

Still crouching, Travis whirled and tried to make out the final gunman through the thick gun smoke. The man had retreated across the street, and when Travis finally caught sight of him, he was already squeezing off a shot. Before Travis could bring his own gun into play, there was a loud report from somewhere off to the left, followed by the sound of the gunman's revolver firing harmlessly into the air as he went down with a bullet in the head.

Travis spun to his left, expecting to see Orion McCarthy with rifle in hand. Instead a young, dark-haired man dressed in black stood holding the reins of a skittish pinto in one hand and a smoking revolver in the other.

As the man slipped the gun into his black holster and approached, Travis holstered his own gun, then checked the bodies and confirmed that all were dead. Turning to greet the stranger, Travis noted the tied-down holster and took him for a gunfighter, the image reinforced by a faint, jagged scar that ran diagonally along his right cheek, the result of either a bullet or a knife. But just now the man's background did not concern him, and he held out his hand in thanks. As the two men shook hands, people ventured onto the street and gathered around.

"I didn't approve of the odds," the man said after Travis thanked him. "Though it looks like you might've handled that last fellow on your own."

"Not if he was a good shot," Travis replied. "Thanks again, Mr. . . . ?"

"The name's Cody."

"And I'm Luke Travis."

Cody nodded, the name apparently not registering as anyone special. He glanced at the bodies in the street. "Who were they?"

"Hired guns. Their boss was trying to encourage me to leave town."

"I guess he'll have to hire some more boys."

"How about letting me buy you a drink?" Travis asked.

"Some other time, perhaps." Cody took hold of the saddle horn and lifted himself onto the back of the pinto. "I've got business of my own to attend to." He tipped his black hat and kneed the horse forward up the street.

Travis watched as the stranger turned right at the corner of Elm Street and disappeared across the railroad tracks. He became aware that there was a substantial crowd on hand now, with people pointing at the bodies and talking excitedly among themselves. He heard the names Kincaid and Donaghue mentioned quite a few times but paid no attention.

"That was some pretty fancy shootin', mister," declared a young man standing nearby.

"They've gone for the undertaker," another commented.

"Hey, you're bleeding," a third man said. "You'd better get that arm seen to."

Travis merely nodded. Glancing down at his left arm, he saw the blood seeping through his shirt and remembered taking the slug. He took a last look at Bridger Kincaid lying on the boardwalk, one foot draped over the railing. Then he turned and walked away.

Chapter Eleven

———◆———

Luke Travis stepped up onto the porch of Dr. Aileen Bloom's office, gripping his left upper arm where the bullet had creased the skin. Though the bleeding had all but stopped and barely showed under his hand, Travis knew the importance of getting the wound properly cleaned and dressed. In his years as a lawman, he had seen more men die from infection than from the actual gunshot wounds.

Still holding his arm, Travis rapped against the door with the toe of his boot. Knocking a second time, he heard shuffling footsteps and assumed it was the housekeeper, Mrs. Finnegan, coming to open the door. But as the door swung inward, a weak but steady voice declared, "What's all the ruckus out here?" and Travis recognized the elderly Dr. Levi Wright leaning on a cane in the shadowed entryway, dressed in slippers and a sleeping robe. He had a bandage around his forehead and looked as if he had not shaved since before his accident. Frowning, though not really looking angry, the doctor continued, "How's an old man to get his rest with all that commotion out in the street? And now someone banging on the door like there's no tomorrow."

"Dr. Wright—" Travis said in surprise. "I thought you were out at the Lanfords'."

The doctor waved his hand and replied gruffly, "That's just what Dr. Bloom would like. Lock me up with a passel of boys and a brand-new screaming baby girl, getting an even worse headache"—he touched the bandage—"while she's in town stealing my practice right out from under me!" He rubbed his grizzled chin and smiled. "The only thing worse than a take-charge woman is an in-charge woman doctor."

"Well, it's good to see you up and about."

The doctor stepped forward into the open doorway and peered more closely at Travis. "Say, I recognize you now. You're the fellow who brought me to the Lanfords'."

"Luke Travis, sir."

"Yes, I remember now. We were introduced yesterday, but I confess it was a bit of a blur at the time."

"How's young Simon doing?"

"Just great. He'll be in bed for a few weeks, of course, but his mother is already having a hard time keeping him there. If there's no infection, I'd say the lad is going to pull through just fine."

"Thanks to Dr. Bloom," Travis said with a touch of devilment in his voice. "She's quite a surgeon."

"Of course she is!" the doctor blurted, again waving off the comment with his hand. "I trained her, didn't I? Hell, she'd better be good with a teacher like me."

From down the hall a woman said, "What's that you were saying?" and then Aileen stepped up behind the elderly man.

Flustered, the doctor glanced over his shoulder and shook his head defiantly. "Just saying you're lucky to have a teacher like me."

"Not that," Aileen went on. "I mean the part about my being a good surgeon."

Dr. Wright squinted one eye at her. "Don't be getting no highfalutin ideas, young lady. I'm the surgeon in Abilene and will be till the day I die."

"And with a head as hard as yours, I'll be an old lady before there's any risk of that!" Grinning, she put a hand on his shoulder. "But I'm still *your* doctor, and I've prescribed a few more hours in bed."

Dr. Wright allowed himself to be led away from the door. He started to shuffle down the hall on his own, then turned, waved his cane slightly, and said, "Remember, young man, what I said about take-charge women!" He grunted and continued down the hall.

"It's good to see you, Luke," Aileen said when they were alone.

"I wish it were under better circumstances." He turned slightly and lifted his hand from his arm, revealing the blood-soaked sleeve.

Aileen gasped, then took his arm and led him inside.

"Just a scratch," he assured her as they passed through the waiting room and into one of the examining rooms.

"How did this happen?" she asked as she helped him lie down on the table. "Bridger Kincaid?"

"He's dead, along with Jeb and two other of his men."

"My God! No one told us." Taking a pair of scissors from the side table, she began to cut away his sleeve.

"It just happened down the block a ways. There was no need for a doctor—just an undertaker."

Aileen shook her head in dismay. "I can't believe such a thing could happen—right in the middle of the street. Didn't the marshal—?"

"He's out of town."

"That figures." Using a wet cloth, she dabbed at the bloody wound. "So you had to face them alone?"

"I had some help. A young fellow by the name of Cody happened by and took care of the last man. Saved my neck."

Aileen straightened and dropped the cloth into a pan of water on the side table. Taking a fresh cloth to dry the wound, she paused a moment, looking thoughtful. "Cody, you say?" she asked, and Travis nodded. "That's strange."

"What do you mean?"

"Judah Fisher has a younger brother named Cody. I've never met him, but I've heard he's a gunfighter. Sort of the black sheep of the family." Shaking her head slightly, she resumed her work. "I suppose it could be somebody else, though it *is* an unusual name."

Travis watched as she gently dabbed at the wound with the dry cloth. He recalled that last image of the gunman named Cody turning his horse up Elm Street in the very direction of Judah Fisher's church. It made sense that Cody Fisher would return to Abilene following his father's murder—perhaps to seek revenge. Travis would have to speak with Judah and find out exactly why his brother was in town—just as soon as he changed his torn, bloody shirt.

"This will sting a bit," Aileen said as she opened a bottle of carbolic lotion and began to smear it on the wound. It did, though Travis gave no sign that he was in pain. "You know," she went on as she returned the bottle to the side table, "it's curious that I didn't hear any shooting. It must have happened while I was down in the cellar checking the medicinal supplies."

"I think the gunfire woke up Dr. Wright," Travis replied. "How's he doing?"

"Very well, but I just couldn't keep him out at the Lanfords'. A bit more rest and he'll be his old self again."

Travis grinned. "Are you sure that's a good thing?"

"Oh, Dr. Wright is as soft as marshmallow. He just likes to talk tough." She finished cleaning the wound and began to unroll some gauze. "You're lucky—you don't even need stitches. But you'll have to keep the bandage clean."

"He said that Simon's doing well, also," Travis commented as she wrapped the gauze around his arm.

"I saw him this afternoon when I brought Dr. Wright back, and he's doing wonderfully. So is his baby sister."

Travis nodded. "They sure were pleased to get a daughter after all those sons. You must be proud to have a little girl named after you."

She paused a moment and stared into the distance. "Aileen Lanford . . ." she intoned. "Yes, it sounds nice." Then she resumed wrapping and tying off the bandage. Suddenly she stopped and looked at Travis. "I just remembered something that might interest you."

"Yes?"

"A couple of the older Lanford boys spend quite a bit of time in town, so when I was there this afternoon

I told them about Cameron running off and asked if they had any idea where he might have gone. At first they said nothing, but when I was packing to leave, one of the boys came up to me alone. He admitted knowing a rough group of kids who hang out down near the stockyards at an abandoned place called The Line Shack—used to be a saloon of sorts." She touched his arm with concern. "The boy said that if he's mixed up with that crowd, he could be in real trouble."

"Do you know what he meant?"

Aileen shrugged. "My guess is the Lanford boy hung out with them once but decided the company was too rough."

"I'll look into it. Thanks, Aileen."

She smiled, then continued tying off the bandage. "Well, that's about it," she said as she finished.

Travis rolled off the table and stood. "How much do I owe you?" he asked, reaching into his pocket.

She placed a hand on his wrist. "Put away your money."

"But I want to pay you for—"

"Don't worry—you'll pay. How about dinner tomorrow?"

Travis grinned. "Seven o'clock?"

"I'll wait for you here," she replied, then led him through the waiting room and out onto the porch. "Good night, Luke," she said.

"Good night," he replied with a self-conscious smile, then headed down the walk.

Cody Fisher turned his pinto up the drive and headed to the front door of the Calvary Methodist Church. It was Thursday, and the sign out front indicated there would be a prayer meeting at eight o'clock that evening. It was almost seven, so he guessed that he would find his brother in the church making preparations.

Dismounting, Cody tied the reins to the iron railing leading up to the front door, then patted the horse and took the four steps in two strides. He reached for the doorknob but suddenly pulled back and stood staring at the door. After taking a few deep breaths, he removed his black hat, turned the knob and entered. There was a narrow vestibule that ran the full width of the building, then another set of windowless doors leading into the main chapel. He pushed on the right-hand door, and it swung open, revealing a simple yet elegant white room with heavy wooden ceiling beams and a central aisle separating two rows of pews.

Cody entered the chapel and let the door swing shut behind him. He looked around for the minister but saw only a group of children of various ages. A couple of the younger ones were occupied with an impromptu game of tag, while the older ones were placing bunches of wildflowers along the aisle in small holders attached to the pews. An attractive, red-haired girl in her late teens had just finished arranging a bouquet atop the altar, and as she turned, she saw Cody standing in the doorway.

The room grew quiet—even the younger children stopped scurrying about—as Cody started down the aisle, his boots reverberating against the wide-plank floor. All eyes were on the dark-haired man, though the older boys were focusing on the low-slung, pearl-handled revolver in his holster, while the older girls were admiring his ruggedly handsome features, made all the more dashing by the faint white scar along his cheek. Cody suddenly felt quite uncomfortable, and he began turning the hat in his hand.

"Are you here for the prayer meeting?" the young woman at the altar asked as she came forward. She smiled coyly, and her fair skin showed the trace of a blush. "It isn't for another hour yet."

"Uh, no," Cody replied. "I came to see the minister."

"He just went over to the parsonage for a moment. My name is Agnes Hirsch." She gave the slightest of curtsies. "I'm helping Sister Laurel bring these orphans to Wichita, and we're staying at the church for a few days. Are you a member of the congregation?"

Cody shook his head and smiled. "No. I'm just visiting, too. My name is—"

"Cody . . ." a voice called from across the room, and Cody turned to see his brother carrying an armload of books through a doorway to the right of the altar. Judah seemed neither surprised nor overly pleased to see his younger brother, and his tone was cautious as he approached around the front row of benches and asked, "What brings you here?"

With a polite nod to Agnes, Cody headed past her to where his brother was standing. Coming up in front of him, he smiled nervously and held out his hand, and there was an uncomfortable moment as Judah shifted the books in his arms, seemingly to avoid shaking hands. Pulling back his hand, Cody said, "I heard about Father, so I came."

Glancing beyond Cody, Judah called, "Would you take the children to the house, Agnes?" As she began to round them up and lead them from the chapel, Judah turned to Cody and said, "I'd have written, but I didn't know where."

Cody nodded, his smile gone as he looked down at the floor. "It was in Tuesday's paper in Hays City. I got here as quick as I could."

"I didn't know if you'd come, so we went ahead with the funeral." There was an awkward silence, then Judah asked, "Any idea how long you'll stay?"

As Cody looked up at his older brother, a fierce light seemed to ignite in his eyes, and he replied solemnly, "As long as it takes."

Judah's jaw tensed. "Just what do you mean?"

"He was murdered, and you and I know damn well the bastard responsible."

Judah flinched at his brother's language. "This is a church—"

"I'm not here for a lecture on profanity. I've come to do something about our father's death."

"With that, I suppose?" Judah nodded toward the gun on Cody's hip.

Placing a hand on the butt of the revolver, Cody replied, "With whatever it takes."

"You know I don't approve."

"You never did."

"And neither would Father," Judah added.

"He's dead. And I'm going to do something about it."

"Cody . . ." Judah said in a gentle tone, placing the stack of books on the bench beside him. He reached out and touched his brother's arm. "Father spent his life upholding the law. He wouldn't want you taking it into your own hands in his name."

Cody pulled his arm away. "I don't suppose the so-called marshal in this town has made an arrest."

"He hasn't turned up any evidence."

"And he won't. But I promise you . . . Marcus Donaghue will not get away with it."

"Cody, let the law—"

"Donaghue *is* the law in this town. Look, I didn't come to argue with you, Judah. I know where you stand, and you may not believe it, but I respect your decision."

"My inaction, you mean."

"You act, but in your own way, and I'm sure it's right for you. But don't try to change me."

"I gave up trying years ago. But I just lost my father. I don't want to lose my only brother, too."

Cody smiled. "No such luck." He turned to leave.

"Cody . . ." Judah called after him, and his brother stopped and looked back. "Don't stay a stranger."

Smiling, Cody put on his hat and headed for the door.

Huddling in the shadows behind the last row of benches, Michael Hirsch ducked even lower so that the man named Cody would not see him. Sure enough, Cody looked straight ahead as he came up the aisle and headed through the doors into the vestibule. The boy waited a moment, listening as Judah Fisher again picked up the books and began placing them along the front pew. Keeping down below the back of the benches, Michael made his way over to the doors, pushed one open slightly, and slipped through. Turning left, he headed to the far end of the narrow vestibule, where a door led to the parking area between the church and parsonage.

Making his way outside, Michael moved to the corner of the church so that he could catch another glimpse of the gunslinger with the pearl-handled revolver. Hiding behind a bush, he stuck his head around the edge of the building and saw the dark-haired man standing beside a spirited pinto. The black-and-white animal was as dashing as its owner, with a long white mane and sleek, muscular conformation. It was wearing a tooled, silver-studded saddle, with the butt of a Winchester protruding from a scabbard on one side. Slung behind the cantle was a pair of leather saddlebags, and completing the gear was a coiled lariat, despite the fact that the rider did not appear to be a cowpuncher.

The man named Cody was about to untie the reins when a voice called his name. Michael could see someone walking up the drive, but it was not until the pinto shifted position that he was able to make out the figure of Luke Travis. Michael noticed at once that he was wearing a gun now, though it was a rather plain-looking one with walnut grips.

As the two men spoke, Michael ventured around the front of the building to a closer position, keeping well hidden behind the bushes. Though he was unable to hear every word being said, the boy could make out enough to know that they had already met, though they did not seem overly friendly with each other. They were discussing a gunfight that had recently taken place, and Michael risked moving even closer and listened with growing excitement. From what he could hear, one or both of them had gunned down the man named Bridger Kincaid and three of his men— perhaps the very ones who had attacked the wagon train earlier that week. Travis was just mentioning the role Marcus Donaghue was playing in Abilene, when Cody, his voice firm with determination, cut in, "That's why I've come."

"To kill the man responsible for your father's death," Travis said flatly, and Cody nodded. "I'm not going to try to talk you out of it, but I think you ought to think this through a little more clearly. If you just rush in there—"

"I've no intention of doing that. Killing him would

be easy—but it's not enough. I first intend to prove that my father was right about him."

"And how will you do that?" Travis asked.

Cody slowly shook his head. "I'm not sure, but I'll figure out a way." He untied the reins, then turned to Travis. "Just what is your interest in this?" he asked.

"A nun and some orphans traveling to Wichita ran into trouble with those fellows we shot, and I've been staying around to see them safely on their way."

"So you'll be leaving now?" Cody asked with an edge of impatience.

Travis shrugged his shoulders. "Not till I find one of the boys who ran off. I just learned he may be at a place called The Line Shack near the stockyards east of town. A bunch of the local toughs hangs out there, and I'm afraid they're caught up in some of Donaghue's operations."

"Kids?"

Travis nodded. "I've been asking around town, and it seems Donaghue is paying some of these kids to cause trouble to local businesses that won't pay for protection."

"Quite a scheme," Cody commented.

"An old and effective one, I'm afraid."

"And you think this orphan boy is involved?"

"Either he joined up with them or he ran afoul of them in some way."

"And was killed?"

"I won't know until I run them down. But even if I do, the boy's sixteen; I can't force him to return with me. And I doubt they'll admit being involved with Donaghue."

"Well, good luck," Cody said, climbing into the saddle.

"One thing," Travis said as the gunman prepared to ride off. "I'd appreciate it if you didn't do anything too final until I've had a chance to find this boy."

As Cody stared down at Travis, a cold light came into his eyes. "Then you'd better find him quickly. My father's been dead since Saturday. That's five days that Donaghue's been walking around without answering for his crime."

"Just don't do anything fool—"

"This isn't your affair," Cody cut in, "so I'd be grateful if you wouldn't tell me how to handle it. No one is gonna stand between me and Marcus Donaghue. I'll do whatever I must to prove him for the scoundrel he is—and then I plan to kill him." With a tip of his black hat, Cody kneed the horse and took off at a trot down the drive, leaving Travis standing there shaking his head.

Michael slipped deeper into the shrubbery and waited for Travis to start back to town. But instead the former marshal headed toward the parsonage, probably to speak with Sister Laurel about the whereabouts of Cameron. As soon as Travis was out of sight, Michael climbed out of the bushes and stood looking down the driveway, thinking about what the two men had said. This Marcus Donaghue was the villain in all that had happened, and apparently Cameron had stumbled upon the key to unmasking the man. Yet Travis himself doubted his ability to make the boys talk, while Cody was riding blindly into danger— perhaps to face a dozen guns alone. If only someone could get the evidence they needed. Then perhaps Travis and Cody would be able to get the law to help them bring down Donaghue and his followers.

Michael frowned and kicked the ground. What

could he do? He was only a boy, and Travis and Cody were up against very evil men. "No!" he suddenly proclaimed as he realized that some of Donaghue's men were actually boys like Cameron. And who better to find out what a bunch of boys were up to than another boy?

With only a glance at the parsonage, Michael took off at a run down the driveway. He had to find that shack those boys had mentioned—The Line Shack, Travis had called it, somewhere down near the stockyards. He passed the spot where Cameron had been beaten up and raced on toward the center of town. *I have to find it,* he told himself. *Before Travis barges in there and ruins everything!*

After being directed to the stockyards, it took him little time to find the dilapidated building. It was already growing dark, and in the excitement of the moment he took no precautions as he ran toward the porch and called Cameron's name. He was greeted by the front door banging open and a young man rushing out.

"Who are you?" the young man demanded.

Michael came to an abrupt halt and stared up in some surprise at the fellow on the porch. He was far bigger than Michael had expected—hardly a boy. Suddenly feeling very vulnerable, Michael said with some trepidation, "I . . . uh, I'm looking for a friend."

"Cameron," the young man said matter-of-factly, and Michael gave a hesitant nod. "Why'd you come here?"

"Where's Cameron?" Michael asked, glancing beyond the bigger fellow and trying to see through the open front door.

"Why d'ya want to know?"

"I've, uh, got something to tell him."

"Like what?"

"It's important," Michael said, his voice growing more steady. "Can I see him?"

The young man eyed Michael for a long moment, then grinned slightly. "Sure thing, kid." He turned to the shack and called, "Cameron, come on out. A friend of yours is here to see you."

After a moment, Cameron appeared in the doorway, looking somewhat perturbed. "What're you doing here?" he asked, then petulantly added, "I'm not coming back."

"That's not why I came."

"Then why did you?"

"I . . . uh, it's j-just that . . ." Michael stammered. Then abruptly he blurted, "I ran away."

"What?" Cameron said in surprise.

Michael smiled and took a step closer. "Yes. I'm sick of being treated like a kid. I thought if I found you . . . maybe I could stay with you."

Standing nearby on the porch, the young man looked from Cameron to Michael, then started to laugh. "You?" he asked, staring down at the younger boy. "You're just a kid."

"I'm thir— I'm nearly fourteen."

"Just a kid," the young man repeated. "Get on home."

"Tell him I'm your friend," Michael implored, looking up at Cameron. "Tell him to let me stay."

Cameron glanced nervously at the older fellow, then turned to Michael. Shaking his head, he said, "I can't, Michael. Ryan's right—you're too young. You don't belong here. You'd better get back."

Folding his arms, Michael said defiantly, "I'm old enough to know what'll happen to you if you make me leave."

Ryan came down off the porch and stepped menacingly toward Michael. "Listen, kid, if you're thinking of causing us any trouble . . ."

"Not me," he replied. "But I know someone who is."

"Like who?"

"Can I stay?"

The young man eyed him closely, then asked Cameron, "Is this kid all right?"

Cameron nodded. "I trust him."

Ryan turned back to Michael. "So what is it?"

"Can I stay?" Michael repeated.

"You tell me what you know, and I'll decide whether you stay or not."

Michael considered his offer for a moment, then making up his mind, he said, "They found out about this place."

"Who?"

"Luke Travis. He used to be marshal of Wichita."

"What's he want with us?"

"He's helping find Cameron."

"Is that right?" Ryan asked Cameron.

"Could be. He's a friend of the nun I told you about."

"And he's on his way over here right now," Michael continued. "I heard him over at the church. That's how I found out about this place."

The young man looked nervously in the direction of town. Suddenly he spun around and crossed over to the open front door. "We're getting out of here," he called inside. "Get your stuff together."

As the other boys started piling out, their few possessions in hand, the young leader told Michael, "Thanks, kid. You'd better be getting home now."

"What? You said I could stay—"

"I didn't say nothing. You're too young."

Michael glared at him defiantly. "I'll follow you."

The young man looked from him to Cameron, who nodded. Facing Michael again, Ryan said, "I bet you would."

"How about it?" Cameron asked, stepping down from the porch and standing beside his younger friend. "Can he come with us?"

"I ought to kick the pair of you out," Ryan said, suppressing a smile. "But you've got spunk. Both of you."

"Then I can come?" Michael asked.

"Sure, kid. Just don't get in the way." Turning to the others, he said, "Let's get out of here. We'll split up and meet by old Meeker's Warehouse." He broke the group into pairs and watched as they ran off in different directions. As soon as they were gone, he shook Michael's hand and said, "My name's Ryan."

"I'm Michael," the boy replied.

"You got guts, kid," Ryan declared as he reached over and patted Michael on the belly. "I don't even need to punch you in the stomach to be sure." He winked at Cameron, who flinched slightly but then grinned in reply.

Cody Fisher dismounted outside the Salty Dog Saloon, tied his pinto to the hitching rack, and stood for a moment in the dark street, watching the activity through the large, right-hand pane window, the edges of which were smudged with putty. Apparently it had been broken recently—no doubt by a saloon brawl,

Cody thought. The entertainment tonight was already in full cry, he noted, the sounds of raucous laughter and clinking glasses blending with the slightly off-key notes of a tinny piano.

Cody instinctively checked the set of the Colt .44 in his holster, then stepped up onto the boardwalk and strode through the batwings. No one paid him much attention as he stood scanning the room. There were at least a dozen tables—all of them occupied—with a good number of men standing around the poker games or lining the bar. The bartender was a bald, bearded man, and there were a half-dozen barmaids working the tables, making sure no one was long without a drink. Cody would have thought it a reasonably respectable place if he had not known Marcus Donaghue was the proprietor.

It did not take long for Cody to decide that Donaghue had to be the big, well-dressed man holding court at a round table near the far end of the bar. Part of what gave him away was that he not only had his back to the wall but was seated in the only upholstered, high-backed chair in the room. Everything about him, from his impeccably tailored brown suit to his smug grin, spoke of a man in charge, with the impression reinforced by the deferential looks of the men seated around the table playing poker. The only part of his attire that seemed at all out of character was the gauze bandage wrapped around his right hand.

Bypassing the bar, Cody headed directly for the table and came to a halt just behind two of the players, from where he had a full view of the man in the plush chair. The man took no notice of Cody at first, and it was not until he raked in the pot that he looked up and saw the newcomer standing there. He proceeded with his deal, but during the next few minutes he occasionally glanced up to confirm that the stranger in the black outfit was still there.

After a few more hands, the man turned over the deal to the player on his left, then took out a long cigar and slowly lit it. Drawing in deeply and exhaling the bluish smoke, he looked up at Cody and said, "You want in on this game, or you just come to look?"

Cody tipped his hat back slightly and replied, "What I'm looking for is a man named Donaghue. They say he owns this saloon—and half of Abilene."

The man squinted his left eye slightly as he removed the cigar from his mouth. Turning it slowly between his fingers, he gave a slight grin. "Some folks say he owns *all* of Abilene."

Cody shook his head. "Not from what I saw today."

The area around the table grew quiet. The man took another puff, let it out, and said, "Just what do you mean?"

"It seems three of his friends were taken down by a single man with a gun. Donaghue sure doesn't own *him.*"

A sudden murmur ran through the crowd, and then someone at the bar stepped over to the big man's left shoulder and whispered something, nodding all the while at Cody. The man's smile suddenly disappeared, and he seemed to be making a supreme effort to control himself as he snuffed out the cigar in the ashtray beside him.

Guessing what had been said, Cody stated what was already being whispered by the people gathered around. "I'm the man who took down the fourth."

The man's voice grated as he asked, "Just what do you want here?"

"Are you Donaghue?"

After hesitating a moment, the man slowly nodded, then said, "I asked you a question, boy."

"The name's Cody," came the reply. Then, using the name he had gone by ever since leaving home several years before, he added, "Matthew Cody." He knew that his reputation with a gun was not yet so great that the name would be common knowledge in Abilene, but at least Matthew Cody was not known to be the son of the late Lawrence Fisher. And since Cody himself had never lived in Abilene, it was unlikely he would be recognized.

"Matthew Cody," Donaghue repeated slowly. "Seems I've heard that name before."

Nodding, Cody replied, "I'm the man who outdrew Josh Weaver in Dodge City."

"Yes!" exclaimed a little man beside the bar. "And Aaron Needleman down in Santa Fe." He started pulling the sleeve of the man beside him as he excitedly recounted having seen the gunfight.

Placing his palms against the table, Marcus Donaghue stared up into Cody's dark eyes and said evenly, "And now you've come to try your luck against me."

Cody saw a couple of men moving closer on either side of Donaghue's chair. Each wore a low-slung gun, and Cody did not doubt they were practiced in their use. He looked at the big man in the high-backed chair and slowly shook his head. "I don't want to kill you," he said in a steady, calm voice. "You're a businessman, not a gunman. I've come to do business with you." When Donaghue just sat looking curiously at him, Cody continued, "I didn't know that those men worked for you. And anyway, I've no use for four men who can't do a job that should only need one. They were amateurs. You'd do better to hire one man like me than four the likes of them."

"You're saying you want to work for me?"

"With four men dead, I figured you might need another gun," Cody replied. From the corner of his eye, he saw that the gunman to the right of Donaghue was looking increasingly edgy, his hand hovering just over his gun butt. Jabbing his left thumb in the man's direction, he said, "Especially if all you've got backing you is the likes of him."

As Cody expected, the man went for his gun. But before his hand had even closed around the butt, Cody had his own gun out and trained on the man's chest. He did not pull the trigger but stood watching the man's shocked expression. As the man slowly moved his hand away from his gun, Cody holstered his own and said, "This time I'm letting you live. I wouldn't want to spoil Mr. Donaghue's card game."

Donaghue began to nod as he looked Cody up and down. "Why don't we step into my office," he said, rising and walking to the door near the table. Opening it wide, he waited for Cody to enter, then motioned his men to remain outside. Following Cody in, he closed the door and circled the ornately carved desk that dominated the room.

"A cigar?" he offered, opening an ivory box atop the desk. When Cody shook his head, Donaghue closed the box and waved his hand toward one of the chairs. "Please, sit down," he said as he sat in his own swivel chair and leaned back. "It's clear you didn't know what you were walking in on this afternoon, Mr. Cody, and I hold you no grudge," he began when Cody was seated. "But you've put me in a difficult spot. You see, I have a job coming up that could be quite lucrative for everyone involved. However, there's a man who's been nosing around too much and may get in the way."

"Luke Travis," Cody stated.

"Yes. The very man whose life you saved today. So you see my predicament. And now, with Travis on the alert, it won't be so easy to get rid of him."

"I saw him in action this afternoon, and he's fast," Cody put in. "Faster than any of your men."

"But not faster than you?" Donaghue said, as much a statement as a question.

"No. Not faster than me."

"Then perhaps there's a way we both could profit," Donaghue continued, and Cody raised an eyebrow. "If you take care of my little problem with Luke Travis, I'm certain there'd be a place in my organization for you. A place that would net you, say, a couple of thousand dollars just for this upcoming job alone—and another thousand for taking care of this Travis situation."

Cody stared across the desk at the man responsible for the death of his father. Now he was offering a substantial sum to remove another problem—Luke Travis. While Cody had no desire to kill an innocent man, he knew that if he agreed he would be given a place within the organization—and the opportunity to unmask the man Donaghue had paid to pull the trigger on his father. And then Cody could kill them both. He would have to go along with Donaghue's offer—at least for the time being—and try to find a way to stall for time.

"When do you need the job done?" Cody finally said.

"By tomorrow night the latest," Donaghue replied. "It's essential that Luke Travis be out of the picture before the westbound train arrives the day after tomorrow."

Nodding, Cody stood and shook hands with Donaghue. He was about to leave, but then he reached over, opened the top of the ivory box, and removed one of the cigars. With a smile, he stuffed it in his shirt pocket and walked out of the room.

Chapter Twelve

———◆———

T he steak's as delicious as you promised," Luke Travis declared as he cut another slice from the huge portion that had been served up at the Sunrise Café. "And it's so tender, I hardly need a knife."

Seated across from him, Aileen Bloom smiled with pleasure. "Then you'll be able to give that arm of yours a rest," she said, nodding at his wounded left arm, which just now was holding the fork as he cut with his right hand.

Glancing down at his shoulder, Travis shook his head. "It doesn't hurt at all." He lifted his left hand and moved his arm in a circular motion as he smiled at an elderly couple at a nearby table.

Lowering her voice so that the other restaurant patrons would not hear, Aileen said, "The shooting was just yesterday. You should rest it for a few more days."

"Anything the doctor says." He gave a mock pout, then continued eating his meal.

Aileen took another bite of the chicken she had ordered, washing it down with some cool spring water. Putting down the glass, she looked up at Travis and said, "You didn't have any luck today, did you?"

"You mean about the boy?" he asked, and she nodded. "It was dark when I got to The Line Shack last night and found it empty, so I gave it a closer inspection today. People have definitely been staying there, though I suppose it could be no more than an occasional vagrant. Still, I wouldn't be surprised if those kids were tipped off and abandoned the place."

"But how would they have found out?"

"It's possible they heard I've been asking questions around town and decided they'd best find a new place. And Abilene is a big town, with plenty of places to hide."

"You still think Cameron is with them?"

"I hope so."

She looked at him curiously as he picked up his fork and stabbed another piece of meat. Then she realized that what Travis had left unsaid was that if Cameron had not willingly joined the gang, he might have been killed in some sort of confrontation with them.

"There's another thing," he said, putting down his fork. "Michael Hirsch has disappeared, as well."

"Michael?" she asked incredulously. "When?"

"Apparently last night. There was a late prayer meeting at the church, and Sister Laurel was so busy helping the minister that she didn't even realize Michael was gone until this morning."

"The poor woman must be beside herself with worry."

"I'm afraid so. She says that Michael is different

from Cameron—that he would never run off on his own like this, unless . . ."

"Unless what?" she pressed, leaning forward and touching his hand.

"Unless he got it in his head to find Cameron himself."

"Oh, dear." Aileen sat back in her chair and folded her hands on the table in front of her, nervously clenching and opening her fingers.

Travis forced a smile. "I'm sure they'll turn up. Now let's get on with this wonderful dinner. We've both got a long night ahead of us."

Aileen picked up her fork and poked at her chicken, but after a moment she put it down and pushed away the plate. Travis watched her but said nothing as he ate a few more bites of steak and then pushed his own plate away, as well.

"You should eat more," she said absently, as though her thoughts were distracted. "You must regain your strength."

Travis leaned across the table and took her left hand. Patting it gently, he said, "I'm all right—really I am. And so are Michael and Cameron. You'll see."

Her lips quivered, and as she nodded, her eyes began to glisten with moisture. "I'm worried," she whispered.

"I know," he replied, giving her a reassuring smile. "So am I. But you'll be fine. Trust me."

Slipping her hand from his, she picked up her cloth napkin and gently dabbed at her eyes with a clean corner. "I know I will," she said at last. "I'm just worried."

"The best way to deal with fear is to face it straight on—like when you operated on Simon. Can you do that?"

She gave a slight smile. "Yes, I can."

"Then let's get started."

Taking his hat from the back of the chair, Travis rose and held out his arm. As Aileen stood and slipped her hand through his arm, he took a couple of coins from his pocket and placed them on the table. Then he led her among the tables and out the door. It was growing dark outside, and the lamps had been lit along the boardwalks on both sides of Texas Street. A few people were walking along the block, but the area seemed unusually quiet for a Friday night.

"Luke Travis," a voice called as Travis and Aileen stepped off the boardwalk and started across the street.

Seeing a dark figure at the edge of the road across the way, silhouetted from behind by a lantern, Travis held up and stared intently at the shadowed face. As the man lifted a thin cigar to his mouth and drew in a puff, the glowing tip reflected in his dark eyes and highlighted a jagged white scar along his right cheek.

Travis grew more accustomed to the lamplight, and he saw the man's right hand hovering near the butt of his holster. Travis's own hand moved instinctively toward the Colt Peacemaker at his hip. "Cody?" Travis asked. "If you've come for that drink I offered—"

"I don't drink with lawmen," came the abrupt reply. There was a brief pause, and then Cody said, "That's what you are, isn't it?"

"I don't wear a badge anymore, but I used to be marshal of Wichita."

"Yes, I've heard of you. I just didn't make the connection yesterday afternoon. And like I said, I don't drink with lawmen—or with men who used to be lawmen."

"I don't understand—"

"You don't have to," Cody cut him off. "Let's just say I've had my own encounters with lawmen—enough to know I don't count them among my friends."

Travis nodded slowly. "You've a right to pick your friends. But I meant it when I thanked you yesterday."

"If I'd have known who you were, I wouldn't have stepped in like that. Still, I suppose it gives me the pleasure of finishing what those fools were unable to accomplish." There was a long pause as the two men eyed each other in the faint lamplight, then Cody continued, "You'd best ask your lady friend to move out of the way."

Aileen looked back and forth in confusion between the two men. Travis patted her hand, then gently removed it from his arm and said, "Do as the man says."

"But I—"

"I'll be fine," he insisted, pushing her away slightly.

Aileen backed away, shaking her head in shocked surprise. Suddenly she turned, saw several people who had gathered on the boardwalk nearby, and started toward them. "Do something. Please. Get the marshal," she implored, repeating it until one of the men nodded and went running down the boardwalk in the direction of the jail.

Across the street, Cody tossed the burning cigar to the ground and walked forward a few paces. Travis, in turn, circled to his left so that the two men would face each other lengthwise along the street, thus reducing the risk to people along the boardwalk or in nearby buildings.

"Don't make this mistake, son," Travis said as he took his stance in front of the young gunfighter.

"They say you're fast. I saw you yesterday, and they're right. But I'm faster—and now I'm gonna prove it."

"You don't have to do this—"

His words were cut off by the movement of Cody's hand toward the butt of his gun. Instantly Travis went for his own gun, cocking it with his thumb as it came up in his hand. The two weapons fired simultaneously, and a woman screamed as Travis staggered slightly. His legs buckled, and he dropped his revolver and went down on one knee. He stared in surprise at the young gunfighter, who stood holding his smoking gun. Then Travis looked down at his chest, saw the blood spreading across his white shirt, and touched it with the palm of his hand. There was another scream, and Travis turned in its direction and brought up his bloody hand, palm forward, as if in supplication. Then he fell face-forward in the dirt.

Screaming again, Aileen Bloom came running down the road to where Travis was lying. Dropping beside him, she rolled him onto his back, her hands holding his cheeks as she called his name over and over. Frantically she looked around and yelled for assistance, and as several townsmen came hurrying over, she wiped at her tears and haltingly directed them to carry Travis to her nearby office. While two of the men were lifting him from the ground, Aileen stood and glanced back down the road, but already the man named Cody had disappeared into the night. "Hurry!" she ordered the men as she led the way toward her office.

Ten minutes later Marshal Stacy Parnell appeared in the waiting room at the doctor's office. There were several townsmen standing around, and as Parnell entered, one of them nodded at the closed door of one of the examining rooms, indicating that the doctor was inside.

"I came as soon as I could," Parnell explained, his breath tinged with alcohol, his entire demeanor giving the impression that he had just been roused from a deep sleep.

Just then the door opened, and Aileen Bloom appeared. Her shoulders were hunched, her eyes swollen with tears. The marshal started forward, then halted as she looked up at him and sadly shook her head.

"Can I see him?" Parnell asked, removing his hat and crumpling it in his hands.

She nodded, then moved mechanically toward the table, on which lay a body covered from head to toe with a white sheet that was stained red over the chest. Closing her eyes, Aileen pulled back the edge of the cloth, revealing Travis's head and upper chest. Directly over the heart, his shirt was soaked with blood, and he was not breathing. His eyes were closed, his expression almost serene.

"I'm sorry," Parnell said as Aileen draped the cloth over the body and started toward the door. He followed her out into the waiting room.

"The name of the man who did this was Cody," Aileen said woodenly as she closed the examining room door.

"Yes, I know. Matthew Cody, I'm told. A young man who's been making a name for himself with a gun."

"Have you arrested him?"

"I, uh, can't."

She cocked her head slightly. "Did he get away?"

"It's not that. It's just—"

"What?" she pressed.

"There were a lot of witnesses, and they all say Travis agreed to the challenge and that it was a fair fight."

"A fair fight?" she said incredulously. "My God, that bastard confronted Travis and forced him into it."

"Now, let's calm down, Miss Bloom," Parnell said, reaching awkwardly as if to touch her arm.

"I'll calm down when you've brought that killer to justice."

"I'm sorry, but I can't do that—"

"What *can* you do?" she blared. "What good are you in this town, anyway?"

"Look, you've got no call—"

"Get out of here!" she demanded, pointing to the door.

One of the other men gingerly stepped forward, hat in hand. "It's like the marshal said, Dr. Bloom. It was a fair fight."

She stared in amazement from one man to the next. Most turned away or looked at the floor. "Get out of here," she said coldly. "All of you. Just get the hell out." She turned away, trying to fight the tears.

The men looked nervously at Parnell, who nodded that they should leave. As they filed out, the marshal turned back a final time as if to speak, but Dr. Bloom had sat down in a chair and was holding her head in her hands, sobbing. He shrugged, clapped his hat on his head, and headed out the front door.

Marcus Donaghue looked up from his desk as Cody Fisher was ushered into the office. Glancing up at the man he knew as Matthew Cody, Donaghue grinned broadly and waved away the bodyguard who had shown Cody in.

"Excellent," Donaghue declared as soon as the door closed and the two men were alone. "A job well done."

"Luke Travis made the mistake of underestimating me," Cody said dryly, sitting across from the burly saloon owner.

"I'll be careful not to make the same mistake," Donaghue replied with a thin smile as he opened the cigar box and held it forth. Cody took one of the long, thick cigars and then leaned across the desk to accept a light from an engraved silver lighter that Donaghue produced from his vest pocket. For a while the two men enjoyed their cigars, gauging each other like a pair of animals trying to determine whether to attack or join forces. Finally Donaghue rested his cigar in a glass ashtray, opened the top drawer of his desk, and removed a long, white envelope. Sliding it across the desk, he said, "You'll find one thousand dollars in there—a token of appreciation for handling that Travis affair."

Without looking inside, Cody tucked the envelope behind his gun belt.

"I said there might be another two thousand in it for you," Donaghue continued. "Are you still interested?"

"Who do you want killed?" Cody asked coldly.

"Not this time. Tomorrow morning there's an army payroll coming through Abilene. It'll be under heavy guard on the westbound train and will be transferred to the Abilene Agricultural Bank. It'll sit there till later in the week, when an army patrol will pick it up. I intend to remove the funds before they arrive."

"And where do I fit in?" Cody asked.

"You'll take Kincaid's place at the bank," Donaghue replied without hesitation. "The bank is closed Saturdays, so the place will be empty once the money is transferred and the bank president locks up and leaves. As soon as he's gone, you and another of my men will be let into the back of the building by a young bank officer on my payroll. He'll open the safe, and you two will empty the treasure box and replace the funds with blank paper."

"And then we bring the money back here," Cody said.

"Precisely. Next week, the army will discover the fraud, and the bank president will be accused of embezzling the funds himself. The young bank officer will serve as a witness against his boss, and the man's fate will be sealed when a portion of the funds turns up at his home."

"Planted there by you," Cody said, and Donaghue grinned smugly. "But why him?" Cody asked.

Donaghue's smile faded. "Because it serves my purpose. He'll take the fall—and he'll pay."

"I don't understand—" Cody began, but Donaghue cut him off with a wave of his hand.

"He was one of the witnesses who sent me to prison three years ago," Donaghue explained. His smile slowly returned, and he calmly folded his hands on top of the desk. The right one was no longer bandaged, though the burned flesh was clearly visible. "He can sweat away in prison while I take his bank out from under him." He gave a slight chuckle, then added, "You'll soon learn that it doesn't pay to underestimate me, either."

"I'll keep that in mind."

Cody started to rise, but Donaghue waved him back down, saying, "Just a minute. I want you to meet someone."

Donaghue stood, circled the desk, and went over to the door. Opening it slightly, he whispered something to the man outside, then shut the door and returned to his seat. A moment later the door opened and a man Cody's age entered. Though on the short side, he seemed muscular and fit, despite his disheveled hair and a couple of days' growth of beard. His clothing was rumpled and his features bland and colorless. The only distinctive thing about him was the six-pointed star pinned to his faded leather vest.

"This is Marshal Stacy Parnell," Donaghue said to Cody, then turned to Parnell and added, "and this is the man I was telling you about."

The young marshal smiled and thrust forth his hand. Somewhat numbly, Cody stood and shook hands with the man.

"So you're the one gunned down Luke Travis," Parnell said animatedly. "I wish I'd seen it."

Cody stood looking between Parnell and Donaghue. As if sensing his discomfort, Donaghue explained, "Marshal Parnell will be with you at the bank tomorrow."

"The marshal? You're kidding," Cody said, not trying to conceal his surprise.

"Who better?" Donaghue asked. "This way you don't have to worry about the law breathing down your neck—unless he leans over your back while you two are opening the treasure box." Donaghue chuckled.

"But a marshal . . . ?"

Parnell looked a bit put out by Cody's attitude, and

Donaghue immediately tried to smooth the situation, saying, "Stacy, here, has been very reliable in the past."

"That's right," Parnell interjected, his tone somewhat agitated. "That's why I'm marshal around here."

Cody looked him up and down again but decided not to comment. Instead he turned to Donaghue and said, "You're calling the shots. If Marshal Parnell's all right with you, he's fine with me." He forced a grin, which seemed to put Parnell at ease.

"Then it's decided." Donaghue stood again and clasped his hands. "You two will meet at the jail in the morning and head over to the bank before the train arrives at nine."

"We'll be there, Mr. Donaghue," Parnell promised.

Donaghue crossed to the door, and as he was showing the two men out, one of his bodyguards approached and said, "Mr. Donaghue, there's a pair of women who insist on seeing you."

"Who are they?" Donaghue asked, glancing beyond the bodyguard into the main room of the saloon.

"Never seen 'em before. And these two I would've remembered."

"Where are they?"

The bodyguard backed from the doorway and waved an arm toward the bar. Entering the main room, Donaghue looked over and caught fleeting glimpses of glimmering red through the press of men that had gathered around the bar. There was some high-pitched laughter, followed by the raucous cheers of several of the men. Donaghue looked at his bodyguard, who nodded that those were the women in question.

"Tell them I'm busy. Have them come back tomorrow afternoon," Donaghue told the man, who started toward the bar. Turning to Cody, Donaghue said, "It'd be best not to hang around here until after the job. The marshal can fill you in on any remaining details." He nodded at the two men, then started back to his office.

As Donaghue was opening the office door, a woman with a stern, commanding voice called, "Mr. Donaghue! I must speak with you now!" He turned to see a somewhat matronly—though apparently once quite attractive—woman pushing her way through the crowd. The woman, whose unusually short hair had been feathered to delicately frame her face, carried a closed parasol and was dressed in a slightly provocative blue dress, hemmed in black lace, which seemed designed for someone in her twenties. Yet it was quite appealing on this woman, who Donaghue guessed to be in her forties, though the subtle use of powder and rouge made her look a good ten years younger. The dress was buttoned in front and corseted to highlight her trim waist and ample bosom—one of Donaghue's preferences in a woman, though he guessed from the lay of the material on her hips that her legs were a bit too ample for his tastes.

The woman sashayed over and came to a halt a few feet away. Planting the tip of the parasol firmly at her feet, she rested her hands on the handle, grinned broadly, and said, "You *are* Mr. Donaghue, are you not?"

"Yes," he replied cautiously. "What can I do for you?"

"Not for me but for my girls," the woman said. Turning and raising her right hand, she called, "Maureen . . ."

There was a stirring at the bar, then the crowd parted enough to let the woman in red pass. She wore a revealingly low-cut dress made from a shimmering red material that clung to her as she moved, accenting each curve of her figure. As she came forward partway, Donaghue found himself mesmerized by her captivating beauty. Her youthful face, set in auburn waves of hair that cascaded around her bare shoulders, glowed like the sun setting in a brilliant wash of reds and oranges. Though her bosom was not yet abundant, her ripening breasts swelled gently as she breathed, like a pair of buds eager to burst forth. He could tell from her finely turned ankles that her legs were long and muscular; they would give a man a firm, steady ride. And though her features were still rounded with a trace of girlish fat, her delicate arms and narrow waist indicated that she was growing into a sleek, beautifully proportioned woman.

"Maureen is just one of my girls," the older woman said, interrupting his reverie. "The others will be arriving by train as soon as I send for them."

"Others?" he asked somewhat absently, pulling his eyes from the younger woman and turning to her older companion.

"Yes. There are six all told. Enough for a good start, wouldn't you say?"

"I'm not sure I understand, Miss . . . ?"

"Maguire. Sadie Maguire at your service." She held out her hand and gave Donaghue's a firm shake. "And service is my business." She winked.

Donaghue narrowed his eyes slightly. "Do you mean—?"

"Precisely. Until two months ago I ran a profitable sporting house in Boston, but of course you've heard of the problems we've had with the revival movement in that town."

Not wanting to seem uninformed, Donaghue nodded that he was well aware of the situation, though in reality he had never heard any such thing.

"When the politicians and the police heeled under to the Christian fanatics and started shutting us down every few nights, I decided I'd had enough of Eastern society. It was time to see a land where men are men, not hypocrites." She waved an arm toward the young woman. "So I packed my bags, picked one of my most delightful and nubile young women, and set out to discover if Abilene really is a place where men are men." She turned to the crowd gathered behind the younger woman. "There *are* real men in Abilene, aren't there?" The response was a chorus of raucous cheers.

Marcus Donaghue found himself grinning. As the noise subsided and Sadie Maguire turned back to him, he said, "That doesn't explain why you've come to the Salty Dog."

"I like a modest man," she replied with a grin. "The fact is that I've had my fill of politicians and lawmen, and I've been told that you are the person to see if I want a smooth-running house."

"You're in need of an investor?" he asked with the wariness that always came when he considered spending money.

"A partner," she corrected him. "A full partner. I'll put up half the money and provide the girls and expertise, while you put up the other half and provide the protection, so to speak. And of course I'll expect your personal endorsement to ensure our success."

Donaghue's lips curled with anticipation as he glanced over Sadie's shoulder at the young woman in the red dress. "I couldn't endorse anything I hadn't sampled myself."

"Of course not," she assured him. "And as a

partner, you'd never be charged for sampling what you already own."

Donaghue's smile broadened. "Sadie Maguire," he pronounced, "I think you and I can do business." He began to shake her hand again, but instead she bent her wrist and gave a delicate curtsy. This was met by a rousing cheer from the future customers of what was already being dubbed Sadie's Sporting House. With the business at hand apparently concluded to their satisfaction, the patrons eagerly took up their drinks and excitedly began to converse about the promised pleasures to come.

Donaghue released Sadie's hand. "If you'll return tomorrow—around two—we can have a late lunch in my office and arrange the particulars."

"I'd be delighted," she replied and curtsied again. She started to turn to leave, but then she looked back and said, "Might I ask a small favor?"

Donaghue raised an eyebrow in caution. "What is it?"

Lowering her voice, she said, "Maureen and I are staying at a hotel until my other girls get here. I've already found a house I'm considering purchasing, and I'd like to have it ready by the time they arrive. Before I settle on a price with the owner, however, I could use the services of a few teenaged boys to help me rearrange some things on the premises."

"That should be no problem. Certainly the hotel could provide—"

"Ah, but you see, my intention is not to make improvements to the property in advance of purchase. In fact, I was hoping for some discreet boys who might be encouraged to do quite the opposite."

Donaghue shook his head. "I'm afraid I don't fully understand . . ."

"There are many things in that house for which I have little use—fixtures and the like—since I'll be installing accoutrements in the finest French decor. But the owner does not know that, since he has no idea of the purpose for which I plan to use the house. And if those unneeded items were discovered to have been vandalized—and you know how irresponsible teenagers are these days . . ." She grinned slyly. "Well, that certainly would help me secure a more favorable purchase price."

Donaghue's smile returned. "Yes, Sadie, I am certain we can do business together. And I have an idea of just the right boys to do the job."

"I must meet with them as early as possible tomorrow, since I have to close the deal later in the day."

"I'll have one of my men arrange the meeting. Where can he find you?"

"How about at the Sunrise Café just after breakfast? Nine o'clock, perhaps?"

Realizing the bank heist would be taking place then, Donaghue was about to suggest a different arrangement, but then he decided that he would rather not draw attention to the time. Instead he nodded and said, "That will be fine. I'll send my bartender around for you at nine."

Sadie glanced at the bar to identify the bald, bearded man, then nodded. "It's been a pleasure, Mr. Donaghue."

"The pleasure is mine," he said grandly.

Turning on her heels, the woman walked over to her companion and took her by the arm. Leading the way through the press of men, she could feel the younger woman's body trembling, and she whispered, "It's all right." Though she could feel her own heart racing, she was certain that no one—Marcus Donaghue included—would ever suspect that a well-dressed sporting-house madam was in reality a Dominican nun or that the young prostitute was her orphan charge.

As they approached the swinging doors, Sister Laurel suppressed a sigh of relief. She knew the danger would not be over until she met with the teenagers, retrieved Michael and Cameron, and got the orphans as far from Abilene as possible. But at least in a few minutes she would be able to get out of her younger sister's constricting dress, which she had kept in her trunk ever since her sister had died two years previously. She wondered if Agnes would so willingly remove the more daring outfit Sister Laurel had borrowed for her from one of the local saloons by claiming it was for a church play. As soon as she had seen her in it, she knew that Agnes was no longer a child and that it had been right to allow her to help find her younger brother. Sister Laurel only hoped that she had not been too hasty in launching this desperate plan without informing anyone else.

Still, Luke Travis has been unable to find the boys, she reassured herself as they reached the batwings. *And I simply cannot wait any longer—until perhaps it's too late.*

Standing partway in front of the swinging doors was a tall, dark-haired man with a low-slung holster and a faint white scar down his right cheek, whom Sister Laurel thought she had seen coming out of the office with the marshal and Marcus Donaghue a few minutes before. The young man reached back and pulled open the right-hand batwing, and Sister Laurel smiled at him and motioned the younger woman toward the boardwalk. But suddenly Agnes halted, her body growing rigid as she looked up at the man. It was as if she had seen him somewhere before, but though he smiled politely at her, he gave no indication that they were acquainted.

"Come along, dear," Sister Laurel urged as she pulled the young woman along, feigning a smile as Agnes at last allowed herself to be ushered through the doorway.

As Agnes was dragged along, she twisted her head toward the saloon, and Sister Laurel had to yank her arm to get her to turn around. The older woman risked a glance over her shoulder and saw the young man looking at them over the top of the batwings. He tipped his hat and turned away.

"What was that all about?" she asked as they headed down the street.

"It was him," Agnes murmured dreamily.

"Who?" she asked in confusion.

"The man I told you about."

"You don't mean Reverend Fisher's brother, do you?" she asked, and the young woman nodded and gave a slight sigh. "My God," Sister Laurel muttered, shaking her head and frowning. "A gunslinger—and right there in Donaghue's office, no less. Thick as thieves, no doubt."

Her eyes half closed, Agnes whispered, "Isn't he beautiful?"

It was Sister Laurel's turn to sigh as she gripped the young woman's arm all the more tightly and fairly hauled her away from the Salty Dog.

Aileen Bloom jumped with a start at the sound of a loud rapping on the door that led from the examination room to the rear hallway. Straightening the bloody sheet that covered Luke Travis's body, she stepped to the door and called softly, "Who is it?"

" 'Tis me—Orion," came the reply, and she pulled open the door. The tavern keeper entered, and she closed the door behind him and stood leaning against it, watching him circle the table on which Travis was lying.

"Look wha' they done t'ye," Orion muttered, stroking his chin and shaking his head as he halted beside Travis's head. Aileen came up beside him and placed a hand on Orion's shoulder. She was a good two inches taller than the squat, burly Scotsman, who glanced up at her and said, "Wha' a bloody mess. An' ye think tha' because I'm his friend ye kin get me t'clean it all up?"

"You're damn right!" a gruff voice called from beneath the sheet.

"Dinna be daft, man!" Orion replied, pulling back the sheet and unveiling a grinning face. "Clean up ye own mess, Mr. Lucas Travis." He pulled the sheet lower to reveal the bloody shirtfront. "An' wha' a mess ye made of it, indeed. Ruined a good shirt, no less."

Travis chuckled as he sat up and unbuttoned the shirt. Underneath, a flat rubber bag hung directly in front of his heart, suspended around his neck by leather thongs. It had a jagged tear in the front, and when Travis pressed it, some more red liquid oozed out between his fingers.

"Very effective," Orion said. "A little trick ye hatched when cleaning up the streets of Wichita?"

Travis shook his head. "It was Dr. Bloom's idea," he explained, smiling up at her. "All it took was this bag of chicken blood and a small surgical blade hidden in my hand."

"Don't forget the blanks in Cody's gun," Aileen put in.

"Aye," Orion agreed with a nod. "Without them, it'd be a real pickle ye'd be in and a real mess I'd be cleaning. How'd the lad do?"

"Perfect," Travis replied as Aileen removed the rubber bag. "It couldn't have looked more real if we'd have used real bullets." He rebuttoned the blood-stained shirt.

"Do ye think Donaghue'll go for it?"

Travis nodded. "He will—because he wants to so badly. We'll know for sure soon enough. I arranged with Cody to meet at his brother's church later tonight—provided he can get away from Donaghue and his men."

"He will," Aileen said. "He's got a good head on his shoulders. He proved that when he came to you with Donaghue's offer to let him in the gang if he killed you."

"Aye, but the lad seems a mite hotheaded t'me," Orion remarked. "Look at the way he barged in on Donaghue in the first place."

"I seem to remember you doing a little arm twisting with Donaghue yourself," Travis reminded him.

"Tha' was different. I had a grudge t'set right, 'n' I only put me arm at risk."

"Cody has an even bigger score to settle—the murder of his father," Travis replied. "I'd expect him to take a bigger risk."

Aileen nodded in agreement. "I only hope it wasn't too great a risk."

"We'll find out when he gets to the church."

"We'd best get ye o'er there, then." Orion moved toward the rear door. "The coffin's on a wagon out back. A plain wooden one, I'm afraid." He gave a mischievous wink. "I'd have brought a fancy brass-fitted one, but in Abilene we dinna let lawmen be buried in style."

"Well, you'd better carry me out there before half the town arrives to pay their last respects."

"Dinna be daft, man! 'Tis plenty dark outside for a corpse t'load itself without risk o' being seen. I'm too old t'be lugging around the likes o' ye."

Travis clapped the Scotsman on the back. "Come along, Charon—it's time to ferry me across the river Styx."

Orion looked up at him crookedly. "The name's Orion, 'n' there's nary a river in Abilene." With a disdainful shake of the head, he muttered, "Ye Englishers surely are a pompous lot."

"I'm an American," Travis declared, "born and bred."

"But it was buttered in England," Orion replied somewhat quizzically. He folded his arms and grinned smugly at their curious expressions, as if his comment had ended any need for further discussion.

Realizing that arguing with the Scotsman was useless, Travis shrugged and turned away, choosing instead to thank Aileen for her assistance in the elaborate ruse that he and Cody had set up earlier in the day.

"It was nothing," Aileen insisted, blushing slightly as Travis took her hands. "I only wish that the victims of every gunfight were patched up so easily."

Travis looked into her soft brown eyes for a long moment, then impulsively leaned closer and lightly kissed her cheek. Letting go of her hands, he turned and followed Orion into the hall.

Standing alone in the doorway of the examination room, Aileen watched the two men head down the hall and disappear through a back door into the darkness of the yard. She followed and stood at the window beside the door. She could faintly see the shadowed form of Travis as he climbed onto the wagon bed and into an open coffin. Stepping up behind him, Orion closed the coffin lid. Then he made his way forward to the driver's seat and picked up the reins, clucking at the horses and leading them around the back of the building and down the alley alongside Orion's Tavern.

Aileen touched her cheek where Luke Travis had kissed her. As the sound of the creaking wagon faded into the night, she pressed her fingers to her own lips and smiled.

Chapter Thirteen

Sister Laurel stepped out of the Sunrise Café at precisely five minutes before nine on Saturday morning and stood waiting on the boardwalk, looking fairly inconspicuous though possibly a bit overdressed in her sister's dark-blue dress. She looked up and down Texas Street but did not see the bartender of the Salty Dog Saloon anywhere in sight.

After leaving the saloon the night before, she and Agnes had returned to the dilapidated hotel next to Dr. Bloom's office, where earlier Sister Laurel had obtained a room so that they could put on their outfits. As soon as Agnes had changed back into her regular clothes, Sister Laurel had sent her to the church with an admonition not to tell anyone where they had gone. Agnes would take charge of the children and pretend the next day that the nun had returned late at night and had gone back out early in the morning. Meanwhile, Sister Laurel would spend the night at the hotel so that she would have no trouble keeping her appointment with Marcus Donaghue's bartender.

Sister Laurel waited a few more minutes, smiling and casually greeting the women who passed along the boardwalk, realizing full well that each was wondering the identity of this new woman in town. A church bell rang in the distance, and Sister Laurel knew that it was the appointed hour. It was followed a few minutes later by the piercing wail of a steam whistle and the sound of the westbound train chugging in at the depot several blocks away.

Sister Laurel grew more impatient as the minutes continued to pass with no sign of Donaghue's man. Then suddenly, as she stood looking down the street, a deep voice called, "Miss Maguire?" and she turned to see the bald, bearded bartender smiling behind her.

"Goodness, where did you come from?" she asked.

"I was inside the café eating breakfast," he replied.

"But I was in there, and I didn't see—"

"I know. I was in the far corner with my back to you." His smug expression made it clear that he took great pleasure in having been able to observe her undetected—and Sister Laurel did not doubt that his boss had encouraged him to do precisely that. "My name's Murray. Shall we go?" he asked, and she nodded and followed him down the boardwalk.

They headed east along Texas Street to a less-developed district just south of the stockyards. The neighborhood was undergoing change and was a curious mix of new buildings going up and old ones ready to come down. The bartender turned right onto an unidentified street, and half a block down he stopped in front of a free-standing brick building that looked abandoned. It was fronted by an enormous pair of doors, capable of allowing entry to the largest of wagons, with the words MEEKER'S WAREHOUSE painted across the front of them in peeling shades of red and blue.

At the right corner of the building was a normal-sized door with a large padlock set in the clasp. Disregarding the lock, the bartender turned the knob and shoved with his shoulder. A second shove forced the door open, and the man turned to Sister Laurel and said, "Right this way."

As she crossed the threshold, Sister Laurel noted that the padlock had not been forced. Rather, the clasp had been disconnected from the door but left attached to the jamb, so that when the door was shut it appeared to be locked. Stepping into the fairly dark interior, she followed the man through what once had been an office and into the open, cavernous warehouse. At the far end of the two-story-high room was a matching pair of loading doors, with a wooden staircase to their right leading up to a loft. Along the left and right walls were high windows—four on each side—through which eight shafts of light spilled onto the hard-packed dirt floor. The dust that swirled in the light beams was so thick that it reminded Sister Laurel of fog rolling across Boston Harbor.

"Ryan!" the bartender called. "It's me, Murray!"

Sister Laurel heard the creak of boards overhead and looked up to see cakes of dust falling from the planks of the loft as someone made his way to the staircase. A moment later a young man came down the steps and started across the room. Sister Laurel guessed that he could be no older than seventeen or eighteen. A second boy appeared at the top of the stairs, came down partway, and stood watching the scene.

"Donaghue's got a job for you," Murray explained as the youth named Ryan came up.

"With her?" Ryan asked warily.

"She works with Donaghue now."

"What kind of work?"

Forcing a smile, Sister Laurel said, "My name is Sadie Maguire. There's a house that I want vandalized. Can you and your friends handle it?"

"Sure thing. But why?"

"That don't concern you," Murray put in. "Just do what the lady asks, and Donaghue'll make it worth your while."

Ryan shrugged. "Just tell me where and when."

"It will have to be today—in the daytime. Is that a problem?" Sister Laurel asked, and he shook his head. "How many friends do you have?" she added.

"Enough. They're upstairs."

"I'd like to meet them. Then I'll take you past the house. All right?"

Ryan shrugged again and turned toward the staircase. "Jake," he called to the youth on the stairs. "Have the boys come down. All of them."

Sister Laurel turned to the bartender. "Thank you so much. I can handle things now."

"Are you sure?"

"Certain. You've been so kind." She moved casually toward the office, subtly leading him from the room.

"If I can be of any further help . . ."

"I'll tell Mr. Donaghue how helpful you've been." She stood smiling as he entered the office, crossed to the street door, yanked it open, and disappeared outside, closing it behind him.

Turning from the office, Sister Laurel kept to the shadows as she approached where Ryan was assembling the boys, who were still coming down the stairs. There were eight of them, and when she saw the last two in line, her heart started to race, and she had to force herself not to call out Michael's and Cameron's names.

Sister Laurel's mind whirled as she tried to figure a way to get the two boys alone and find out if they were there voluntarily or against their will. In either case, she was determined to bring them back to the church —and then as far from Abilene as possible. Just as she was deciding what she would do, the two boys looked up at her. Their expressions shifted rapidly from curiosity to uncertainty to shock as they realized who she was.

The nun frowned and tried to communicate with her eyes that they should remain quiet. She had hoped her disguise would be more convincing, and now she could only pray that they would not reveal her true identity. She saw a glint of awareness in Michael's eyes, and he nodded slightly, as if signaling that he understood her intentions. But just as he leaned toward Cameron to whisper something, the older boy stepped forward and asked, "What are you doing here?"

Michael tried to grab his friend's arm, but the boy pulled away and came halfway to where Sister Laurel was standing. "I'm not going back!" he declared indignantly as the woman raised her hand, urging him to be quiet. "I'm old enough to lead my own life."

"What's going on?" Ryan demanded.

"It's Sister Laurel—from the orphanage," Cameron explained, while Michael pulled at his sleeve and told him to shut up.

"A nun?" Ryan said in disbelief, staring at the

well-dressed woman. Suddenly he realized they had been duped, and he turned to the other boys and shouted, "Take them!"

"But I'm part of the gang!" Cameron protested as the boys surrounded him and Michael and took hold of their arms. "I'm the one who told you who she is!"

Ryan was paying him no attention. Instead he pulled a knife from his boot and started toward the woman, a wicked gleam in his eyes.

Realizing that her plan had come apart, Sister Laurel resorted to more persuasive means. She slipped her right hand through a small opening she had made in one of the seams of the dress and grasped the butt of the Smith & Wesson .38 that was holstered to her thigh. As Ryan advanced, knife in hand, Sister Laurel drew out the weapon, cocked it, and said calmly, "Put that thing down."

Ryan came to an abrupt halt and stood gaping at the revolver in her hand.

"I said put it down," she repeated, and he hesitantly complied, letting the knife drop to the ground. "Let them go," she added, waggling the gun toward the boys who were holding Cameron and Michael. It took no further prodding.

"What kind of nun are you?" Ryan muttered. "You're bluffing. You wouldn't—"

"Yes she would," Michael cut in, edging closer. "She once shot a dog for barking during Sunday services."

"A nun?" Ryan said, unconvinced. "You're crazy."

"Sure," Michael continued. "Stuff like that is all through the Bible. Don't forget Abraham sacrificing his own son and Solomon cutting that baby in two."

"Enough," Sister Laurel said, secretly pleased at

Michael's spunk. "Let's get out of here." Michael quickly came forward, but Cameron held back. "Come on, Cameron. You don't want to stay here, do you?" she asked as the older boy looked from the nun to the other boys. "Friends wouldn't have turned on you," she pointed out.

Cameron glanced at Ryan a final time but saw no sympathy in the young man's eyes. Looking down in dismay and embarrassment, he came forward to where Sister Laurel and Michael were standing.

"Let's get out of here," she said, backing toward the office door.

"Not so fast," a voice called from behind her, and she whirled around to see the bartender standing in the doorway with a revolver aimed at her. "Drop it," he demanded.

Sister Laurel had moved the barrel of her gun away from Ryan when she turned, and now there was nothing she could do but comply. With a frustrated sigh, she carefully released the hammer and placed the revolver on the ground beside her.

Murray came over, picked up the gun, and stuffed it behind his belt, then called to Ryan, "You shouldn't have let her get the drop on you. You can't trust anyone—least of all a woman. That's why I waited outside." Smirking, he turned to Sister Laurel and said, "We'll let Mr. Donaghue straighten this whole thing out."

"Let the boys go," she said firmly, placing a hand on each boy's shoulder. "They've done nothing."

"Donaghue will decide that. Now move." He waggled the gun and forced Sister Laurel and the two boys through the office and out into the street. As he led them down the secluded road, he gripped Michael's collar with his left hand and kept the gun pressed against his back, warning all of them that he would kill anyone who tried to get away.

The bartender kept to the back streets and alleys as he led his prisoners toward the Salty Dog Saloon. They were coming up an alley between Texas and Railroad streets, approaching the rear entrance of the saloon, when without warning Michael swung his arm and dropped to his knees, knocking aside the gun as he yanked his collar out of the man's hand. With a curse Murray swung the gun back, but before he could bring it to play, Michael spun around and leaped at the man's knees, knocking him onto his back.

"Run!" Michael shouted at the others as he crawled up over the man and scrambled for his gun hand. He heard the click of a hammer being cocked and found himself looking down the barrel of the gun.

"Don't shoot!" Sister Laurel cried with a gasp, reaching to help Michael off the man, who stared up at the boy in fury, his finger whitening on the trigger. "Please don't shoot him," she begged, and slowly the man's finger relaxed, and he lowered the hammer.

As the bartender clambered to his feet and dusted himself off, he looked around and suddenly realized that only the woman and the younger boy were present. "Where is he?" he demanded, turning in place and looking both ways down the alley for some sign of Cameron. When Sister Laurel merely shrugged, Murray grunted and waved the gun at her and Michael. "Get moving!" he ordered, jabbing at the air with the gun barrel and motioning them forward. "Mr. Donaghue'll have more than a few questions for you."

Wrapping her arm around Michael, Sister Laurel

gave him a reassuring squeeze, and together they continued down the alley toward the rear entrance of the Salty Dog.

A few blocks away, on Mulberry Street between Texas and Second, Cody Fisher and Marshal Stacy Parnell stood on the porch in front of Hazlett's General Store, sharing a smoke and discussing the relative merits of Cody's pinto and Parnell's big gray gelding, which were saddled and tied to the hitch rail in front of the store. To any store patron or casual passerby, it sounded as if they had met outside town that morning, had challenged each other to an impromptu race to Abilene, and now were debating which animal had performed the best. In truth they were making up the whole thing as they focused their real attention on the Abilene Agricultural Bank, across the street and halfway down the block.

The bank was closed this Saturday morning, but there was a flurry of activity inside the brick building. Fifteen minutes after the westbound train had pulled into Abilene, a wagon with four men on board had appeared, flanked by four heavily armed horsemen. The wagon had been empty save for one large wooden box, which had been lifted off and carried inside under the direction of the bank president, who was on hand to supervise the transfer of the army payroll. Now two of the horsemen stood on guard at the door while the others deposited the funds in the bank vault.

A few minutes later, the guards emerged from the bank. Four of them climbed into the empty wagon, while the others mounted their horses and started up the street. The driver turned the wagon in a tight circle, and the procession headed back the way it had come.

Marshal Parnell smiled and nodded as the riders passed, muttering under his breath, "Pinkertons."

"I'll be glad to see them gone," Cody replied just as quietly, referring to the fact that the Pinkerton guards were scheduled to return to Chicago within the hour on the eastbound train.

The two men switched their conversation to the weather as they waited for the bank president to leave. Five minutes later he emerged from the building, locked the front door, and headed up the street.

"Morning, Mr. Crowell," Parnell said casually as the man walked past.

Nodding, Crowell said somewhat curtly, "Marshal."

"Everything go smoothly?"

Crowell allowed a faint smile. "All's secure until the army arrives next week."

"Good. Then I guess I can get back to my other work." Parnell tipped his hat slightly.

The bank president nodded perfunctorily and continued up the road. As soon as he had rounded the corner of Texas Street, Parnell and Cody untied the reins of their horses and led them down the street past the bank. At the next corner, they turned right, then doubled back along an alley that ran behind the bank. Partway down the alley, they tied the horses near a pile of trash behind one of the buildings and pushed aside a couple of wooden crates to reveal a pair of carpetbags they had hidden there earlier. Each taking one in hand, they continued down the alley on foot.

"There he is." Cody nodded toward a small man at the rear of the Agricultural Bank.

"Hello, Wade," Parnell said as they came up to the young man, who could not have been much over twenty.

Wade silently nodded, his eyes darting nervously between the marshal and Cody and then up and down the alley. Finally he turned to the rear door and fumbled in his pants pocket, his hands shaking noticeably as he withdrew a key. He took a deep breath to steady his nerves, then inserted the key in the lock and turned it to the left, triggering the spring action and unlocking the door. Turning the knob, he shouldered open the door and waved the men inside.

Carrying the carpetbags, the two men followed Wade through the bank to the closed walk-in vault, which had a six-foot-high iron door with a large tumbler lock.

"You got the combination?" Parnell asked, and again Wade fumbled in his pocket, this time withdrawing a slip of paper with several numbers on it. "Where'd you get it?" the marshal inquired as Wade gingerly took hold of the lock and began to spin it to the right.

"Crowell's daughter," the young man replied, looking over his shoulder. For the first time a trace of humor touched his eyes.

"She just up and gave it to you?" Parnell asked.

"She gave it to me, all right—but not the combination." Wade smirked, then went back to his work. "Gave it to me good one weekend when her folks were away. After we was done about the third or fourth time and she was sleeping, I slipped into the old man's library and found it in his desk drawer—along with the key. I traced a picture of the key real good and later filed myself a copy. That's when I come to Mr. Donaghue."

"You did right, boy," Parnell said, clapping him on the back. "You'll earn a lot more from Donaghue than that Crowell fellow will ever pay you."

"Too bad Mr. Donaghue don't have a daughter, too," Wade said mischievously.

"You just mind your work," Parnell replied, adopting what passed for a stern tone.

After a final spin of the tumbler to the right, Wade grasped the handle beside the lock and pulled it to the left. There was a loud click, and then the door swung free.

"Good work," Parnell declared, pulling the door open wide and stepping inside. "You keep watch," he added to Wade as Cody followed into the vault.

The two men placed their carpetbags beside the wooden strongbox, which sat on the floor to the right of the door. As Parnell opened one of the bags and withdrew a small crowbar, Cody checked the strongbox and discovered that the bank president was so confident of his vault that he had not bothered to lock the box after examining the contents. Waving away the crowbar, Cody pulled off the open padlock and lifted the lid.

The box was filled with federal notes—at least thirty or forty thousand dollars, by Cody's estimate— and for a few seconds the two men just stood looking down at them. Then they grinned at each other and went to work emptying the money and replacing it with blank, bill-size stacks of paper from inside the carpetbags. Once the real money was loaded into the bags and replaced with worthless paper, they closed the strongbox and picked up the carpetbags.

Wade appeared at the open vault door, grinning as he took one of the bags from Parnell, who followed him out. "Got it all?" he asked eagerly, and Parnell nodded.

Cody was coming out with the second bag when he heard what sounded like a door closing. The other two men heard it at the same time, and they all looked out into the main room of the bank just as a man locked the front door behind him and turned to face them. It was not the bank president but a younger man—perhaps in his forties.

"Wade . . . what are you doing here?" the man asked in confusion. Seeing the marshal, he said, "Marshal Parnell. I don't understand. Has there been trouble?" He started across the room toward where the three men were standing.

"M-Mr. St-Sterns," Wade stammered.

"Marshal . . . ?" Sterns repeated as he walked closer. As he took in the open vault door and the carpetbags held by the marshal and the stranger dressed in black, he slowly seemed to realize what was going on. Suddenly he blurted, "My God!" and turned to run, fumbling in his pocket for the key.

Before the man made it to the door, Parnell had his gun out and shouted, "Hold it, or you're a dead man."

Sterns glanced over his shoulder and saw the marshal's gun trained on his back. For a moment it looked as if he was considering making a break for it anyway, but then he reconsidered and reluctantly dropped the key in his pocket.

"That's better," Parnell said as the man turned and raised his hands. "Get away from that door—over here," Parnell ordered, and the man walked slowly toward them.

"What'll we do now?" Wade asked, his voice trembling with fear.

"Shut that vault," Parnell told him. When it was done, he added, "Now get out of here, Wade, and let us handle it."

"But—"

"Do as I say," Parnell ordered. "We'll take care of

Sterns and make sure everything is locked up when we go."

"Yes, but—"

"Get out of here! Now!"

Wade stared nervously between the marshal and Cody, carefully averting his eyes from the man named Sterns. Then hesitantly he backed down the hallway and slipped outside.

"Now what?" Cody asked, putting down the carpet-bag and drawing his own gun as Parnell motioned Sterns into a corner where they could not be seen from the windows.

"We've no choice," Parnell said flatly. "Pete Sterns, here, is vice president of this bank. He's got to go."

"You mean kill him?" Cody asked, wincing slightly. He saw that the man named Sterns was biting his lip but attempting to look as unafraid as possible, as if biding his time until he could think of some way out of this.

"What else can we do?"

"But that'll ruin our whole story," Cody argued, attempting to buy time as he frantically tried to think of a better solution to their quandary. "Everyone will know Crowell didn't embezzle the money."

Parnell began to smile. Looking over at Cody, he said, "Not necessarily. All we've got to do is make it look as if Crowell did the shooting." He nodded as the plan took form in his mind. "Yes, that's it. We kill Sterns, dump his body somewhere, and leave the gun at Crowell's house along with some of the money. Then we get Wade to say that Sterns found out about the embezzling and had gone to confront Crowell about it. It'll look as if Crowell killed him to shut him up." Parnell turned to Sterns, grinning broadly. "Yes, that's what we've got to do."

"Look, Marshal," Sterns said. "You don't have to do this. I don't care about the money. I'll get out of town. You don't have to—"

"We got to." Parnell shook his head and looked at him almost sympathetically. "Sorry, but we just got to."

"But not here," Cody put in quickly. "It's got to be done somewhere else."

"Right," Parnell agreed. Suddenly he began to look quite nervous, as if the reality of his decision was just hitting home. A few beads of sweat trickled down his forehead, and he wiped them with the back of his gun hand as he muttered, "Somewhere else."

Cody had been about to offer to do the deed, figuring that he could let Sterns go once they left the bank. But looking at Parnell now, Cody detected some hidden meaning in the man's changed demeanor, and he decided to press him. "I'll bring the money to Donaghue," he suggested, "while you take care of this fellow. All right?" When no reply was forthcoming, he added, "You can handle it, can't you?"

Parnell glanced at Cody, his left eyelid quivering slightly. "Uh, sure. But maybe . . ."

"It's your idea. You should have the pleasure of executing it. That is, unless you don't think you can—"

"It's not that. It's just . . ."

Cody looked him squarely in the eye and said in a somewhat derogatory tone, "You've never killed anyone before, have you?"

"Yes I have," Parnell insisted. "Uh, once, that is."

"It gets easier."

"Maybe if they're shooting back at you. But the first fellow wasn't armed—just like Sterns here."

Cody felt a coldness shudder through him. Struggling to steady his emotions, he said tonelessly, "You're the one who shot Judge Lawrence Fisher, aren't you?"

"Donaghue forced me to. He found out the judge had tried to telegraph the governor. The message wasn't sent, but Donaghue knew it was only a matter of time before Fisher arranged a full investigation. I didn't want to kill the old man, but Donaghue said that if I didn't, he'd make sure I was the first one to go to prison."

Cody felt every muscle in his body straining as he struggled against turning his gun on Stacy Parnell and pulling the trigger right then and there. Clenching his left hand into a fist so as not to squeeze the trigger with his right, he said abruptly, "I better handle this Sterns fellow, then. You take the money."

Looking clearly relieved, the marshal holstered his gun and went to retrieve the two carpetbags. Meanwhile, Cody stepped up to the bank officer and grabbed his collar, yanking him down the hallway a bit more forcefully than necessary. When they reached the rear door, Cody glanced back at Parnell, who was approaching with the carpetbags, and said, "You'll have to walk. We're taking the horses."

Parnell nodded. "I'll see you at the Salty Dog," he said, adding, "And thanks, Cody."

Cody's response was to shove the bank officer through the rear door and down the alleyway.

"Where are you taking me?" Pete Sterns asked as he rode down Second Street alongside the gunman dressed in black. The reins of the marshal's gray gelding were tied to Cody's saddle, and Sterns had to grip the saddle horn to keep his seat. His eyes kept darting to the gunman's holstered revolver, as if he was debating whether or not he could leap from the horse and get away before Cody would be able to draw and shoot him in the back.

"I'm not going to kill you," Cody said flatly. He looked over at Sterns, who seemed quite confused by the comment. "Parnell and Donaghue know me as Matthew Cody. My real name is Cody Fisher. My father was Lawrence Fisher."

"The judge?" Sterns asked in surprise, and Cody nodded. "That's ridiculous. The judge's son is the minister of—"

"You'll see in a minute," Cody cut in, turning his horse right onto Elm Street and kicking it into a gallop toward the railroad tracks.

Sterns gripped the saddle horn tighter, deciding that it was better to remain with this possible madman for now than to risk getting shot in the back or breaking his neck by leaping from a galloping horse.

It took but a minute to ride up Elm, past Mud Creek, and onto the drive that led to the Calvary Methodist Church. The horses pulled to a halt in front of the church, and Sterns watched in amazement as Cody leaped from his pinto and shouted, "Judah! It's Cody!" A moment later the minister emerged from the church.

Sterns stared at the two men in a near state of shock, then muttered to Judah, "This is your brother?"

"Yes," Judah replied. "What happened?" He turned to his younger brother.

"A little hitch in the plan. Mr. Sterns walked in on the robbery, and I had to pretend I was going to kill him."

Judah looked up at Sterns and grinned. "He didn't, obviously." Sterns just nodded numbly.

"Is Travis still here?" Cody asked.

"He and Orion left for Donaghue's a few minutes ago."

"Damn! They expect me to be inside the saloon when they make their play. I better get going." Cody untied the reins of the marshal's horse and handed them to Judah, then turned to Sterns. "You have to wait here until it's over."

"What's going on?" the bank officer asked as Cody climbed into the saddle of his pinto.

"Judah will explain. Just remember—if anyone asks you, you're dead!" He smiled at the man and turned his horse to ride away. Then he pulled on the reins and looked back at his brother. "One other thing, Judah," he said, his voice breaking with emotion. "It was Marshal Parnell who pulled the trigger on Father."

Judah's jaw dropped. "Are you sure?"

"He's right," Sterns put in. "I heard it myself."

"What will you do?" Judah asked, stepping closer.

"If he's not dead when this thing is finished, I'm going to kill him."

"Don't. Let the law handle it."

Cody laughed humorlessly. "I thought Parnell *was* the law in this town." He patted the revolver in his holster. "Well, he's gonna discover another law right here."

"Don't do it. Travis can arrest him, and he can be held until a new marshal is appointed."

"Not good enough," Cody said bluntly. "And if you weren't hiding behind that collar, you'd agree."

"It's not the collar—"

"Before that it was the bottle," Cody continued. "It's the same thing. You talk a good line, but when it comes down to it, you're just afraid. That's why you're

227

staying here while I finish what should have been done days ago."

Judah shook his head and looked down at the ground.

"Don't worry," Cody said, starting his horse forward at a walk. "Father would have understood. It's just your little brother who doesn't." He slapped the reins and took off at a gallop down the drive.

Judah watched him disappear down the road in a cloud of dust. Then he sighed and turned back to the horse. Holding the animal steady while Sterns dismounted, he said, "Come over to the parsonage, and I'll tell you what's going on." He tied the horse to the railing beside the front steps, and then the two men headed to the minister's residence.

Judah was still explaining how his younger brother and Luke Travis had joined forces against Marcus Donaghue when the front door burst open and a teenaged boy came racing into the front parlor.

"You're Cameron, aren't you?" Judah said, jumping up from his chair.

"It's Sister Laurel!" the boy blurted. "And Michael. They've been taken prisoner!"

"What are you talking about?" Judah asked, approaching the boy. "Sister Laurel went shopping this morning, and—"

"No—she came to where we were hiding. They found out who she is and took her to see somebody named Donaghue."

"But that's impossible," Judah insisted. He was about to say something more but stopped when he saw the oldest of the orphans—the red-haired young woman named Agnes—step into the doorway behind Cameron.

"No, it isn't," Agnes pronounced, her expression a mixture of concern and guilt.

"What's going on?" Judah asked, looking back and forth between Cameron and Agnes.

Coming forward into the room, Agnes said, "I think I'd better start at the beginning."

Chapter Fourteen

Just what the hell are you up to?" Marcus Donaghue bellowed, standing up from his chair and smashing his fists against the desktop.

Sister Laurel glanced around the office and out into the main room of the Salty Dog Saloon, as if looking for help. But it was still before ten in the morning, and the saloon was closed to patrons; the only people on hand out there were half a dozen of Donaghue's hired men. Facing the saloon owner, she held her head high and said nothing.

"Do you really want me to have one of my men beat the answer out of you?" he asked, his fists clenched white as he leaned over the desk. When she merely narrowed her eyes at him but did not reply, he looked at the boy beside her and said, "Or would you rather we beat it out of him?"

"No! Don't do that," she quickly said, stepping

closer to Michael and putting an arm around his shoulder.

"Then talk." Donaghue's hands relaxed somewhat, and he placed them palm-down on the desktop and sat down.

"It's exactly as your bartender said. I'm a Dominican nun bringing a group of orphans to Wichita. Two of my boys ran off and joined that gang, and I wanted to get them back. I thought if I could find them and talk to them, I could convince them to return with me."

"So you dressed up as a whore?" he said dubiously, clearly unconvinced.

"A madam," she corrected.

"And who was that young trollop you brought along?"

"One of the orphan girls."

"You really expect me to believe this fairy tale?"

"It's the truth."

"And a nun wouldn't lie, I suppose." He gave a mocking laugh. "Then what about last night?"

"I'd do anything to protect my children," she said firmly.

"Even strap a gun to your thigh." Shaking his head in disbelief, he picked up the Smith & Wesson revolver that the bartender had taken from Sister Laurel. He spun the cylinder a few times, then casually pointed the gun at her. "You'll have to come up with a more convincing story," he said, swinging the gun toward Michael. "Or this boy dies."

"It's the truth," she insisted. "Send someone to the Methodist church and check it out."

Donaghue tapped the fingers of his left hand on the desk, as if in thought. Then with a contemptuous sneer he said, "I think I'd rather beat the truth out of you."

"Don't hurt Sister Laurel!" Michael shouted, wrapping his arms around the older woman's waist.

"You just better hope I don't hurt you," Donaghue shot back. As he put down the gun and stood, one of his men appeared in the open doorway. "What is it?" Donaghue asked.

"Parnell's here."

"Good," he declared, his expression brightening as he came around the desk. "You stay here with these two," he told the man, who drew his revolver and stepped into the office. Then Donaghue headed out into the main room and shut the office door behind him.

Stacy Parnell was standing beside the saloon owner's usual poker table, having placed the two carpetbags on top. He grinned as the big man approached. Opening the top of one of the bags to reveal that it was stuffed with money, he announced, "We got it all, boss."

Without bothering to respond to the marshal, Donaghue opened the second bag and pulled out a bundle of federal notes. While examining the money, he said, "How did it go?"

"Uh, all right," Parnell replied cautiously.

Donaghue looked over at him, reading the man's eyes. "What do you mean? Where's Cody?"

"Everything went perfect—until we were getting ready to leave and Mr. Sterns walked in on us."

"The vice president?" Donaghue asked, and Parnell nodded. "Go on," Donaghue demanded bluntly.

"Well, he saw what we were about, and we couldn't just leave him." Parnell paused, as if considering whether or not to take full credit for what came next.

Apparently deciding to risk it, he plunged ahead. "I told Cody to take him somewhere and kill him. We can plant the gun with the bank president and make it look as if he killed Sterns when Sterns caught him embezzling the money." Seeing the way Donaghue's eyes narrowed as he weighed the plan in his head, Parnell quickly added, "Wade can back us up on it. He can say Sterns told him he was going to confront Crowell."

Slowly Donaghue began to nod his head. Then he smiled broadly and pronounced, "A good plan, Stacy. Couldn't have come up with a better one myself."

Parnell grinned with relief. "Cody'll be here as soon as the job's done," he said, and then, to cover his own position further, he added, "I had him take care of Sterns 'cause I didn't want to leave all this money with a new man."

"You did right," Donaghue assured him, turning his attention to the money. "Let's see how much you boys got."

Just around the corner from the Salty Dog, Cody Fisher stood with Luke Travis and Orion McCarthy, the three men checking their weapons as they debated altering their original plan. Cody had caught up to the two men just as they were preparing to burst into the saloon, expecting Cody to be inside with Parnell and Donaghue. Now they had just about decided to scrap that plan and simply burst in as a threesome, when suddenly a voice called out, "Travis! Cody! Wait up!" They turned to the left to see Judah Fisher running down Railroad Street from the direction of the church, practically in sight of the saloon, which was in the next block to the right.

Travis frantically waved Judah closer to the buildings, motioning him to be quiet. The minister seemed to understand and hugged the buildings as he came the last fifty feet and rounded the corner of Cedar Street.

"What's wrong?" Cody asked as his brother rushed over.

"Ev-everything!" Judah stammered, struggling to catch his breath. "It's S-Sister Laurel—and M-Michael." He doubled over slightly and gagged a few times; it was evident that he had run the entire way from the church.

"What about them?" Cody pressed, grasping his older brother's forearm.

Straightening and looking up at Cody, his eyes spoke his fear as he said, "They're in the saloon with Donaghue."

"Are ye daft?" Orion interjected.

"It's true. Apparently Sister Laurel got it into her head to find Cameron and Michael on her own, and she used Donaghue to get to them. She pretended to be a madam looking to open a brothel—with Agnes acting as one of her girls. She asked to hire some boys to help her set up shop, and Donaghue had one of his men take her right to them. The plan worked—until Cameron blurted out who she really is. She and the boys were dragged to the saloon a little while ago, but Cameron escaped and came back to the church."

"Damn!" Cody cursed. "I saw them last night—but I had no idea. I should've recognized that young redhead."

"Forget that now," Travis told him. "We've got to get them out of there. We can't just barge in there until we're sure they're out of the line of fire. We've got to get them out of the saloon or at least into the back office."

"I could go in first," Cody pointed out. "They're expecting me, anyway. It'll look as if I'm just coming from killing Sterns."

As Travis was nodding in agreement, Judah suddenly called, "What are you doing here?" and the other three men turned to see Agnes come racing around the corner.

"I want to help," the young woman declared, panting but apparently in better shape than Judah.

"You shouldn't have followed me. This is no place—"

"It's my brother in there," Agnes reminded him.

Cody stepped forward, a faint smile on his lips as he said, "So you're the lady in the red dress. You had me fooled—Donaghue, as well." As she blushed, he added, "But my brother is right. This is no place for a—"

"For a girl?" Agnes cut in.

"I was going to say *woman*." Cody flashed a disarming smile.

Composing herself, she said, "I did all right last night. You said so yourself."

"Yes, but that was different. There wasn't the risk of gunplay. Today—"

"Wait a minute," Judah interrupted. "She may have a point. You can't make your move until you know where Sister Laurel and Michael are being held. They could be in a back room or even upstairs under guard. You go in with guns blazing, and who knows what'll happen? They could be shot before you ever find them. No, we've got to find them first, then make sure they're out of danger."

"Aye, we know tha' already," Orion said impatiently.

"And I think I know a way Agnes and I can help," Judah pronounced.

"You're not talking about the two of you going in there, are you?" Travis said dubiously. "There are already too many civilians at risk."

"You're forgetting that you're a civilian, too," Judah reminded him, adding, "We've got just as much at stake here as any of you."

Travis saw the unwavering look in the young minister's eyes, then turned to Agnes and saw an even more determined light. He slowly nodded and said, "Perhaps you'd better tell us your plan."

Marcus Donaghue closed the carpetbags containing the army payroll and eagerly clapped Stacy Parnell on the back. Nearby, the bartender stood beside the closed door of the office, in which another of Donaghue's men was guarding Sister Laurel and Michael. There were four other men in the main room— all hired guns—two standing opposite the bar at the far end of the room and two seated at a table near the large double doors that were closed against the batwings.

When someone started pounding on one of those doors, Donaghue signaled one of the men at the table to check the window. The man stood and glanced outside. "Looks like a minister and a girl," he said with a shrug.

Arching his eyebrows in surprise, Donaghue motioned the man to unlock the doors and let them in. Donaghue then placed the carpetbags on the floor and was moving away from the table when the doors swung open and Judah came barging in, dragging behind him a young red-haired girl in a rather plain-looking brown dress. Closing the doors behind them, the two gunmen who had been at the front table took up positions in front of the doors, their weapons still holstered but their gun hands at the ready.

"Is she here?" Judah blared, looking around impatiently as he circled the room, finally bringing the girl to an abrupt halt in front of Donaghue. "Where is she?"

"What are you talking about?" Donaghue asked.

"The woman," Judah said flatly. "The one who calls herself Sister Laurel—or Sadie Maguire—or whatever name she's using today." He roughly shook the girl's arm. "Tell him!" he demanded.

"I-I'm Ag-Agnes," she muttered in fear.

"Or Maureen or Darlene or whatever else suits your purpose," Judah said with a sneer. He turned to Donaghue. "I've been duped, plain and simple."

Donaghue was about to speak, but he held his tongue, preferring to let the minister play his whole hand first.

"Go on, tell him!" Judah repeated, again shaking the girl. "Tell him the way you and that phony nun came to my church and pretended you wanted to set up an orphanage—even had a few kids along to make it look good." Facing Donaghue again, he continued, "But they're just a bunch of swindlers. That so-called nun hoodwinked me out of five hundred dollars of the church's money. Then this young trollop here . . ."

Turning to Agnes, Donaghue commented with a smirk, "You looked far more appealing in that red dress last night."

"She knows how to be appealing, all right," Judah said bitterly.

"You speak from experience?" Donaghue asked with a touch of amusement in his eyes.

"You're damn right I do. And I was a fool. She

knows how to slip into a man's bed—and slip all the money out of his wallet when he's not looking. I wouldn't put it past her to slip a knife in his back, if she had the chance!"

Donaghue's smile faded. "I know what you think of me," he said to Judah. "You blame me for your father's death. So what are you doing here now?"

"That lady and this—this whore took my church for over five hundred dollars. And I expect you to pay."

"Me?" Donaghue asked incredulously. "You're mad."

"They work for you, don't they?" Suddenly he turned and slapped the young woman. "Tell him!"

Holding her stinging cheek, Agnes fought her tears as she stammered, "I h-had to t-tell him, Mr. Donaghue. He—he beat me." She broke down sobbing.

Judah let her go, and she buried her face in her hands. "She told me everything," he declared. "They're not here to open an orphanage but a whorehouse—and you're backing the whole operation. So I expect you to pay back every last penny the church lost. Call it a business expense."

"You've got to be crazy to ask me for money."

"You owe me!" Judah raged, his eyes wide with anger.

Donaghue tried to read the message behind Judah's words. It was clear that this was about more than just the money the woman had stolen—yet five hundred dollars was a small price to pay if it might also satisfy the minister regarding his father's death. But could there be any truth to what Judah was saying? Donaghue did not think for a moment that the older woman was actually a nun, but now he was equally sure she was no madam. More likely she was a swindler, just as Judah claimed. But what was her game?

Turning to the bartender, he said, "Bring her out here, Murray," adding, "The boy, too."

In the confusion, no one noticed that the gunman named Cody had entered the saloon through the still-unlocked front doors, leaving them slightly ajar. He caught Donaghue's eye and signaled that he had successfully completed his assignment. The saloon owner seemed preoccupied with the two intruders, so Cody circled the room to where Marshal Parnell was standing near the bar. "It's finished," he whispered to Parnell, who understood and smiled.

When Sister Laurel and Michael appeared at the office door, the young boy immediately recognized his sister and went running across the room into her arms.

"Now you're gonna tell us who you really are," Donaghue said to Sister Laurel. "And what you really want."

"I already told you," she began, not realizing the story Judah had made up. "I'm a Dominican—"

"Enough of that!" Donaghue shouted, losing his temper.

"But it's the truth," she insisted.

Judah Fisher rushed past Donaghue and shook a finger at the nun. "The truth is that you're a liar and a thief! Pretending to be a nun—taking advantage of our church!"

"What?" she gasped, her face whitening with shock.

Cody came forward from the bar now, his revolver held loosely in his hand. "I wouldn't trust any of them," he remarked. "Least of all this preacher man. The marshal, here, tells me you had him kill the man's father. Ain't that right, Stacy?" He glanced at Parnell, who looked both uncomfortable and angry that Cody had betrayed his confidence. Turning to Donaghue, Cody continued, "Who knows what a preacher with a grudge might do to get even?"

Donaghue was nodding, as if he had been having precisely that same thought.

"Give me five minutes alone with him—with all four of them—and I'll get the full story," Cody said confidently.

"Yes, I'd like that," Donaghue agreed, coming to a decision. "Take them in there." He motioned to the large back office. The man who had been inside guarding Sister Laurel and Michael came out now and moved over beside Murray at the bar. "Go with them," Donaghue ordered the marshal, who drew his revolver and approached from the bar.

Cody and Parnell herded Judah, Michael, and the women toward the open office door. When Sister Laurel started to protest and hold her ground, Cody shoved her roughly, and Agnes took her arm and gently urged her to comply. As the four prisoners were ushered inside, the marshal started to move past Cody into the room, but Cody abruptly pulled the door shut, closing Sister Laurel and the others in the room alone. Before anyone realized what was happening, Cody turned his gun on Parnell and shouted, "Drop it!"

Freezing in place, Parnell stared in bewilderment at the young gunman, his own gun pointed down at the floor. Across the room, the two men near the front doors were the first to realize what was happening, and they clawed for their guns. But the doors behind them burst open simultaneously, and a gruff voice with a Scottish brogue called out, "Dinna even try it!"

His comment was punctuated by the sound of the Winchester in his hands being levered.

The two men stopped in place, their hands hovering over the butts of their guns. Donaghue's other men must have felt more confident about their positions, because the three gunmen drew their revolvers, while Murray leaped behind the bar to snatch up the shotgun that he kept there. As the two men across the room from the bar brought their weapons to bear on Orion McCarthy, one was met by a blast from the Winchester, which blew away the side of his face and sent him sailing over one of the tables near the wall. The second man was drawing a bead on Orion as the Scotsman levered the rifle, but before he had the squat tavernkeeper in his sights, a door in the corner behind him was kicked open, splintering the door and shattering the jamb. Luke Travis fired his Colt Peacemaker from the alleyway beyond the door, catching the man in the back and knocking him off his feet. Immediately Travis burst into the room and was greeted by a shotgun blast, which peppered the shattered door with buckshot.

Seeing Travis roll and come up unharmed, Murray swung the shotgun and squeezed the trigger of the second barrel, but the shotgun jerked up in his hand and fired harmlessly at the ceiling as a slug from Cody's revolver tore through his neck. Murray dropped the shotgun and clawed at his neck, turning and staggering as blood sprayed across the mirror behind the bar. Gasping and spitting up blood, he grabbed at the shelf in front of the mirror, his hand knocking off bottles as he fell to the floor.

One more man was foolish enough to make a play—the one who had been in the back room earlier and now was standing in front of the bar near Cody and Parnell. He had already drawn his weapon, but in the first few seconds of confusion he had not known where to fire. Now, as Cody turned his revolver back on the marshal, the man by the bar swung his gun toward him. He was met by a blast from Travis's gun as the former lawman regained his feet. The bullet tore into the man's right shoulder, throwing him against the bar.

Travis kept his revolver trained on the man, who was trying to bring up his gun as he slid to the floor. Travis shook his head and started to say, "Don't," but when the man did not give it up, Travis was forced to pull the trigger again. This time the bullet centered the man's chest, killing him instantly.

It was over in less than five seconds. Parnell was still holding the revolver in his hand, while the two men in front of Orion had never even drawn their guns. Donaghue had retreated behind his usual chair but had not risked going for the gun under his coat, preferring to rely on the derringer up his sleeve when the moment was right—or his political connections, if it came to a trial.

Orion stepped up behind the two men he was covering and snatched the revolvers from their holsters, tossing them across the floor. "I did'na let these two even raise a hand," he boasted as he prodded his prisoners toward the bar with the barrel of the Winchester. Glancing at the four bodies scattered around the room, he shook his head and declared, "'Tis a shame the same kinna be said f'ye, Lucas, nor f'ye, Cody, me lad."

Donaghue cautiously opened the flap of his coat and stood waiting to be disarmed. "A miraculous recovery," he said with a trace of a smile as Travis came over and snatched the short-barreled revolver from his shoulder holster. "Your death was staged for my benefit, no doubt."

"And my resurrection," Travis said coldly.

Nearby, Cody Fisher stood holding his revolver on Parnell. The marshal still had not dropped his gun, and Cody seemed in no hurry to demand that he do so. Suddenly Parnell realized that he was at risk of being shot, and he slowly knelt and placed the weapon on the floor. As he stood and held his empty palms open at his sides, he noticed that Cody's gun hand was shaking slightly, as if some force within him were struggling to pull the trigger. Parnell quickly raised his hands to show he had surrendered.

Sneering, Cody muttered, "You filthy bastard." As Parnell stared in terror at the gun in Cody's hand, Cody added, "You're the bastard that killed my father."

"Your f-father?" Parnell stammered. "I don't know—"

"I'm Cody Fisher. My father's name was Lawrence," he said evenly. "You can carry that to your grave."

"Don't do it," someone urged from behind him. Cody did not have to turn to recognize the voice of his older brother, who had just emerged from the back office with the others. "Father would want a trial," Judah told him.

"Father's dead."

"And you're about to put another bullet in him."

Cody's finger tightened on the trigger, and he raised the revolver until the barrel was pointing up the marshal's nose. Beads of sweat poured down Parnell's forehead, and his lips quivered as he begged, "P-please . . . don't—"

Cody smiled and pulled the trigger. But there was

no explosion and the gun did not buck in his hand—
only the metallic sound of the hammer dropping on
an empty chamber. It was enough to make Parnell's
knees buckle as he nearly fainted with fright.

Cody was grinning as he holstered his gun and
turned to face the others. "Just thought I'd let him
know how it feels," he said, approaching his brother.
There were tears in both men's eyes as they embraced.

As Travis led Marcus Donaghue toward the bar, the
saloon owner paused in front of Sister Laurel and said
in a surprisingly good-natured tone, "I must compliment you on your performance. I take it you *are* a
Dominican?" When she nodded, he added, "A most
resourceful order, I see." He smiled pleasantly, nodded, and continued over to Parnell, who was holding
himself steady against a table. Grasping the marshal's
arm, Donaghue helped him over to where Orion was
guarding the other two men. His expression remained
peaceful, as if he saw this incident as a minor setback
that would soon enough be set right.

Marshal Parnell did not have any such illusions.
Instead he saw himself hanging by the end of a
rope—or spending the rest of his life in a rat-infested
prison. Neither prospect was acceptable, and as Orion
motioned the four prisoners toward the front doors,
Parnell glanced through the windows at the gathering
crowd outside and tried to think of a way out of this
predicament. If only he had a weapon—perhaps he
could take a hostage out there and make an escape.
But it would have to be before they were brought to
the jail and he was locked inside one of his own cells.

Parnell's legs went rubbery again, and Donaghue
grasped his arm and yanked him upright. In so doing,
Parnell felt something hard brush against his arm, and
suddenly he remembered the derringer Donaghue

always kept up his sleeve. He started to sweat even more profusely as he realized why the man seemed so relaxed.

Donaghue'll save his own hide, Parnell told himself, realizing that the outlaw leader would take no extra risks to help him. *Now . . . I've gotta do something now.*

It was when they were passing through the doors that Parnell made his move. Orion McCarthy was at the head of the group, with Travis and Cody bringing up the rear. As Parnell stepped out onto the boardwalk, he pretended that his legs were giving way beneath him, and when Donaghue propped him up, he grabbed the man's sleeve and yanked at the derringer hidden behind a leather wristband. Before anyone could react, Parnell had wrested away the small gun and was pointing it at Donaghue's head.

"I'll kill him!" Parnell shouted as he stepped behind Donaghue and grabbed hold of his collar, pressing the gun against the base of his skull. He pulled the big man back along the boardwalk, the crowd behind him scattering.

Orion pushed the other two prisoners off to the side and covered them with the rifle, while Travis and Cody confronted Parnell, who was effectively using Donaghue as a shield. "Don't be a fool," Travis said, keeping his gun ready but making certain not to aim it directly at them.

"Put it down," Cody added, taking a step forward until Travis caught his sleeve to hold him back.

"I won't go to prison!" Parnell whined. "I won't hang!"

"No one's going to hang you," Travis tried to convince him, raising a hand to calm him down.

Marcus Donaghue seemed more disgusted than

afraid, and he shook his head and blared over his shoulder, "You idiot! You've got one damn bullet in there. What good'll it do? You think they care if you shoot me? And if you do, they'll just take you anyway, and you'll hang all the same. Put it down. I know a lawyer—"

"Shut up!" Parnell yelled, pressing the derringer more tightly against Donaghue's skull. His hand shook with fear as he looked over at Cody and said, "I . . . I d-didn't want to kill the old man. Donaghue made me do it."

"I know," Cody said as convincingly as he could manage.

"It's Donaghue's fault. I wouldn't have done any of it if it wasn't for him."

"I know that," Cody added. "Just put down the gun."

"I—I can't. I can't hang."

"Just put—"

Suddenly Parnell pushed Donaghue at Cody and Travis. By the time the big man had dropped to the boardwalk to get out of the line of fire, Parnell had the derringer pointed into his own mouth. Backing up along the boardwalk and waving his free hand to keep everyone away, he looked over at Cody, his eyes beseeching the other man for forgiveness. Then he pulled the trigger and blew away the back of his skull.

There were screams from the crowd, followed by the sound of several women sobbing. Cody and Travis walked over to where Parnell was lying on his back, his head cradled in a spreading pool of blood, his bulging, sightless eyes facing the boardwalk overhang above.

Kneeling, Cody closed Parnell's eyes. "I forgive you," he whispered, shaking his head as he stood and looked down at the man. "You damn fool."

Travis placed a hand on Cody's shoulder. "Come on," he whispered, and the two men turned and walked side by side back along the boardwalk.

Chapter Fifteen

◆————◆

After breakfast at the Sunrise Café on Monday morning, Luke Travis climbed up into the saddle of his brown gelding and started down the street. Two days had passed since the arrest of Marcus Donaghue, who was being held at the local jail awaiting trial. He was being guarded by a force of a dozen men, working in two shifts, who had been deputized by the mayor as a temporary police force pending the appointment of a new town marshal.

As Travis rode along Texas Street, he saw Dr. Levi Wright bending over beside a chair at the edge of the street in front of his office, struggling to lift what looked like the sign that usually hung on the post at the end of the walkway. Dismounting in front of the Grand Palace Hotel, Travis tied the reins to the hitch rail and approached.

"Oh, thank you," the doctor said as Travis came up

and hoisted the sign for him. Travis held it in place under the perpendicular wrought-iron arm, while Dr. Wright climbed up onto the chair and attached the hooks at the top edge of the sign to the pair of short chains hanging from the arm.

"The wind knock it down?" Travis asked as the old man climbed off the chair.

Stepping back to admire his handiwork, Wright shook his head. "It's a new one. Ordered it on Friday." He raised his thumb like an artist to examine the proportions of the sign and determine whether or not it was hanging straight. Nodding in satisfaction, he continued, "It'll take a little getting used to, but I'd say it looks just about right."

As Travis moved back slightly to read the sign, he remembered that the former one had a smaller board hanging below on which Dr. Aileen Bloom's name had been painted. That was gone, and Travis assumed Dr. Wright had added her name to the main sign. Sure enough, there it was in simple, bold letters. He started to smile, and then suddenly he realized that hers was the only name listed and that her title now read PHYSICIAN & SURGEON.

"Where's your name?" he asked Dr. Wright in surprise.

"Where it ought to be . . . retired."

"Are you really giving up your practice?"

"I've been practicing so many years, I figure I must have gotten it right by now, so why not give another person a chance to make her own mistakes?"

From down the walkway, a woman said, "I hope you'll still be coming around to set me right when I do."

Travis looked over to see Aileen approaching.

"Don't you worry about me," the elderly doctor

told her. "I'll be nosing around enough to set you straight when you need it. And remember, I've got an investment in you."

Aileen came up to where the two men were standing. Turning to Travis, she explained, "Dr. Wright will still be a partner, though he won't be working actively —unless, of course, I need to call on his services."

"I'm not talking about that kind of investment," Wright said gruffly. "I mean the twenty dollars you owe me." As Aileen started to grin, he turned to Travis and added, "The lady stole my twenty-dollar gold piece and hammered it into some fool boy's head."

"I've offered to pay you back," she reminded him.

"It wouldn't be the same. That was my lucky coin, and I want the same one back."

"You'll have a long wait," Aileen teased.

"I can outlive a young whippersnapper like Simon Lanford—and like you, too."

"It will be good to have you around," she replied.

Shaking his head, Dr. Wright picked up the chair and started up the walkway, calling back, "I'll just leave you young folks to your own devices. And take your time—I'm not officially retired until Friday!"

Aileen and Travis watched the old man head up the steps and into the house. Then Aileen turned to Travis and said, "I was just waiting for Sister Laurel to bring Michael over. I want to make sure his cut has healed properly before they set out for Wichita."

"I'll be sorry to see them go," Travis replied.

Aileen nodded, then remembered that Travis had planned to accompany the orphans to Wichita. She was about to ask if his plans had changed when a young voice called their names. They turned as a large, two-seated buggy driven by Judah Fisher pulled up with Michael at his side and Sister Laurel and

Agnes Hirsch in the rear seat. The nun was wearing her habit again, her face beaming with pleasure from under her wimple.

"How are you feeling?" Aileen asked the boy as he climbed down.

"I feel great."

She gave his forehead a cursory examination. "There's really no need to go inside. I can already see that there's no infection." Reaching into the pocket of her white jacket, she produced a shiny penny. "This is for being such a good patient," she said, handing it to the boy.

"Why, thank you, ma'am," Michael said, taking the coin and staring at it in surprise.

"That's so nice of you," Sister Laurel told the doctor. Turning to Michael, she said, "Would you like to go buy yourself some candy?"

"Maybe later," he replied, turning the penny over and over in his palm. He glanced at the Colt Peacemaker strapped to Luke Travis's waist and thought, *Only seventeen dollars and thirty-six cents to go!*

Luke Travis was helping Sister Laurel down from the buggy when she asked the doctor, "Would you like me to bring Michael back in a few days, just to be certain?"

Aileen shook her head. "You needn't delay your journey any longer. You can always see a doctor in Wichita."

"What makes you think we're going to Wichita?"

"I don't understand . . ."

Judah Fisher was helping Agnes down from the other side of the buggy. He turned now and said, "Go on, Sister Laurel, don't keep her in suspense."

"You tell her," the nun insisted. "After all, it's all your doing."

Coming around the buggy, Judah said, "The credit really belongs to my congregation. At our business meeting last night, it was decided that we would offer Sister Laurel our support in setting up an orphanage here in Abilene—provided she will run it."

"Won't that be something," Sister Laurel declared, clasping her hands. "An orphanage run jointly by Catholics and Protestants—for children of any race or religion."

"We'll be using the parsonage," Agnes put in.

"Delightful," Aileen said. As she turned to Travis, her smile grew more bittersweet. "It looks as if you'll be going on to Wichita alone. We'll all miss you."

"Haven't you told her?" Sister Laurel asked.

"I was about to when you rode up."

"Tell me what?" Aileen pressed.

Grinning, Travis reached into his pocket. "I was keeping this as a surprise." He opened his hand to reveal the silver badge of Abilene's town marshal.

Reaching out and touching its shiny surface with her finger, Aileen muttered, "Do you mean . . . ?"

"I accepted the job yesterday. I like this town, and I want to do what I can to make it a better place to live."

Aileen looked up at him and smiled.

"You're not upset, are you?" he asked. "I mean, given your concerns about lawmen, I wasn't sure—"

"In your case, I'll make an exception." She leaned forward and kissed his cheek. "I'm delighted," she said, taking his hand in her own. Then she lifted the badge and pinned it to his shirt, as Michael and Agnes clapped.

"It looks right on you," a new voice pronounced, and everyone turned to see Cody Fisher sitting on his pinto beside the buggy. There was a bedroll slung behind the saddle and a pair of leather bags draped on either side.

"Are you leaving already?" Agnes asked, her voice betraying her disappointment.

"Time to move along," Cody declared, dismounting.

"Where will you go?" his brother asked.

"Wherever the road takes me."

"You've always got a home here."

"I know that, big brother. And thanks." He walked up to Judah, and the two men embraced. Then Cody whispered, "And thanks for showing me that there are many kinds of courage. Father would've been proud of you."

"Of the both of us," Judah corrected him.

"What will you do now?" Travis asked as Cody started back to his horse.

"I'll just head west and see what comes along."

"The way you've been going, the only thing that'll come along is another gunslick out to make a name for himself by killing Matthew Cody."

"I'll have to handle that when it comes." Cody climbed up into the saddle and tipped his hat.

"Why not try being Cody Fisher for a while?" Travis suggested. When Cody held up on the reins and looked down at him questioningly, Travis went on, "The road you're riding leads straight to the cemetery. And since all roads lead there eventually, anyhow, why not ride yours to uphold the law, rather than to skirt around it?" Approaching the pinto, Travis reached into his pocket and produced a second badge, engraved with the words: DEPUTY MARSHAL, ABILENE, KANSAS. He held it out to Cody. "It'll look just as good on you as this one does on me."

Cody stared down at the badge in Travis's hand,

then looked over at his brother, who was smiling and nodding his approval. Hesitantly the young gunman reached down and took the badge. Holding it against his chest, he glanced over at Agnes and said, "What do you think, pretty lady?"

Beaming with pleasure, Agnes said, "It makes you look even more handsome, Deputy Fisher."

"You can call me Cody," he replied, pinning the badge to his shirt. Leaning down from the saddle, he shook Travis's hand and said, "It'll be a pleasure to work with you, Marshal. But one thing confuses me."

"What's that?"

"How come it took you so long to ask? For a minute there, I thought you'd actually let me ride out of here."

"You wanted the job all the time?"

"Not the job. Just the shiny badge." Tapping the silver star on his chest, he turned to Agnes Hirsch and proclaimed, "It does make me look handsome, doesn't it?"

The reply came in a high-pitched screech as an eerily human voice called out, "Dinna be daft, man!"

All eyes turned to see Old Bailey perched atop the shoulder of Orion McCarthy, who stood at the edge of the boardwalk in front of his tavern. The burly Scotsman had his hands on his hips and was rumbling with laughter as the parrot fluttered its wings and squawked, "And may the Devil be damned!"